I0579625

EAGLETOWN

FRED JUST

KITSAP
PUBLISHING

KITSAP PUBLISHING

Eagletown
First edition, published 2017

By Fred Just

Copyright © 2017, Fred Just

Cover Illustration by Wanbao - http://wanbao.deviantart.com

ISBN-13: 978-1-942661-45-0

Published by Kitsap Publishing
P.O. Box 572
Poulsbo, WA 98370
www.KitsapPublishing.com

Printed in the United States of America

TD 20170327

100-10 9 8 7 6 5 4 3 2 1

CHAPTER 1

"I reckon it's about time we make our annual trip down to Vancouver to gather another year's supplies." Nat remarked to his wife who was sitting on the couch sewing up a pair of his pants.

She smiled and nodded as her thoughts turned to the sights and sounds of the city. Once a year they went down to Vancouver to pick up staples such as sugar, flour, spices, etc. Nat would pick up any needed hardware for repairs and some grain for the stock.

Nat broke into her thoughts, "It's been a long year this time without the radio working. I've kind of missed keeping up on the news every evening. Funny how that thing just up and quit working. It was fine one day and static the next. We'll take it with us and get it fixed or get a new one. You know---you would think it would have had the decency to go on the fritz just before we were going down for supplies, instead of a week after getting back."

She noticed his coffee cup was empty so she put down her sewing, and rising, picked up his cup, and headed for the kitchen to get another cup. Next month would be their twentieth wedding anniversary, and maybe she could find something special for her husband while they were there. They usually spent two days but this year he promised to stay three so she could do more window shopping.

As Nat's wife was setting the coffee down beside him he heard the motor of a boat coming into the secluded, almost hidden, cove where they lived. "Unusual time for a person to out in in a boat, as its neigh on to eleven o'clock," he said as he arose and went to the window to look out, "and it's darker than hell. Can't see a thing. No lights on the boat. I don't like it!"

He turned on the outside lights and looked again. "I can see the boat heading for the dock." Nat walked over to the gun rack and took out his rifle and started outside. "I'm going to throw the flood lights on them as they land." He proceeded to the where he had attached the switch box for the lights. As he opened the box to throw the switch he looked toward the dock and could make out that someone had stepped off onto the dock and was tying the lines.

He threw the switch and the area on and around the dock, burst into a brightness of light. Nat's first thought was 'My God – What is it?' There were two figures, one on the dock and one standing on the bow of the boat. They looked like creatures out of a nightmare. The creatures tried to shield their eyes from the light, and began shooting haphazardly at the lights. Nat came quickly to his senses aiming carefully and fired at the one standing on the bow. The bullet caught the creature in the head killing it instantly. When it hit the water it splashed water on the other creature which in turn dropped its rifle and tried to wipe the water off frantically. Nat again shot, killing it quickly.

All was silent as Nat carefully watched the boat for further movement. Seeing none he headed for the house to have his wife stand by with a gun while he walked down to the boat to look it over. As he neared the house he saw his wife's body lying on the ground a few feet from the porch. Fearfully he dropped to his knees beside her and held her in his arms as he realized she was dead. She had evidently run out of the house when she heard the shots and one of the creature's bullets had caught her through the right eye, killing her outright.

Nat gently laid his wife back down, stood up, fighting to control his emotions, then went into the house exchanging his rifle for a shotgun. Picking up his high intensity portable light he cautiously headed for the dock and looked closer at the body. It almost made him nauseous. It was basically shaped like a human being but hands and face almost looked like blackened raw flesh that had been diseased, and the eyes looked like they had been partially pushed out of their sockets.

Shining his light on the body in the water he realized it looked more gross, as the face looked like it was already starting to rot.

Nat suddenly felt a chill go up and down his spine as he realized that there might be another one in the boat. He quietly listened for any sound that might give him a clue. Then in the silence he heard a thump, but he wasn't sure if the noise was from inside the boat, or only the boat bumping against the dock. Being extremely cautious, Nat stepped on board the boat. It was about a thirty foot cabin cruiser and appeared to be well out-fitted. 'A lota' money tied up in this one.' Nat thought. He slowly tried the door that went down to the living quarters. It was locked. Putting his ear to the door he listened for any sound on the other side. Nat listened for what seemed like several minutes, and then he heard what sounded like a muffled moan. Not knowing what he was getting himself into, he stepped back and with one solid kick, battered the door open and jumping to one side instantly. There were no shots and nothing came flying out as he crouched down to one side of the doorway. Then he heard what sounded like muffled yelling. Bringing his shotgun to his waist, as he stood up, he stepped into the doorway, shining his light inside the cabin ready to shoot.

But what Nat's eyes beheld, was not what he expected. Bound and gagged were three women lying on the floor. He quickly scanned the cabin for any danger before proceeding further. Seeing none he set his shotgun down, and drew his hunting knife, and cut the ropes loose from the first one. As soon as she got her gag off she threw her arms around him and started crying and thanking him for saving her. Nat, prying her arms from around him, told her to try to control herself, and sit down, so he could free the other two women. He cut the ropes on the second one, and she also was crying as she just sat there thanking him over and over,. The third upon being freed only very graciously said thank you, as she softly sobbed.

When he started to question them about how they came to be victims of the creatures, the first two he had freed started talking at the same time. Nat held up his hands. "Now wait just a minute! One at-a-time!" Pointing to the first one he had freed, "What is your name?"

"Sarah! They captured me while I was sleeping."

He pointed to the next one. "What's your name?"

"Ellen! I was looking for a place to spend the night when they jumped me."

"Looking for a place to spend the night? Were you lost?" He pursued.

"No. They had burned my house down the night before, but I was hiding in the woods so they wouldn't find me."

"This still doesn't make sense to me." Nat nodded to the last one. "And your name?"

"Lisa." She said softly.

"Next question! Who or what are those things that I killed out there?" Sarah asked. "You don't know?"

"If I knew, I wouldn't be asking."

"The war did that to them." Ellen said.

"War? What war?"

The three women looked a each other not knowing what to say. Ellen finally spoke up. "I don't know how come you didn't hear about it, but almost a year ago there was a nuclear war killing almost everybody. Those things you killed were humans that were exposed to a lot of radiation and lived."

Nat was stunned. "My God! Were there many survivors?"

Sarah shrugged her shoulders. "Who knows?"

Ellen continued, "There are two types of people left. Those that were affected by the radiation and those that escaped it. The affected ones have been hunting down the people that weren't affected, and capturing or kill-ing them. They had captured my husband a couple of months ago. I doubt if he is still alive."

"Well---we'll finish this conversation later. Follow me." He escorted the women off the boat onto the dock. As they approached the body on the dock they stopped to look at the figure lying there. Nat noticed the hatred in Lisa's eyes as she looked at it. Turning to her he spoke. "Ugly son-of-a-bitch, isn't he?" She just spat on him and turned to walk away. Nat shoved the body into the water and headed toward the house.

When they arrived at the house he told them to go in inside as he knelt down beside his wife's body. The women stopped to look "My wife! Just go on inside and I'll be in after a while,"

As the women went into the house, Nat picked his wife up and carried her to his workshop. Inside the workshop, he placed her body upon the workbench, and took down some cedar boards he had stored in the rafters.

Nat set about the task of building a coffin for his wife's burial. With his agile hands he carefully built the coffin, sealing all seams and joints with tar to prevent any type of seepage. When he had the coffin finished, he went into the house, and got a sort of blanket made out of beaver pelts that had been his wife's favorite, and brought it out to the workshop. After lining the coffin with the blanket he placed his wife inside. Tar was then applied to the rim, and after taking one last look he placed the lid on top, fighting back his emotions as he fastened it down. He had constructed the coffin using no nails, only wooden pegs because nails rust and start wood rotting,.

Nat knew nothing about preserving a body, but he was going to make an effort. He drilled a small hole in the top and using a vacuum pump he had, he pulled as much air as he could out of the coffin then quickly sealed the hole. Next he took some large sheets of plastic and made huge plastic bag and fitted it around the coffin. Again he used the vacuum pump and drew the air out of the plastic bag, and sealed it.

Checking the time Nat realized it was almost five o'clock, and he started to feel the weariness creeping into his body. As he entered the house he noticed the woman had fallen asleep in the living room on the couch and chairs. Being very quiet he turned out the lights and went into his den and started a fire in the fire place.

Settling back into the easy chair his thoughts went back to when they had first came to the cove. It had been in the spring eighteen years ago. He had bought the land because of the hidden cove and the privacy it offered. The first thing they built was a one room log cabin for shelter, then a dam to control the stream and to run a small generating plant. They didn't build anymore that first winter as it was an exceptionally wet one. Come spring they started building the house. The two of them worked side by side digging out the dirt for a basement by using shovels and a wheelbarrow. Nat brought sacks of cement in by boat and they mixed their cement using sand and gravel from a nearby pit. It took all summer just to get the basement in. The following spring he went to Vancouver and purchased the making for a small sawmill. Using the mill he cut all his own lumber for the house. His wife had worked right beside him all the way. They used wooden pegs made out of maple instead of nails to construct the house. Wiring, glass, plumbing, etc. had been brought in from Vancouver.

Two fireplaces were built, one at each end of the house. The living room floor was built two feet lower than the rest, giving it a sunken look. Dining room and living room covered one end of the house, and his den, rather large, covered the other end. In between, were the kitchen, bathroom, and laundry room on one side, and the bedroom and entranceway on the other side.

Besides the house, they had built a shed for the cow, and a workshop for Nat. It had taken them six years to build the house. Having their own electricity, he bought his wife a washer and dryer and electric cook stove. They were able to have any of the modern conveniences they so desired to have.

As Nat was thinking about the hard times, and good times, they went through, he drifted off to sleep as the fire slowly burned itself out.

"It's almost noon. Do you want any breakfast?"

Nat's eyes shot open as he felt a hand on his shoulder. Jerking his head around, he saw Lisa standing there. Then it all came back to him. His wife's death, the creatures, rescuing the women, and building the coffin. "You startled me." He said. "I don't know if I can eat anything, but a cup of coffee would sure help me."

"We fixed you some breakfast anyway. You should try to eat something. It would do you some good."

Arising from the chair he started for the dining room. "I suppose I should."

Lisa took hold of his arm. "I'm sorry about your wife. I know how you feel."

Nat growled at her. "I doubt it." He then saw tears forming in her eyes. "I'm sorry. Thank you for your concern. I'm just upset I guess."

"That's alright. Just try to eat something."

They went out to join the others at the table. Nat sat down and took a sip of coffee, looking at the breakfast. Pancakes, small steaks, and eggs. Suddenly he started to feel a little hungry.

Nothing was said during breakfast. After he finished his food and coffee, Ellen poured him another cup. Nat took a big swallow, and then broke the silence. "What do you gals plan on doing now?'

Ellen spoke. "We don't know. None of us have any place to go. No friends or relatives to go to. Our homes are gone.

"What she's trying to say," Sarah said, "Is, could we stay here for right now. Even for a little while as we decide what to do?"

He knew he couldn't just say no. They weren't capable of making it on their own. Somebody had to look after them. "I think we can work something out."

Nat rose from the table. "I've got to do something right now. We will talk later." He grabbed his coat and went outside.

It was a clear day and the sun was bright. With a purpose in mind, he went to the shop and got a shovel. The sun was hot as he dug his wife's grave. He removed his coat and continued to dig,. Digging, with his mind on thoughts of his wife he didn't even notice his pet raccoon as it ambled over to watch him. He had raised the raccoon from a little tyke. Its mother had been killed by a wolf, or some other predator. They had called it Bandi, short for bandit, because it was always trying to steal food off the table when it was in the house. Nat had dug down far enough that his shoulders were about even with the top of the grave, so Bandi jumped onto his shoulder It startled Nat, but he knew it was his friend right away, "Hi Bandi." He took the raccoon into his arms. "I'm pretty busy right now, and besides I don't feel like playing." He just held the animal close to his chest. The raccoon sensed things weren't right. Bandi nuzzled Nat's neck, and then licked his face. Setting the animal back over on the side of the grave, he gave it a couple of pats. "Now you just let me alone, so I can get this done before dark. Why don't you go up to the house and maybe you can get some goodies."

He knew he wasn't going to get finished today because he got such a late start. It was just getting dark as he finished building the forms in the bottom of the grave for pouring concrete to make a liner for it. Tomorrow he would pour the concrete, and if the weather held, it wouldn't take too long for it to set. He turned and walked to the house, feeling his muscles starting to ache from all the digging of the day.

As he entered the house he noticed the woman had started supper. Not speaking he hung up his coat and went to wash up. After drying his hands and face he went out to the kitchen.

"It will be about a half hour before suppers ready." Ellen stated.

"Okay. I'll be in the den. Just let me know when, and I'll come out and eat." He went into the den and started a fire then sat down to rest.

Sarah came in with a cup of coffee. "Here, you look like you might want this." She sat the cup down next to him.

"Thank you."

"I want to thank you again for letting us stay here. The house is really beautiful. It looks like a lot of work went into it."

"A lot did. My wife and I did all the work ourselves."

"Well, suppers just about ready, so I had better get back and help them put it on the table."

A few minutes later he heard Ellen yell. "Suppers on the table!"

They had taken a grouse out of the freezer and fried it up, along with mashed potatoes, gravy and green beans. Nat bit into a piece of the grouse and thought. 'Somebody sure knows how to cook.' He stuffed himself, but it was just too good to stop eating. After finishing his last bite he looked at the women. "That was one fine meal. Thank you."

"Lisa found some blackberries in the freezer, so she made a pie." Sarah stated. "Want some?"

"I couldn't eat another bite. But, later I'll take you up on it." He picked up his coffee cup and went into the den, while they cleared the table and cleaned the kitchen up. After putting more wood on the fire, he lit up his pipe and sat down in his easy chair to think.

They would have to talk this evening to make some kind of arrangements for their living conditions. The bed was large enough for three people, so they could sleep in there. He would sleep out on the couch, that way he could be more ready for trouble if it should come.

After the kitchen was done, Lisa brought him a cup of coffee. "Here you go. Anything else I can get you?'

"No. This is fine."

From the looks of all the books, you must do quite a bit of reading. Have you read them all?"

"No. Not quite." It was true; he had a lot of books. In fact one wall and part of another were bookshelves, filled with books.

"I noticed a piano over there. Do you play it?"

"No, but I was going to teach myself someday. Just haven't got around to it."

"I do! Maybe some time when I feel up to it, I'll play some, if it's alright with you."

I'd love it some evening, but for right now, will you get the others to come in here so we can talk?"

Lisa went out and asked the others to come into the den. They all found a seat, and waited for him to start.

"The house is small for us, but I think we can work things out. I'll sleep out on the couch and you three sleep in the bed. It's plenty big enough for the three of you,. I've noticed that all of your clothes are torn and in pretty bad shape. Now---you all look about the same size as my wife, so feel free to go ahead and wear any of her clothes that fit you. Sarah, you look like maybe you're just a little fuller than the others. There are some clothes in there that were a little too big for my wife, but I think they will fit you."

"Out in the garden are plenty of vegetables for food. In fact, some are ready to be picked and canned. Can any of you do canning?"

Lisa spoke up. "I know how."

"Good! You can teach the others so you don't have to do it all. Now---if you would like, you can go ahead and get cleaned up and change your clothes."

Later that evening they talked about their past and Nat learned more about the women. Sarah was twenty-two years old and had never been married. She had been staying at a small fishing village up north when the war had happened. The day after the bombs had fell, she had went out into the woods to pick berries and got lost. It took her fourteen days to find her way back to the village, and when she got back everybody was dead or dying. Evidently the winds had carried the radiation into the village while she was lost in the woods. She had been lucky to be lost at the time.

She had managed to stay alive by taking canned foods from stores and homes. A man had drifted into town and told her about the creatures, but after a few days he up and disappeared. How the creatures knew where she was she didn't know. They had come early in the evening and grabbed her while she was sleeping.

Ellen was twenty-five and she and her husband lived not to far up the coast from Nat. About a month after the war a boat had stopped at their place with three men on board. After telling them about the war they offered to take them with them, but her husband decided he would stay where they were. The creatures had showed up a few months ago attacking them during the night, but her husband had managed to run them off. Then one night they heard someone calling for help. At first they were afraid to go out and see who it was. The voice sounded so desperate that her husband decided to look into it. She watched her husband go to the edge of the woods toward the voice, and as he got to the woods, two of the creatures attacked him. Ellen shot a rifle in their direction, but not at them as she was afraid she might hit her husband. That was the last she seen of them until a few nights ago. They came back to get her.

She heard them calling for her to come out or they were going to burn her out. Being afraid of them she went out a back window and hid in the woods while they set the house on fire. When she didn't show, they started looking in the woods so she just started running. She didn't know how far she ran, but by morning she was exhausted. That day she took naps where ever she could find a place to lie down. Then last night she was walking along the beach hoping to find a house or someplace to spend the night. The creatures seemed to come from nowhere and grab her.

Lisa was thirty and a widow, as her husband had gotten killed three years ago in a logging accident. She didn't want to talk about her being captured. All she said was they had set her house on fire.

It was getting late so they decided to turn in and get some sleep. Nat was extra tired so he had no trouble going to sleep.

Nat was awake at the crack of dawn so he got up and made some coffee. After having a couple of cups, he went outside and started mixing and pouring concrete for the liner in the grave. The sky was clear so he knew it was going to be a warm day. 'Good!,' he thought to himself. 'The weather will sure help set the concrete up. Maybe I'll be able to place the coffin in the grave day after tomorrow.'

Just then he heard Ellen call out to him. "Breakfast is on the table. Are you going to come in and eat:"

I'll be right in. Just as soon as I put the tools away." He took the tools to the shed and put them away before going into the house. As soon as he stepped inside he smelled the bacon, and it did smell good. Nat washed up and joined them at the table. "It looks like the day is going to be a good one. Not a cloud in the sky."

"We are going to start doing the canning." Lisa said, "but you're going to have to show us what is ready to be picked."

"I'll be glad to, but I'll need somebody to help me clean out the screens on the dam."

"I'll help!," volunteered Ellen. "Just tell me what to do, and I'll do my best."

After they finished eating he went out to get the things ready that would be needed on the dam, while the women cleaned up after breakfast. When they were finished he took them out to the garden and showed them what to pick for canning.

While Sarah and Lisa started picking, Nat and Ellen went out to the dam. He had brought his rifle as was his custom when going too far from the house. As they walked out on the dam Nat spotted a big buck standing close to the woods on the other side. He quickly took aim and shot it. They went over to the deer and in one swift motion he drew his knife and cut its throat, then castrated it so it wouldn't be gamy tasting. He also cut the scent glands off the hind legs. He had hit the deer right in the ear.

Ellen looked at the deer in amazement. "You're a pretty good shot."

"I have to be, or I'd go hungry. With four mouths to feed I figure we could use the meat."

"But the freezer looked like it had quite a bit of meat in it."

"It may look that way, but it doesn't last all that long when you start using it to feed four."

Ellen helped him gut the deer and carry it back to the house. After they had it hung, they returned to the dam to do what they had started out to do.

It took about three hours to get all the screens cleaned and back into place. When they were finished, Ellen went to help Sarah and Lisa. Nat checked on the grave and then went to the wood shed and split wood for the rest of the day.

As the sun was getting low he decided to quit. He put the axe away and headed for the house. On the way he came across Bandi. "Hello Bandi. Where have you been hiding? I'll bet you haven't met the gals yet, because I haven't heard a word from, them about a, mischievous raccoon yet. I think it's about time they met you." He bent over and picked Bandi up in his arms and went inside.

"I don't believe you gals have met our resident bandit. Ladies, this is Bandi. He's a mooch and a thief. If you put any food on the table be sure you watch it closely, because if you turn your back the food will disappear.

The women all took turns holding Bandi and fussing over him. He was at the height of his glory with all the attention he was getting not to mention tidbits.

Nat went on in to clean up. Afterwards he came out just in time to see Sarah put a plate of bread on the table then turn back to the sink board. Out went Bandi's paw and down went all the bread onto the floor. None of the women had seen what happened. A couple of minutes later, Ellen put the vegetables on the table. "Sarah! Didn't you put some bread on the table?"

"Why, yes I did." She turned and looked. "Well the plates right there." Walking around the table she spotted Bandi and the bread on the floor.

Nat walked over. "You should have heeded my warning about him."

Sarah bent down and picked up Bandi, and his booty, and put both outside. "We'll just have to leave him out there while meals are being prepared."

After supper, Nat retired to the den and built a fire then lit his pipe, and settled back in his chair. It sure helped having the women around as it kind of took his wife's death off his mind and made it easier to cope with.

All of the sudden Bandi jumped up on his lap. "Looks like they gave you a reprieve and let you back in. Maybe they are getting wise to you. If they are, it's going to be hard for you to steal food with three women watching you." Bandi nuzzled his neck and beard, then licked his face, and cuddled up in his lap.

The nest day Nat was up early to check the concrete. He felt that it wasn't set enough for him to handle the lid to the liner, so decided to put the burial off another day. The day was spent making a marker for the grave.

After checking the concrete the following day he decided he could finish burying his wife. First he built a tripod over the grave. Then using a sled he brought the coffin out to the grave. By using a block and tackle he lowered his wife's body into the grave. It was difficult for him to control his emotions as he did this task. Next he put tar around the top of the liner, and then lowered the lid down on it. As he got ready to throw the first shovel load of dirt into the grave, his emotions almost came out, but he suppressed them. Nat finished covering up the grave then took down the tripod, and went and got the marker. As soon as the marker was implanted he stepped to the foot of the grave and looked at it.

BELOVED WIFE

NANCY C. SARGENT

OCT. 19, 1960

SEP. 13, 2000

Nat noted the sun was starting to set as he knelt down and said a prayer for his wife. Then all of his emotions burst loose as he sobbed uncontrollably.

He didn't know how long he had been kneeling by the grave when he felt someone drape his coat over his shoulders.

Lisa knelt down beside him. "It's getting chilly out here." She reached out and put her hand on his. "I know your sorrow, because the night I was captured, my only child, a boy, was killed. We had run out of the house to escape the fire, and we were jumped by the creature. My son managed to squirm loose. He ran back into the house, but as he stepped back out on the porch he had his father's rifle. Being only eight years old he could hardly point it. One of the creatures shot him as I watched, not being able to do anything." Lisa's eyes started to water. "The bullet caught his head and blew the top off of it, throwing him back into the burning house."

Nat put his arm around her and they just sat there for awhile. Later they arose and went into the house.

They all sat down to eat, but nobody could eat much. All seemed to be having their own thoughts. Then like a shot, Nat's fist came down on the table. "God-damnit! They're going to pay for this!"

"How?" Asked Sarah.

"I'm going out hunting for the bastards!"

The women looked at each other then Ellen spoke. "We're going with you!"

CHAPTER 2

The night Nat buried his wife was a very disturbing one for him. At first anger kept him awake. Anger at the creatures for what they did to his wife. The more he thought about that night of hell, the more anger that flared up in him.

Finally giving up on the idea of sleep, he got up and lit a fire in the fireplace. Setting on the couch, watching the fire, his anger turned to a sense of loss. Never had his mind held such a turmoil as it was having this night. There was no doubt about it, he longed for his wife deeply.

Nat hadn't heard anything, but he sensed that somebody was watching him. At first he listened, but only heard the crackling of the fire. Instead of turning around and looking, he dismissed the feeling, thinking it was all in his head. Then he heard the floor creak right in back of him. His muscles tightened as he prepared to take action. Before he had the chance he felt a hand softly on his shoulder.

"Nat, it's me, Lisa. I couldn't sleep, and I noticed that you had a fire going. May I sit with you for a while?"

He turned and looked up at her. The fire cast enough light on her face, that he could see a troubled look in her expression. Giving her hand a pat, he nodded for her to sit down.

Lisa sat down next to him, and just stared into the fire. After a few minutes she turned to him. "I'm scared!"

Nat put his arm around her shoulders. "You have every right to be. You've been through a lot. We all have."

Softly she asked. "Can I hold on to you for a little while?"

"Yes. If you think it will help, go ahead."

She put her arms around his waist and laid her head on his chest feeling his strength. No more was said as they both drifted off to sleep.

The singing of birds outside woke Nat up. Lisa was still asleep in his arms. He slowly loosened her arms, and gently laying her down, he got up. As he lifted her legs up onto the couch her robe fell open exposing her shapely thighs. Nat couldn't help but notice the shapely beauty of her legs as he pulled her robe back over her nakedness. After standing up, he paused and admired her Eurasian beauty.

Later that day he gathered the women together to explain what they had to prepare for in the future. "If we are going to be going after those creatures, we're going to have to be prepared"

"We're going to have to watch out for each other, and help each other. I'll teach you what I can about fighting. It's up to you to learn it as best you can. While in the military I was assigned to a special attack team. I'm going to attempt to teach you some of what I learned. Later it may come in handy."

Their training started the next day. First thing on the list was how to shoot a rifle and hit what you were shooting at. Lisa and Ellen had shot guns before, so it was easy for Nat to teach them to be good shots. Sarah, on the other hand, had never shot a gun in her life. She was a good student tho' and learned quickly once she got used to it.

When it came to learning how to go up and down a rope, the women had a difficult time of it, as their arms were not the strongest part of their bodies. Once, Sarah, after climbing to the top, and starting back down, happened to grab the rope and her shirt at the same time. The shirt tore open, exposing her ample breasts.

After reaching the ground and covering herself she stated embarrassingly. "I hope I never have to crawl down a rope again"

We all laughed, and Ellen said "You might have to. But next time don't get it tangled up with your shirt."

After a couple of weeks they were progressing very well. The next incident was not expected in the least. The women were learning to walk across a narrow log which Nat had suspended over the stream. Ellen got about half way across, when Bandi showed up. Now, Bandi thought that if she could walk on the pole, he could too. The only trouble was that he started from the other end, and met Ellen over the water.

While she was balancing herself, she yelled at Bandi, "Get out of the way!" Bandi stood his ground. He wasn't going to try to turn around and go back.

"Bandi! Go back!" She pleaded.

Pretty soon she lost her balance, and into the water she went. The raccoon looked down at her as to say. "What are you doing down there?"

As the water was only about three feet deep, Ellen stood up and looked at Bandi. "Damn you! Look what you caused!" She splashed water on Bandi, and he quickly finished crossing the log and headed for the woods,

Lisa and Sarah were laughing at her as she waded out of the stream. Before Sarah knew what had happened, Ellen had a hold of her and threw her into the water. Lisa braced herself, but Ellen won and Lisa also landed in the water.

Ellen hollered. "How's the water girls?"

"Wet!" answered Sarah. Then they all started laughing.

During the night a few weeks later, Nat had gotten up and lit a fire because he couldn't sleep. He heard one of the women come out of the bedroom and come into the den. Looking up he saw it was Ellen.

She knelt down on the floor beside the couch. "Nat." She said softly as she put her hand on his bare chest. "I need a man's touch."

Nat didn't answer, but put his hand out and stroked her hair. Suddenly he felt the need, and desire, for sex was burning in his loins. As he let his hand slide down past her neck to one of her breasts, he felt her undoing his pants and caressing him.

He helped her slide his pants off, then she stood up and let her robe drop to the floor. The light of the fire on her totally nude body drove Nat's passion to a higher peak. Standing up he took her into his arms and kissed her, feeling her warm flesh against his. Slowly they sank to the bearskin rug on the floor letting their passions build, as they tenderly fondled and kissed each other's bodies. Soon their bodies were filled with an overwhelming urgency and they came together in a sexual embrace.

They both climaxed at the same moment and afterwards they caressed and kissed each other's bodies, as they let their passions subside.

Later, Ellen arose, put on her robe, kissed Nat, and then looked deep into his eyes as if to express her thanks. Then, turning, returned to the bedroom.

As Nat lay back on the couch, he was a little concerned over the incident. He hoped the other two did not find out about what had happened, and start competing for him, as it would cause problems for everybody.

The next day there were no indications from any of the women as to what happened, so he felt a little more at ease,

When it came to learning how to use a knife for fighting, they seemed to have a hard time of it, but they managed pretty good after a while.

To learn about using a grappling hook they had to hike about three miles back into the woods where there was a rock outcropping., Nat had each one of them throw the hook up, and after it caught on the top, they had to climb up, and stand, then come back down.

Lisa got about fifteen feet up the rope when the hook came loose. After she hit the ground, the hook came down just missing her. As she started to get up she found that her ankle hurt too much to stand on it.

Nat looked her ankle over and thought that it was only sprained, or may- be cracked,. He then showed them how to make a litter using two poles and their jackets. Putting Lisa on the litter he then took the front while Ellen took the back. Later Ellen and Sarah traded off,.

After getting back to the house and soaking the ankle for a while it start- ed feeling better.

A couple of days later she was up and limping around with a cane. While she was healing, Sarah and Ellen took over all the household chores.

One evening Lisa decided to play the piano for them. It didn't take her long to get used to playing again, and everybody loved it. Nat had two favorites; 'Walk in the Wild Wood', and 'Music Box Dancer', and she knew them both. After that she played almost every evening. She would always start out with 'Walk in the Wild Wood', and finish up the evening by playing the other one.

Somehow Bandi had got into the house after lunch one day. With every- one gone he managed to get the refrigerator door open. In the course of raiding the frig he had dumped one of the shelves over on top of him, and he was covered with milk, jam, gravy, and berry pie.

When Nat and the women dame back into the house, there was Bandi, sitting right in the middle of the mess, eating berry pie. They all formed a half circle around Bandi, and he just looked up at them, then he wasted no time in returning to his meal.

Ellen spoke first. "Bandi, just what in God's name do you think you're doing? Look at this mess!"

Nobody wanted to pick him up, because of the gooey mess that covered his hair.

Ellen kept after him. "Listen to me you little imp. Who's going to clean this up, or clean you up for that matter?"

Bandi looked up at her, sensing that he was in deep trouble, scrambled for Nat's leg, and started climbing up. Nat put his hand down and stopped him. "Whoa! I don't want you getting me covered with that stuff too"

"Well, somebody has got to." Lisa said as she went and got a towel. "Come here Bandi, and I'll take you outside." She wrapped the towel around him, and went outside heading for the stream. When she got to the stream she tossed him in. "Now I don't want to see you again until you have cleaned yourself off." She then turned and headed back to the house.

By the time she got back in, the other two had started cleaning up the mess. "I don't think we should let him back in for a few days." Sarah said, and the rest agreed.

The time finally came when Nat felt that they were trained enough to set out to wage their war against the creatures. Before going he wanted to test the women to see how well they had learned what he had taught them.

To test them, he decided to make an obstacle course, and time them. The course started out with lying on the ground. At the signal to start, the person running the course had to jump up, run about fifty feet, drop to the ground, fire three shots at a target shaped like a person, then jump up run about twenty feet, leap over a three foot log, draw their knife and stab a dummy shaped like a person. After using the knife they would run to a tree, climb up the tree, come down a rope, and then proceed down a well marked trail.

The trail contained several obstacles, such as going over and under logs, crossing a small swamp, running down a bank and at the bottom, turn a sharp left and out on a log which was suspended across the stream. Once across the stream, they had to run down the stream for about a hundred yards. At this point there was a rope tied to a branch out over the water. They had to figure out how to get the rope, and then swing across the stream. After that it was back to the starting point.

Each woman would run it by themselves, and Nat would time them individually,. He would not tell them their time, so one would not feel she was better than the others.

The day of the test, Nat arose early and went out to mark the course. He got back to the house before the women got up. After breakfast he told them what was in store or them. They were excited as he explained the course to them. "When you get to the small swamp, it is up to you to find out how to get across to the other side of it. You will each carry a rope, knife, and rifle with you. As the rifle we took from the creatures, don't have shoulder straps on them, and mine does. You will have to use mine each time."

The women drew straws to see who went first, and Ellen was to go first, then Sarah, and Lisa last.

Ellen got into position and waited. On the signal to go she jumped up and ran. Nothing was said as they awaited her return, but as she came back into view toward the finish, Lisa and Sarah were cheering her on. When she crossed the finish line she was so winded she couldn't talk.

When Lisa asked her how the course was, Ellen just said. "Uh-uh! You'll find out when you run it."

Sarah was next. On the signal she got off to a good start alright, but as she jumped over the log she tripped. Before Nat could holler to ask if she was alright, she had gotten up and continued on. As she crossed the finish line, Nat was surprised at her time. She was only three minutes behind Ellen's time. For some reason he felt that it would be Ellen, Lisa, then Sarah. Sarah's finish had surprise him, but it was a good surprise, and he was proud of her.

When Lisa took off, Nat was surprised at her quickness. She seemed a little more nimble than he expected. Upon coming down the rope Lisa didn't wait until she reached the ground, but dropped from about six or seven feet. Nat knew that would pick her up a few seconds there.

Nat was talking to Ellen and Sarah, not watching for Lisa yet, when Sarah yelled. "Here she comes!"

They watched her heading for the finish line, and he noticed that she was as quick on her feet as a deer. Upon her crossing the finish line, Nat was downright amazed. She had beat Ellen's time by five minutes. He didn't know how she did it, but the fact remained, she did it.

Nat was curious about how long it would take him to run the course. He knew the course, so he felt he would be able to run it considerably faster than the women.

Ellen gave him the signal to go, and off he went. As he got to the swamp he didn't have to stop and ponder on getting on the other side, because he knew which limbs to grab and swing across like a monkey to get on the other side.

He had chased enough animals through the woods, so he breezed over and under the logs, and through the brush without any trouble. When arriving at the rope over the water he didn't climb the tree to get the rope. Instead, he took the rope he had with him, tied a stick to the end of it, and twirling it around, and feeding it out slowly until it wrapped itself around the suspended rope. Then he pulled the rope in and swung across. As he crossed the finish line, he checked his time. It was the same as Lisa's time. Well, so much for thinking he had the advantage.

Later Nat found out that Lisa had the ability to reason and figure things out better than he gave her credit for. As she was approaching the swamp, her eyes were already looking the situation over. Just as she arrived at the edge of the swamp, she had spotted the limbs, so didn't have to stop. When she got to the rope over the water, she had done the same thing Nat had to retrieve the rope.

That night, Nat announced that the next couple of days they would be preparing to set out on their war. They had to button up the house and pack their supplies. He had decided to take the cabin cruiser that the creatures had used, because it was outfitted better than his.

The next day they started loading the boat with supplies, and on the following day they moved as much as possible down into the basement.

When they had everything moved into the basement, Nat removed the trap door and built a false floor over the opening.

That night Ellen came to Nat again for sexual comfort. They both realized that this could be the last time they were able to come together, because after setting out on their venture anything could happen. Their love-making, lasted nearly half the night.

Nat was up early, and restlessly he went down to the boat and rechecked everything. Being satisfied with the boat, he rechecked things around the house and other buildings. Everything seemed to be in order, so he then went to his wife's grave. Standing over the grave, he again swore vengeance on the creatures for her death.

While standing there, Lisa walked up beside him, and putting her arm through his said. "It's hard to accept, isn't it?"

Nat didn't say anything, just nodded in agreement with her.

"I can tell you loved her very much. She must have been wonderful woman. I wish I could have met her."

Nat looked at Lisa."I wish you could have too. She was a little bit like you in a way."

"Let's go in and have breakfast." She said. "Sarah and Ellen are up and it's just about ready."

Breakfast was very quiet as nobody felt like talking. They all had their own thoughts, and ironically they were the same. 'What lies ahead for them?'

After boarding the boat, and casting off, they headed out of the hidden cove. Once hitting open water, Nat told the women that they had to each learn how to handle the boat. Each one was to run the boat for an hour at a time.

Nat stayed with them during each one's first hour, teaching them how to steer by compass, use the automatic pilot, read the gauges, and explaining how important it was to watch for floating logs, and other debris.

During the second turn at the helm they were by themselves. While one was steering the boat he would teach the other two about tying ropes, and reading charts, and maps.

Later in the afternoon a storm started to come up, so Nat took the helm.

The wind was picking up rapidly, so he knew he had to find a place to pull into to wait out the storm.

The rain was coming down so hard that visibility was restricted dramatically. Pulling in as close to the shore as possible, he knew that they could hit a rock just under the surface, but he had no choice if he wanted to watch for a cove or inlet.

Every so often a wave would splash over the boat, but so far the bilge pump was keeping up with it. It took all of Nat's strength and skills to keep the boat on course. Just as he felt the storm was winning, and they were getting dangerously close to the beach, he saw up ahead what looked like a cove or inlet. It was a narrow slot with huge rocks on both sides. As they came abreast of it Nat turned the boat and headed for the slot. He hoped for two things. One, that it was deep enough, and two, that the storm didn't crash them up against either side.

Just as they approached the slot, Nat gunned the motor. A large wave caught them from the back, and they quickly shot through the slot. The cove was plenty big for the boat. He rapidly put the boat into reverse, and they came to a stop. Putting it in neutral, Nat looked the cove over carefully. The cove was about two hundred yards deep and a hundred yards wide.

Over to one side they noticed a dock, and up on the bank a house. Nat eased the boat over to the dock. As they came along side of the dock, Ellen, and Sarah, leaped on it, and tied the boat securely.

Nat looked up at the house, then turning to the women said. "We better check that out. No telling what's up there. I'll go first, and then Ellen you follow me. Lisa, you and Sarah wait a few minutes then follow Ellen."

He started up the trail being very cautious as he crept forward. Arriving at the front of the house he noticed that some of the windows were broken out, and the door was open about five inches. As he went onto the porch from the side, he noticed Ellen waiting by the edge of the clearing with her gun ready. Pushing open the door he noted that the hinges squeaked loudly, like they hadn't been oiled for some time.

Entering the living room he saw that it had been totally ransacked. Then he checked the kitchen. It too, was a mess. Nat then slowly worked his way down the hall, checking the bathroom next. Seeing nothing in the bathroom, he proceeded to the end of the hall. There were two bedrooms, one on each side of the hall. Both doors were about half way open, and he could see that the one on the right had been used recently.

Using he barrel of his rifle, he pushed the door to the one on his right open all the way. Nat sensed something was wrong but he didn't know what. Thinking it must be his nerves, he cautiously stepped into the room to check it out.

Nat felt something against his back, and heard a man's voice at the same time. "Make one slight move and you are a goner."

CHAPTER 3

Nat calmly spoke. "Mister, you're making a mistake." He knew that as long as whoever it was, kept the gun up against his back, that he could spin around and disarm them before they could react. But, the trouble was, he didn't know if there was only one person or more. If there was more than one, it would be foolish to try anything.

"No, you made the mistake by coming in here." The man retorted.

The Nat heard Ellen's voice. "Freeze! Or I'll blow your head off."

That answered Nat's question as to how many there were.

The man spoke. "Looks like we have a stand-off here. If you shoot me my reaction will cause me to pull the trigger and blast your companion's guts out. So who is going to win?"

Nat spun around catching the man's rifle with his elbow, and in the same motion brought his rifle barrel up under his chin. "You lose!" Nat said. Taking the man's rifle from him, Nat looked him over. He was in is early twenties, about five foot ten, and had a lot of fear in his eyes.

Nat looked him in the eye. "Now you have a shotgun against the back of your head and a three hundred savage poking you in the throat. Are you planning to try anything foolish?"

After he said no, Nat continued, "All you have to do is walk over and sit on that bed when I remove the barrel from your throat. Then we'll talk."

Nat lowered his rifle, and the man walked over to the bed and sat down. He looked up at Nat and said. "You know. If I had known that there were two of you, I would have had the upper hand,."

Just then Lisa and Sarah came into the room. "What's going on?" Asked Lisa.

"Not much," said Ellen. "This guy here thought there was only one person, and then he thought there was two and now he just found out that there are four."

"How come you thought I was by myself?" Nat asked.

"Well, I just figured if there were two that they would be sticking together. When I heard the front door squeak, I peeked out and saw you just as you went into the kitchen. Then I went into the other bedroom thinking that when you came down the hall and saw that someone had been staying in this bedroom, you would check it first. In that case your back would be towards me and I could make my move"

"What's your name?" Nat asked.

"Arn."

"Well Arn. We have no axe to grind with you, so here is your gun back."

Arn didn't understand. "What did you come here looking for?"

"We came by boat. The storm was getting to rough, so we pulled into this cove. Upon seeing the house we decided to check it out."

Nat told him about their war against the creatures.

"Well, there are plenty of them around, and it's not too hard to find them. If you can see good at night."

"What do you mean?" inquired Nat.

"I can see that you don't know too much about them."

"No. But I reckon' I'll find out. What can you tell me about them?"

"Quite a bit. They only come out at night because the sunlight blinds them. In fact any bright light affects their eyes, so they shy away from the sunlight. Somehow tho' they can tolerate the light from a fire. The reason I know this is because they use fire for cooking. Another thing that keeps them inside is the rain. When they get water on their skin, it acts like an acid, and burns them. What it boils down to is that you are only safe from them when it rains, or during the day."

Nat thought back to that night of hell, and realized why they had reacted to the flood lights the way they did. It also explained why the one had panicked when the water had splashed on its skin.

Arn continued. "The only trouble is that it's come down to a kill or be killed world. The mutants, as I call them, hunt you down at night, and the normal people hunt you down during the day. I've had to kill both just to survive."

Ellen asked. "Why are the so-called normal people killing each other off?"

"I don't know," Arn answered. "It's just became a way of life. Not all the normals are like that. Some are just trying to survive the best they can. One time I came up to the top of a small hill, and looking down into a clearing I saw a couple with two children around a fire fixing something to eat. Thinking that maybe I could get to know them I started down. I hadn't gone but a few feet, when I heard gunshots. Stopping to look, I saw all of them get killed. Three men then came out of the brush and started going through what few things the family had."

Not liking what I saw I crept down to the edge of the clearing, and then shot them."

"Good for you!" Sarah said. I would have done the same thing."

"Why are the mutants, as you call them," Nat asked, "trying to capture the normals?"

"To eat 'em. They've became cannibals."

Ellen quickly put her hand over her mouth and ran for the outside.

Arn looked at Nat, "Weak stomach huh?"

"No. They captured her husband. She figured he was dead, but I don't think she ever conceived what his fate might have been. How do you know they are cannibals?"

"One day I came upon an old two story house. As I was sneaking up to check it out, I came across several human heads that were lying in one spot. A couple hadn't been there to long, but the others were in different degrees of rotting. When I worked around to the front of the house I saw where a fire had been, and all around it were bones. I'm not so dumb that I don't know human bones when I see them."

"What did you do?" Sarah asked.

"I figured that several of them might be staying in the basement, so I set fire to the front and back of the house. As old as the house was it burned like paper. As the house collapsed I could hear the screams from the mutants as they burned alive. It didn't take long for the house to burn."

Nat had heard enough for right now,. "Let's go down to the boat. I could sure use a cup of coffee. Would you care to join us for coffee, and maybe a bite to eat?"

Arn looked up at him. "You really mean it?"

"I wouldn't have offered if I didn't."

They all went down to the boat. Arn was surprised at the boat. "This is really nice. You have everything here you need."

Lisa and Sarah fixed the coffee and some sandwiches, while Nat and Arn talked about the mutants.

"How much destruction was done by the war?" Nat asked.

Not as much as you would expect. At least around the outskirts of Vancouver. I've been there, but I didn't go any farther south. It's probably about the same elsewhere. Most of the roads and highways are passable. There are even vehicles to get around in, but getting out in the open, like in a car going down the road, is dangerous. If you do, you're likely to run into a road block and get your head blown off."

"How about aircraft and military basses?"

"I don't know about the military bases, as I haven't been to any yet. But I've seen airplanes setting at an air strip north of Vancouver. Evidently nobody so far has come along that knows how to fly them."

After eating Nat got the maps out to plan their future movements, and Arn kept Sarah's attention by telling her about his experiences after the war. For some reason she was a captivated audience.

Ellen hadn't eaten, and Lisa was trying to talk to her to help her feel better, but she was so upset about what her husband's fate most probably had been, that Lisa was having a hard time getting through to her.

Nat decided that they should go to Nanaimo first to see what they could find there. They would have to go in during the day because there were too many buildings that the mutants could be hiding in the basements of. After that, they would work their way down the coast of the island, checking the villages along the way, and winding up at Victoria. From there they would go over to Vancouver to see what's left. After leaving Vancouver they would head south into the Puget Sound area.

It was starting to get late so they decided they had better get some sleep so they could get an early start. If they left early enough they could get to Nanaimo before noon weather permitting.

The boat slept eight people, so Nat invited Arn to stay aboard for the night, and he readily accepted, as it gave him a little sense of security being around the others.

During the night Nat suddenly woke up. Laying there he just listened. Then it dawned on him the wind had stopped blowing, and the rain had quit. Quietly he got up to look outside. Moving so as to not awaken the others, he headed for the door to check outside.

"Where are you going?" It was Arn.

"To check outside." Nat whispered.

"Just a minute. I'll go with you."

They both went out onto the rear of the boat. Nat looked up at the sky. "That storm sure cleared out in a hurry. Look at that, hardly a cloud in the sky."

"This is the kind of weather the mutants like, and I don't."

Looking at his watch, Nat observed. "There is still about five hours of dark left. We better keep a guard for the rest of the night. I'll take the first watch, you go get some more sleep."

"Alright, but if you start feeling tired, wake me up."

Arn went back inside, and Nat went on shore just a few feet from the dock, and then stepped into the bushes. He felt that if anybody came down to the dock that they wouldn't expect anybody to be hiding in that spot.

As daylight started to break, he went back to the boat. Arn came out onto the deck, looked around, and stretched. "Morning Nat. You know, that has to be the best night's sleep I've had in one hell'va long time."

Nat smiled at him. "A good night's sleep is probably one of the best things for a body."

"Well, I sure feel good. Either I slept awful hard or you're awful quiet. I didn't even hear you moving around"

"Shouldn't have heard me. I stayed up there in the brush."

"Well, that explains why I didn't hear you moving around."

"Right! Now let's get the gals up and have some coffee."

The women got up, and using the camp stove fixed some breakfast. While having breakfast, Nat outlined what he had planned,

Arn listened intently, and then asked. "Do you mind if I throw in with you?"

Nat looked at him. "I don't mind at all. In fact, I was kind of hoping that you would. We can always use another gun. Besides, you have a better knowledge of what we're up against."

The water was a little choppy but the winds were relatively light, so they made good time. Just before noon they pulled into Nanaimo and tied up.

The town looked awful quiet. So quiet that it was scary just looking at it. They decided that Nat would go first and then Ellen and Lisa would follow, with Sarah and Arn pulling up the rear always keeping each other in sight.

As they worked their way up the streets, it was quite evident that everything had been ransacked. After about an hour, Nat noticed a man and woman duck into a restaurant. He let the others catch up to him, and told them what he had seen.

"Arn! You and Sarah go around to the back of the building,. If they come out the back door, catch them. Don't shoot unless you have to."

Arn and Sarah quickly moved to take up their positions as Nat and the other two got closer to the front. Ellen stayed on one corner of the building while Lisa crawled down to the other corner, so they both could watch the entrance. Nat then crossed the street and by going around back of some shops came through the one just across the street from the restaurant.

A few minutes later the couple came out of the restaurant. As soon as they had taken a few steps Nat hollered. "Freeze right where you're at!"

The couple stopped and didn't move. Then Ellen stepped out with her gun pointed right at them. Nat then came across the street to talk to them. "We're not going to kill you. In fact I'm not even going to take your guns away. I just want to talk."

The man nodded. "Go ahead. Talk."

Nat explained to them about their war against the mutants, and why they had came to Nanaimo.

The man thought for a bit before speaking. "You sound like you're telling the truth, and you look like an honest man."

He continued. "This is Alice, and we hide out with another six people about twenty miles out of town. The only reason we came into town was to scrounge around for more food."

Lisa had gone around back and gotten Arn and Sarah.

Arn asked. "Are there many mutants around here?"

"You betcha'. It's been a constant battle for our lives. Why don't you find a car and follow us out to our hideout?"

Nat told the others to return to the boat, and if he wasn't back by dark to get the boat out of the harbor and find a cove for the night, then come back in the morning.

Since the others weren't going, Nat rode with the couple. He noticed that there were several cars along the road either out of gas, or just broke down. A few were off the road, and he noticed one had been shot up. "What happened there?"

"Not sure." The man answered. "But I think the mutants caught some body going down the road one night and opened fire on them. I looked it over and saw a lot of blood, but no bodies."

It took almost an hour to get where they were going. The hideout was a one story house in the middle of a field. As they pulled into the yard, two men carrying rifles came out to meet them.

Getting out of the car, Nat's escort spoke to one of them. "Jim, this guy I brought, came to talk to us. He's different from most. I feel we can trust him."

The man stuck his hand out. "Hi! My name is Jim. This is Phill." He nodded to the other man that had come out of the house with him. "If Hank says you can be trusted, then that's good enough for me."

"My name is Nat. I mean you and your group no harm."

"Well Nat. Come on inside and have a cup of coffee, and tell us about yourself."

While the coffee was being poured, Nat noticed there were two more women and a boy about twelve years old. Hank had said there were eight people. One was missing.

Nat had a feeling. "One person is missing. I have a feeling I'm being watched in case I start something. Which I have no intention of doing."

Jim smiled. "You're pretty cautious aren't you?"

"That's how I stay alive."

Jim raised his voice. "Okay Sam! Come on out! He knows you're here!"

A tall willowy man with a mis-shappened jaw and distorted mouth came out. Jim nodded toward him. "Sam can't talk. He took a bullet in the face and it put a stop to his speech. It happened one day when a group of men attacked the house about a month after the war."

Jim went on. "At first there were seventeen of us, but the attacks have taken their toll. That particular attack took two of our group. The other seven were killed by attacks from the night people."

"Sure sorry to hear that," Nat said. "I think it's terrible that we have to fight our own kind as well as the mutations."

Phill spoke up. "I agree, but that's the way it's become."

The more they talked, the more they became relaxed with each other. The group told Nat about their plight to survive in a world that had became almost animalistic. Nat in turn told them about Arn and the women, and how they had came together, and now were waging a war against the mutants.

Hank spoke up. "I'll say one thing. You got guts. You're up against almost impossible odds. The mutants out number us. In town alone there are probably at least two hundred of them"

Nat looked at him. "Why sit and let them come pick you off one at a time?" Why not become the hunter instead of the hunted?"

"He's got a point there." Jim said. "But they have an advantage. They can see at night and we can't. And during the day they go into hiding."

"That's true," Nat said, "but on the other hand we have something to our advantage also. If I understand right, they can't stand bright lights, or water. That's two weapons we have besides our guns."

Jim nodded in agreement. "That's an interesting idea. I hadn't considered using them as weapons, but you're right. They would make damn good weapons."

Nobody had thought about the time, and then Nat noticed that daylight was starting to fade. "It's getting to late for me to get back to town, so do you mind if I bunk down here for the night?"

"You're more than welcome. We'll make up a place for you to bed down." Jim said, and turning to one of the women he spoke. "Alice, see what you can come up with for our guest."

After having a meal of delicious stew and more talk, Nat got ready to turn in. They had given him one of the beds, but noticing they only had two beds, he declined so one of the women didn't have to sleep on the floor. Alice insisted that he take the bed, but he wouldn't hear of it. She finely gave up and gave him some blankets. He found a spot and stretched out to get some sleep.

Nat hadn't been asleep long when a gunshot woke him up. He jumped up and ran into the living room. Seeing Phill, he asked. "What the hell is going on?"

"It's those goddamn mutants again!"

A small flash of light appeared at the edge of the field. Jim, Phill, and Alice started shooting at it, and it went out. Jim explained. "That was a flaming arrow they were going to shoot. We watch for them to light one, and then we all aim at that point. Sometimes there are more than one at a time, and it gets touchy."

Another light appeared and Nat brought his rifle up and shot before the others, and the light went out.

"Goddamn!" Jim said. "You're a hell-of a good shot!"

Nat smiled. "Just lucky that time. But if you want to save ammo, wait a second when you see the flame and then shoot directly below the flame and a hair to the right. That way they will be drawing back to shoot and you know that they are almost directly in line of the flame."

Just then another appeared. "Watch!" Nat said. He paused, took aim and fired. The flame arched for a short distance and then hit the ground.

Then all of the sudden there was three flames. Phill said he had the middle one, and Jim said he had the one on the left. The three men fired at the same time, and two of the flames arched for a short distance, and the other just dropped.

After about two hours the shooting stopped, and Hank spoke. "Well, that's it for the night."

"How do you know?" Nat asked.

"It's always the same. They give up after a while and move on. We still stand guard tho', because they could always change their minds."

Nat had trouble getting back to sleep, and when he finally did, it was a troubled sleep. The smell of coffee brewing woke him up. As he got up he noticed that the women had already arisen and Hank and Sam were in the beds. They must have been who stood guard last night he assumed.

Upon coming out of the bedroom, they all bid him a "Good morning." Alice gave him a hot cup of coffee.

He sipped at his coffee then asked. "Has anybody gone out and counted how many we managed to kill?"

Jim answered. "Wouldn't do any good, because they always take their dead with them."

They talked about the fight during the night over coffee, and then Nat announced that he had to be getting back to his group on the boat.

After a short silence Jim spoke up. "We have been thinking about what you said yesterday. You know, about becoming the hunter and all that. What do you think about all of us joining up with your group?"

Nat didn't have to think it over. He had hoped they would want to. "I think it would be a good idea, and safer for all of us."

Phill got up. "I'll wake up Hank and Sam, and then we better pack what we want to take with us."

Jim turned to Nat. "Want to help me load the ammo and guns?"

"Sure!" Jim led the way down into the basement that Nat hadn't realized was there. He was surprised at the amount of weapons, and ammo, they had amassed. "Looks like you have built up quite an arsenal here."

"We did that shortly after the war. It was Hank's idea, he foresaw what was coming, and I'm glad he did. He still goes out looking for more quite often."

Besides the car they had a pickup, and they loaded the guns and ammo in the back, leaving very little room for anything else. After getting loaded they headed into town. Jim drove the pickup and Nat and the boy rode with him. Shortly after pulling out onto the road, Jim commented, "Sure hope nobody decides to take a pop shot at us, 'ause if they were to hit that stuff in the back it would be the end of us. I don't know whether you noticed it or not, but there are 14 boxes of dynamite packed in there."

"I noticed it." Nat said. Nothing more was said the rest of the trip.

As they pulled down by the water front Nat saw the boat tied up, but he didn't see anybody around it. He was afraid something had happened to them as he opened the door and got out. Looking around the area for any movement, he walked around to the front of the pickup. Just as he headed for the dock, Arn' head popped up in sight from inside the boat. Hi Nat!"

Nat waved. "Come ashore! We need your help!"

Arn and the others came up to the pickup, and after introductions were made, Arn turned to Nat. "You missed the excitement last night."

"That's what you think." He went on to tell them what had happened out at the house during the night. "Now, tell me about the excitement that I missed"

"Well, we pulled out of here and went up the coast a few miles and found a little cove to anchor in. A little before midnight we heard a boat. At first I thought it was going to go on by without seeing us. They didn't tho', and turned in toward us,. We waited until they were about twenty yards or so away then shined the spot light on them and opened fire at the same time. They didn't have a chance. The one at the controls evidently fell against the throttle, because the boat all of the sudden started picking up speed, and shot right past us and ran aground so hard it killed the motor"

"We checked it out this morning when it got light, and there were two mutants on board. I didn't look to close, but I could tell we had hit them several times. Also we got a couple more guns and some ammo."

Nat chuckled. "Wait till you see what we got in the back of the pickup."

Arn walked around to the back of the truck and looked. "Wow! There is enough stuff there to blow the hell out of anybody!"

"These folks have elected to join us in the battle against the mutants." Nat answered. "I see there are several cabin cruisers tied up here. Let's check to see if by any chance there are any keys in one or two of them."

I already did that," Arn said, "and there isn't any."

"Well then we will have to hot-wire a couple of them."

Jim spoke up. "Maybe we can take the ignition switches out of the car and truck, and then wire them up to the boats."

Nat gave it a thought. "It sure won't hurt to try. Go ahead and pull the ones out of the car and truck while Arn and I pull some out of a couple of boats."

Nat picked two boats that he felt would be the best ones. After removing one of the ignition switches, Hank showed up with the one out of the car. It took a little figuring, but he finally got the car switch to work. The next one went easier. Evidently the mutants had been using the boats, as the batteries were fully charged.

After getting everything loaded aboard the boats, Nat asked Hank. "Is the water system in this town still hooked up?"

"I think so, let's check,."

They got a big pipe wrench and opened a fire hydrant. Water shot out with plenty of pressure. After shutting it off, Nat explained his plan.

"Now we know what water does to the mutants. If we find a fire department in this town, we can take the hoses, hook them up to the hydrants, and then pump water into some of these buildings. The water will find its way into any basements, and hopefully drive the mutants out into the open. We can pick them off as they come out."

Everybody agreed that it was a good idea, and as good a time as any to start their battle against the mutants.

"Hank volunteered. "I know where a fire station is, let's go."

They all headed for the station, and upon arriving, found just about everything pretty much in order.

"Guess what!" Arn stated. "The trucks still have the keys in them."

Jim turned to Nat. "Well, what are we waiting for? Any suggestions as to where we start?"

"As a matter of fact I was thinking that maybe the theater. It's designed to be dark inside, so probably there are several holed up in there."

There were two trucks, so Jim drove one and Nat drove the other, while the rest climbed on.

Upon arriving at the theater they discovered two hydrants near-by, which they hooked the hoses up to.

Nat and Hank took one hose, while Jim and Sam took another. The rest took up positions by the exits. Phill turned the water on, and when Nat gave the signal, Alice shot the locks of the doors. As they rushed in, they took one hose to the right and the other to the left. Bursting into the auditorium, Nat realized how right he had been. A volley of shots was fired as the mutants ran for the exits. Their screams were deafening as the water hit them. Shots were being fired outside as some mutants tried to make an escape out the exits. Lisa stepped up beside Nat and started firing into the auditorium. The whole episode lasted about fifteen minutes.

Nat went outside to see if any of their group had been hit.

CHAPTER 4

Hank had gotten his arm grazed by a bullet, but everyone else was fine. Lisa went over and helped Alice put a wrap around Hank's arm.

They took a count of how many mutants they had killed. Seventy-one. Nat stood looking down at a couple of the mutants. He thought to himself. 'What a pity and disgrace that mankind had to do this to its-self. Man, with the ability to think and reason, had not the foresight to realize that as long as he had the technology to destroy the world, he was bound to do it. Now man is pitted against man because of that lack of foresight.'

Lisa walked over to him. "What are you thinking?"

Nat turned his head and looked at her with sadness in his eyes. "Just what man has done to mankind."

Lisa put her hand on his arm. "Yes, it is a shame, but we have to worry about the future now."

They turned and walked to the others. Nat told them to gather up what they thought were the best weapons, and head down to the boats.

They packed everything they felt was important for their journey. It was getting late when they pulled out of the harbor. A couple of hours later they dropped anchor in a small cove for the night.

Taking turns through the night at watch things went smooth. Twice a boat went by, but didn't even slow down.

The next day they pulled into Victoria. Nat felt that this place would be a hotbed of mutants, so he cautioned them to proceed very slowly, and, to keep their eyes peeled for any movement what-so-ever.

Nat decided to send them out in teams to look the town over for mutants, but not to do anything except come back to the boats. They all agreed to be back an hour before dark. Arn led one team, with Nat and Jim leading two others.

Approaching the Empress Hotel, Nat, noticed that most of the windows had been broken out, but otherwise it was still in good shape.

As they stepped into the lobby Lisa said. "Kinda' scary isn't it?"

Nat nodded in agreement and signaled for her to be quiet. Looking around, he sensed that there were others present in the building. He stopped and listened closely for a while, then crept over to the elevator and put his ear up to it. After listening a couple of minutes, he signaled for the others to go outside.

Outside he explained that he had heard movements that sounded like people moving around, and a noise that sounded as if something had been dropped. He then surmised that this might be a large gathering of the mutants.

They then proceeded up and down the streets, checking out the various shops and stores, realizing that mutants could be in the basement of any one of them. All of the places had been pillaged and broken up.

Upon returning to the boats, Nat related what they had seen to the others. After a general discussion, it was agreed that if anybody had survived the radiation and the mutants they would be on the outskirts of town, but they had to do something about the mutants.

Nat decided that the others should take the boats to some cove for the night and he would stay in town to watch and observe the mutants to make sure this was a strong hold, and tomorrow they would decide what to do about them.

Arn wanted to stay with Nat, but Nat vetoed that, but agreed to let Ellen stay with him. Any more than two would be dangerous.

As the others left, Nat and Ellen made their way up to the top of the Parliament building. After making sure they were in a place where no one could sneak up on them, they settled in for the night.

Shortly after dark the moon cast enough light so Nat could make out just about everything around the area. It wasn't long before the mutants came out of the hotel and were milling around. Mutants started coming from other parts of town also, so that meant they were all over, several of them left in boats to pull their nightly raids, Nat assumed.

Nat and Ellen decided to take turns watching what was going on while the other one catnapped.

Nat quickly awoke as Ellen touched his shoulder. "Nat! Look! One of the boats just came back, and they have some hostages!"

Tasking the binoculars, he looked down at the scene a little closer. They had a man and woman and a girl about twelve or thirteen years old. All had been stripped and hands tied behind their backs, and were being pushed along. The girl tripped and fell to the ground, and one of the mutants started kicking her until she go up. At the same time the man tried to charge the one that was kicking at the girl, while the woman was screaming at the mutant to stop. Two mutants started to beat on the man with rifle butts, knocking him to the ground. They then picked him up and gave him a shove toward the hotel. Other mutants came over to gather around and look, occasionally one would reach out and probe or feel the captives.

As Ellen watched in horror, she knew that there was nothing they could do to help the people, but she asked anyway. "Isn't there anything we can do to save them?"

Nat's muscle tightened. "No, nothing." He knew what their fate was, and it made him mad and sick at the same time. A short time later they heard the screams of agony as people were being tortured to death.

Three more boats brought back people, and the scene was the same each time. Neither one of them slept the rest of the night.

As soon as it was daylight they went down to the dock to await Arn and the others. A half hour had passed before they showed up. On board the boat Nat related what they had seen during the night. All agreed that something had to be done that day.

Arn suggested that they flood them out like they did before, but Nat pointed out that the way the building was they could avoid the water. Jim thought they could set the building on fire, but there was no guarantee that the fire would get to them down where they were at.

Lisa spoke up. "We have that dynamite we picked up in Nanaimo."

"Right!" Arn said. "We could blast them out."

"Not quite." Nat responded. "But we could bury them."

"I think I see what you mean." Said Jim, in deep thought."

Nat arose. "Let's go look the building over."

They spent the next two hours looking the building over for the right places to set the dynamite.

It will take most of the dynamite we have." Nat stated, "But I think we can do it."

It took another two hours to set the charges. Nat cut all the fuses the same length to be lit at the same time.

"Okay, Now everybody that's lighting a fuse. Set your watches to be exactly the same time. Those of you lighting the ones on the inside will have ten minutes to get out. So run like hell, and don't fall down. I'm going up on the third floor and set a fire, and then I'm getting my ass out of there, so it will be up to you to get the fuses lit on the first try. I should be out of the building before you light them, so don't worry about me."

A time was agreed on and Nat took off to set the fire,. Upon reaching the third floor he got sick to his stomach at what he found. There were seventeen bodies hanging like beef carcasses from the ceiling. On the floor was blood and guts that stunk so bad he could hardly stand it. Mixed into the innards were several dozen heads of men, women, and children. Some of the bodies were missing arms and legs.

As quickly as possible, Nat found as much furniture as he could, and piled it in the room and set it on fire. When he was sure the fire would keep going he started outside to safety. Just as he was starting down the stairs he tripped and fell. He felt his left leg and left arm break as he was tumbling down the stairs. The pain was excruciating as he came to a stop.

Looking at his watch he realized they were going to light the fuses in fifteen minutes, so that only gave him twenty-five minutes to get out. He didn't want to holler for help because that would ruin their whole plan. If he hollered the mutants would hear him and know something was up. The others would not light the fuses as planned and take time to get him out. It was too close to dark to postpone it.

He had to try to get out on his own or die along with the mutants. It took him about seven minutes to crawl down the rest of the way to the second floor. The pain was so great he had to stop for a minute to rest. Nat then pulled himself up onto his right leg and hopped down to the landing just above the main floor. As he was hopping down the rest of the way he fell and rolled down the remainder of the steps. Laying there in a state or pure pain he was ready to concede that he wasn't going to make it and closed his eyes to accept his fate, Just then Arn came running around the corner, but didn't see Nat in time, and tripped over him.

It didn't take Arn long to realize the situation. He helped Nat up onto his right leg, but the pain was so great that Nat couldn't even hobble along. Nat told Arn to leave him and get out. "No way!" Arn said.

Arn then put him over his shoulders and started to carry him out, but Nat was such a big man that Arn could hardly carry him. Arn struggled but managed to keep going even tho' it was slow. Just as they started out the door the dynamite blew. The blast knocked them down the steps and glass and debris was flying all over them. Nat passed out from the pain, and Arn was hit in the head and knocked unconscious by a flying piece of debris.

When Nat came to, he realized that his leg and arm had been set and he was in a berth aboard one of the boats. He sensed that someone was beside him and he turned his head. It was Lisa.

"You had a close call." She said.

"Yeah, I guess I did, but I made it. Thanks to Arn. Is he alright?"

"He's okay, just a few cuts and bruises, Sarah patched him up."

"Good! I'll say one thing! This is the sorest I've ever been in my life. I think every part of me hurts."

"What happened up there anyway?"

The scene of the bodies flashed through his mind. He decided not to tell her about that. I tripped just as I started down the stairs. I hopped, crawled, and rolled down to the first floor. That's where Arn found me."

"Arn said he tripped over you"

"That's right. He was running so fast he didn't have time to stop."

"Well, it's a good thing he found you."

"By the way." Nat asked, "How successful was we anyway?"

"Mission completed! If there was anything living in that hotel, it's dead now. After the blast the fire took over and completely destroyed the building. It was starting to get dark so we got out of there."

"Where are we now?"

"Heading for a cove on the mainland to give you a little time to heal."

They reached the cove the next morning which was located north of Vancouver, and almost completely hidden.

While Nat was recuperating the others went out a few at a time and brought back food and managed to find more survivors. By the time three months had passed, their party had increased to over a hundred people. They all seemed to look to Nat for advice and leadership.

When Nat felt he was well enough to travel he felt they should work their way south into the Puget Sound area.

That morning everyone gathered around Nat to hear what he had planned for the next leg of their uncertain journey into the unknown.

Nat, raising his hands for silence, spoke in a voice that was not loud, but carried to the farthermost person. "From here we are going to travel south into the Puget Sound area to see what is left, and if there are any survivors such as ourselves. If there are any, shall we say, normals, and then it is up to us to find them, and help them. Look around you. What you see is a small drop of people compared to what was. From what we have seen, the mutants outnumber us by a very large percentage. If we stick together, we can survive. Any of you that want to stay, can. Those that are going, gather up your things and get aboard the boats"

Turning around, Nat headed for his boat without looking back. If he had of he would have seen every person picking up their things and heading for a boat. The people wanted to follow Nat. To them he was their leader no matter what happened in life or death.

Like a small armada they pulled out of the cove and headed south. The weather was perfect for traveling by boat even if it was still winter. As they passed Vancouver a lot of them got their first view of a city that took a direct hit with a nuclear bomb. The city looked like a pile of rubble from a distance. Nothing was standing for miles. Ships had sunk in the harbor, buildings and trees were flattened. An eerie quiet death seemed to hang over the city.

Not one person spoke as they viewed what was left of a once large, thriving city full of Lile. Nat went to the side of the boat and started vomiting over the side. The whole scene had made him sick.

Lisa came over and put her hand on his shoulder. "Anything I can do?"

Nat turned and looked at her. His complexion was pale as he spoke with a twisted face. "Not unless you can take us all back in time. Before this happened, and prevent it."

She really didn't know what to say or do. A tear came to her eyes as she put her arm around Nat, and she spoke more to herself than to him, "I wish I could."

It was almost dark when they reached Whidbey Island. After finding a place to spend the night, some went ashore to check the area out for safety. Some of the women went ashore and started fires to fix supper for everyone, and the rest secured the boat by tying them together and dropping anchors.

After supper most returned to the boats, but a few pitched tents preferring to sleep on solid ground. Guards were posted and everybody settled down for the night.

Nat was having a tough time getting into a sound sleep and kept tossing and turning in his berth. His restlessness was keeping Ellen awake, as she slept in the berth above him. After a couple of hours she slipped out of her berth and lowered herself down as quietly as possible. Nat, who always seemed to hear any movement out of the ordinary, came wide awake, listening for what could have caused Ellen to get up.

She knelt beside him and ran her hand over his chest. "You're not sleeping well." She whispered.

He didn't answer as she slid under the covers next to him. Ellen was already naked and, Nat could feel her warm soft body next to him. His passion mounted as her hand gently skid down his bare chest to his belt. She undone his pants swiftly and reached for his manhood. Lifting his body slightly he helped her remove his clothes. They came together in a heated passion, releasing their frustrations and tensions.

A heavy rain had started to fall on the deck above them, but neither heard it. Afterward, they lay side-by-side exhausted. Nat turned toward her. "It's raining pretty hard," he whispered, "that's good."

She didn't answer him, only smiled and thought to herself. 'He's a beautiful man. Always aware of everything and is so compassionate.' Rising she kissed him lightly on the forehead, noticing that he was already asleep, and returned to her own berth.

Later on in the night, Nat came awake with a start. Listening, he couldn't tell what could have awakened him. He then remembered that he had been dreaming about his wife, and that fateful night. It also dawned on him that the rain had stopped. Quietly he got up, pulled his pants on, and went outside. The sky was still heavily laden with clouds, but the moon was getting ready to break out of them. He lit his pipe and went over to the side of the boat, and just looked into the dark murky water, thinking about his wife.

He thought about the good times. Of how they always did things together, like going hunting, and walking on the beach. How they laughed at dumb little things, and each other's little mistakes.

Nat remembered the time when they came upon a dead seal that someone had shot, and she cried over the senseless killing and insisted that he bury it. Nat refused to bury it, but dragged it down to the water, and explained that by doing that he was helping other lives to live. He told her that the scavengers like crabs and birds would feed upon it. They had just as much right to live as the next. Then she understood what he was saying and stopped crying.

For once, Nat was so deep in thought, that he didn't realize that someone was approaching from in back of him.

CHAPTER 5

Suddenly he snapped back into the present. Nat didn't hear anything, but he sensed he was not alone. Just as his muscles tensed he felt a pair of hands on his shoulders.

The hands were soft and gentle, as they slid down his back and around his waist. Lisa laid her cheek against his back and held him tight. "It's cold out here. You should have a shirt on."

He felt her warmth against his back. "I didn't plan on being out here long."

"You have been out here for a good half hour."

"I guess I just forgot about time."

"What's bothering you? Are you alright?"

He turned in her arms, and put his around her. "I'm alright. Just memories."

Lisa looked up into his face, and tears came to her eyes. "I know. It happens to me too."

He reached up, and wiped away her tears and kissed her on the forehead. "I guess we just have to learn to live with them. It's hard at times, I know, but if we work at it we can learn to appreciate the fact that we are able to have the good memories and blank out the bad."

"I guess I'm still trying to learn how to do that. Could you teach me how?"

"No---you have to learn that yourself. Nobody can teach you."

Nat had a special feeling for Lisa because he knew she had been through a lot. He bent over and kissed her trembling lips. The kiss was tender, but with deep feelings. Nothing more was said as they went back inside to get some sleep.

The next morning everybody gathered on shore for breakfast which consisted of coffee and stone cakes. Everybody talked amongst themselves except Nat. He was off to one side deep in thought. Arn came over and sat down next to him. "Something bothering you?"

"Sort of. I'm trying to decide about all of our futures."

"Boy! That's a tough one."

"Yeah! But I think I got an idea. I just hope that everybody agrees with me."

"Arn slapped him on the back. "Nat---if it's your idea, every one of them will go along with you. You are their 'El Cid'."

"Well I wouldn't say that, but I know they all listen to what I have to say. I just hope they agree with me on this one."

Arn stood up. "Let's go find our!"

Nat got up and walked over to the others. After pouring another cup of coffee he held up his hand to get their attention. When everyone had quieted down he started to speak. "I have been doing some deep thinking, and I foresee some problems coming up. Right now I know of four women that are pregnant. Being on the move all of the time is not going to be easy on them. Another thing, and I'm not trying to frighten anybody, is that we don't know how much radiation the mothers were exposed to. I think we all hope the babies are born healthy."

"Now, one thing we are going to have to do is find a place to settle down. A sort of a home base. This many people on the move could work against us. As far as we know, the mutants have not organized into large groups. The time may come when they do. If this were to happen, we would lose, because they out number us. So, what it boils down to is this. We have to have more security."

"I have given several places some thought, and feel there is only one place that stands out as a good possibility. That one place is deep in the Olympic Mountains. If we can find a good valley to settle in, we can build us a town, so-to-speak."

"The snow in the winter will help to protect us from the mutants. In the summer the fertile ground will help us to raise crops, and there is plenty of game around for meat. We can gather up some cows and chickens for our dairy products."

"I'm sure we can find a portable sawmill to cut the lumber for our homes. We have the manpower to build that town, and enough ingenuity to work out any other problems that we come across. Also a dam can be built for water supply and electricity."

"This will give us and our children a place to call home. I have built a home in the wilderness, so I am aware of the problems that have to be overcome. The secret of this being a success is that we all work together towards a common goal."

"Now, I want you all to think about what I have just said, and talk it over amongst yourselves. When you have decided what you want to do, let me know." Nat then sat down.

Jim got to his feet, looked around at the people, then back at Nat. "Well, the way I see it, is this. You have drawn us a picture, and if anybody here can't see it, they are either dumb or blind. I feel I am speaking for the rest, when I say, what are we waiting for? Let's go build us a town! A town that we can all be proud of!" He turned back to the others. "Am I right?"

Everybody voiced their agreement, and gave three cheers for Nat.

Arn slapped Nat on the shoulder. "What did I tell ya?"

Nat smiled. "Well, I guess you were right." He was pleased that they had agreed with him. Now they had a purpose and a reason to survive.

Lisa and Ellen walked over to Nat just as a young couple came up to him. The young man stuck his hand out and shook Nat's hand. "My name is Will, and this is Jenny. We would like to know if you will marry us?"

Nat was dumbfounded. He looked at Ellen, then Lisa, and both were smiling. Looking back at the young couple, he put a hand on the young man's shoulder, and the other on the girl's "The fact that you two want to join together and build a life for the future, is one of the most beautiful things I've heard for a long time now. You two have just proven to me, that there is a true hope for a future of mankind. It's that hope, I think we all have been looking for."

"I want you both to face each other, and hold each other's hands." They turned and done as he told them. "Now!   Deep down in your hearts, tell yourselves that this is what you truly want, and that you love the other. Now seal it with a kiss."

As they completed their kiss, Nat looked at them with warmth. "You are now married, and I wish you both a very happy life together."

Will shook Nat's hand. "Thank you sir."

Jenny reached up and pulled Nat's head down and kissed him on the cheek. "We will never, never forget you, for the rest of our lives. If our first born is a boy, we will name him after you." They both then turned and left to start getting their things together.

Nat turned and looked at Ellen and Lisa. "Well, it probably wasn't the best wedding, but it sure was my first time at doing that sort of thing."

Ellen smiled. "It may not have been a long one, but I think it was the most beautiful one I've ever seen."

Lisa had tears rolling down her cheeks. "I think so too."

Nat was concerned. "What's the matter? Why are you crying?"

Lisa wiped at the tears. "I always cry at weddings"

"Oh." He said feeling awkward. "Well, we better get a move on. Everybody is just about ready to pull out."

After everybody got ready to set out, Nat looked the boats over. Not too far away, he saw Will and Jenny in a small, beat up boat. He turned to Arn. "See that little dilapidated boat with the young couple in it?"

Arn looked where he was pointing. "Yeah."

"That boat will not make the trip out in these waters. Flag them over here, and tell them to join us. We have enough room."

"I see what you mean. It wouldn't make it a mile out before it sank." Arn hollered and motioned them to pull over next to them as Nat went below to study some maps.

When they got close, Will asked Arn. "What is the matter?"

"You got orders to abandon ship and come aboard this one, because that one won't make the trip in one piece."

Will knew that it might not, so he tossed their gear over to Arn. "You sure you got enough room for us? We don't want to crowd you folks."

"Don't worry about it. We got lots of room to spare. And besides, its orders from Nat."

Will helped Jenny over to the other boat, and then came over himself. "We sure do appreciate you folks doing this."

Arn grinned. "Remember---we help each other. That's how we are going to make it. My name is Arn. What's yours?"

"I'm Will, and this is Jenny. Nat married us on shore just before we set out."

Arn hadn't known about the wedding until now. "Well, I'll be damned!" He then grabbed Will and pushed him towards the helm. "Congratulations! I'll be back in a minute!" Turning quickly he headed down below.

"Well, well, Preach. You didn't tell me that you performed marriages."

Nat looked up from the maps,. "I didn't know myself, until today"

Ellen turned around and spoke. "I might add that it was one fantastic wedding. Short! But fantastic!"

Arn sided over to Nat and spoke low, so that only Nat could hear. "Damn! You don't suppose you could do it again do you?"

Nat knew what was coming. "I can't hear you. Can you speak a little louder?"

Now Arn started to fidget, and turned red. "Can I talk to you alone for a minute?"

"Well, we don't have any secrets around here." He turned and looked a Lisa, Ellen, and Sarah, then winked. "Don't the rest of you agree?"

"Ah! Come on Nat!" He was getting desperate. "It's kinda personal."

"Okay. Let's go to the forward cabin."

As soon as the door closed Arn spoke up. "Listen! I want to get married. Would you do it?"

Nat was enjoying the whole thing. "Oh---I suppose I could. Who is the lucky lady?"

Arn's mouth dropped open, "You!---You!---Oh shit! You know damn good and well it's Sarah! Who else could it be?"

"Well, you're a young buck, and I don't keep tabs on you. Maybe you were getting around when I wasn't looking."

"Oh come on now! Sarah and I have always been side-by-side, and you know it. I love her, and I wouldn't even consider any other woman."

"Have you asked Sarah about this?"

"No. I want to surprise her."

Nat got a knowing smile. "Oh."

Arn pressed. "Well? Will you do it?"

"I suppose I could. But there is a slight problem here."

"Huh? What problem?"

"If I marry you now, we will have two sets of newlyweds on board, and we only have this one room that's private."

"Oh shit! Sarah and I are not virgins by any means. They can have the room. We don't care."

Just then a knock came at the door. Nat opened it, and it was Lisa. "Storms coming up. Ellen has gone topside to take over the helm."

"Thanks." Nat answered. "Let's go Arn."

As soon as they got topside Nat looked out toward the storm. It was coming out of the west, right down the Strait of Juan de Fuca, and looked like it was going to be a good blow. He turned to Arn. "Signal the other boats to pull in closer so we can render any help if needed." He then headed up to take over from Ellen.

When he got there she let him have the wheel. With a sigh of relief she commented. "Glad you're here. I don't think I could have handled this one."

"Sure you could have. Now go down and help the others watch for any other boats that might need help."

She hurried to join the others as Nat prepared to fight the storm out.

"Boat floundering off the right side! People are in the water!" Arn yelled.

"Is anybody close to them?" Nat yelled back.

"It looks like Jim is closing in on them! Yeah! It's Jim! I think he's going to get to them in time!"

"Let me know how he's doing!"

"Will do!"

Nat was too busy fighting the wheel to be able to watch the rescue operation. He hollered down. "How many in the water."

Arn tried to count but couldn't tell. "I don't know! At least five! Jim just fished one out of the water! No, make that two!"

A few minutes later Arn yelled again. "I just seen one go under, and I haven't seen him come back up! Jim just got another!"

"Damn-it-all." Nat thought to himself. "I sure hope we don't lose any more!"

Nat heard Lisa yell. "There he is! Jim is trying to get a line to him!"

The Sarah yelled. "I think there are two people still hanging onto the boat!"

"I see 'em!" Arn yelled. "I don't think Jim can see them tho'!"

Nat knew he had to do something and do it quick. He slacked off on the throttle and let the storm carry him closer to the floundering boat. If he misjudged, his boat would slam into the troubled boat and probably cost those two peoples lives that were hanging on. Nat's boat started to turn sideways to the storm. Quickly he opened the throttle full speed and it started to straighten out again. He ventured to take a quick look for the other boat. No-where could he see it.

Suddenly he heard Arn yell. "Hold it there if you can! We are right beside them!"

Nat was working the throttle and wheel with all he had in him, praying he didn't slam into the other boat.

"We got them on board! We got them! We got them!" They were all hollering.

Nat felt a jolt, and knew he had just slammed into the other boat. Shoving the throttle to the full speed position, he hoped his boat didn't get damaged from the collision.

Lisa appeared at his side. "The other boat just went down. I think when we hit it that finished it."

"Could anybody tell if it did us any damage?"

"I don't think so. Our back corner is what hit it. It would be too risky for anyone to try to lean over and look."

"I know. I hope no one tries. If we start taking on water, we will know then. How are the two we saved?"

"Cold, wet, and grateful. They will be all right. Ellen and Jenny took them below."

The storm lasted for another two hours, and Lisa stayed with Nat. When the winds started to die down, Arn came up and offered to take over.

"You sure as hell can take over. I've had it." He took two steps and fell down.

Lisa was right there. "What's a matter? Are you all right"

"To tell you the truth. I haven't got any strength left in me."

"What do you want me to do?"

"Let me lie here, and go get me a cup of coffee."

She was only gone for a few minutes. "There was still some left in the thermos. Here."

"Thank you. Now, would you be so kind as to find me a blanket: I feel awful cold."

When she left, Arn asked. "Are you going to be all right?"

"Oh yeah. I'll just lay here for a bit and relax my muscles. Give me a half hour and I'll be up and around."

Lisa returned with a blanket and a pillow. She put the pillow under his head, then put the blanket over him and tucked it in around him. "This should help. Ellen has put on some fresh coffee. As soon as it's ready I'll bring you some."

"If I had the strength I'd kiss you."

Arn chirped up. "Man, you must be weak."

Lisa laughed. "Well, I'm not!" She bent over and gave him a deep warm kiss.

Nat got a sheepish grin on his face. "I feel better already."

She bent over and gave him another, lighter kiss. "That's from everybody else, for a job well done. I think everyone felt a lot safer through the storm knowing you were at the controls."

"Well, I thank you for the vote of confidence. Did we lose any other boats?"

Arn spoke up. "I'm counting right now."

Nat looked at Lisa. "You know you don't have to stay up here, if you want to go below."

I know, but I want to stay here in case you want anything. How are you feeling?"

"I'm starting to feel a little better already."

"Looks like we lost two more." Arn reported, "But I don't know who yet."

"Lisa, help me try to stand up. I got to have a look.

Arn turned around. "You just stay put! There is nothing you can do now. Besides, Jim is edging over towards us. Maybe he knows."

"I still gotta' get up,"

"Oh no you don't!" Lisa glared, "If you try, I'll sit on you, and I'm not a light as I look."

Nat decided that since it was put to him in that manner, he had better stay put. He felt Arn idle the boat down to a slower speed. A few minutes later he felt the boat bump against something.

Arn turned to Lisa. "Will you take the wheel? I'm going down to get Jim. He just came aboard,"

"Sure! I'll be glad to."

He headed down below, and in a few minutes he returned with Jim.

When Jim saw Nat he looked shocked. "What happened? You get hurt?"

Nat looked up at him and grinned. "Naw! Just laying down on the job."

Kneeling down, Jim looked at him closer. "Cut the kidding. You don't look so good."

"Well, I'm alright. Just a little weak. I was at the helm all through the storm, and it just wore me out. I'll be alright in a little bit."

"I hope so." Said Jim, showing his concern. "That was really some rescue operation you pulled off today. I don't think I could have handled a boat like you did. Especially a boat this size"

"It wasn't because I knew what I was doing. I just figured I had to do something, and I got lucky."

"Well, either luck or skill, it worked. We lost two other boats, but saved the people off them. One of the other boats lost a man overboard. I haven't found out who yet, or which boat. That guy with the thirty-eight footer. What's his name? Ken! Well, he said he has lots of room if you want to transfer those two you saved over to his boat."

"Sure, that's fine. Arn can go ahead and take care of that. What about the ones you took on?"

"Three of them are going over to Ken's boat. By the way, where are we going to go ashore on the Olympic peninsula?"

"I figured we could take shelter behind the Dungeness spit for the night, and then go into Port Angles tomorrow morning."

"Isn't that kind of a risky place to take shelter? There could be quite a few mutants around the Port Angles area."

"Damn good chance of that. We will have to post extra guards during the night, but I feel it's just as safe as any place else. I figure we can find some trucks in Port Angeles, and then we can drive up the Elwa River as far as possible, then hike in to where we feel is a good spot to build and then build a road to that spot."

"Sounds okay to me, but I'm still nervous about tonight. Well, I had better get back to my boat. I'll talk to you at Dungeness."

"Okay. Take it easy."

Jim headed back to his boat, and Arn took over the helm from Lisa.

Lisa came over and sat down beside Nat. "Feeling any better?"

"Yeah. Help me sit up."

She helped him sit up and he leaned against the side. "Thanks. This beats the hell out of laying flat on your back. I could go for another cup of coffee too."

"Sure. I'll be right back." She jumped up and headed down below.

Arn turned his head. "Ken is starting to close in on us. Where is Lisa?"

"She went to get me a cup of coffee."

"When she gets back she can take over, and I'll go below and get ready for the transfer."

Lisa was back in short order. "Here's some fresh coffee."

"Thanks. Arn wants you to take over for him so he can go down and help transfer those two we saved over to Ken's boat."

"What do I do?"

"Just keep a steady speed, and a straight course. The other boat will do the rest."

"I'll try." She stood up and took over the helm while Arn went below.

The transfer only took a few minutes, and Arn returned to Nat and the helm. "It went beautiful. They said to give you there grateful thanks, and hope you feel better quickly."

"I feel pretty good right now. Lisa. Would you help me stand up? Once I get up I think I'll be alright."

She helped Nat to stand up. "You gonna be okay?"

"Yeah. A bit wobbly, but I'll make it now."

"I'll help you down below anyway."

Upon joining the others, Nat promptly sat down. All wanted to know how he felt, and he assured them that he was doing fine.

Sarah came over and put her arms around him and gave him a kiss on the cheek. "Want something to eat, or a cup of coffee?"

"Just a cup of coffee will do."

When she went to get him a cup of coffee, Arn returned down below.

Nat asked. "Whose is at the helm?"

"Lisa."

Arn turned to Nat. "You never did answer me for sure whether or not you would do you-know-what."

Nat then remembered the conversation before the storm came up. "Well, I don't know. I'm still thinking."

"Oh come on! I know you! You don't have to think long to make a decision."

Sarah came back with two cups of coffee and gave Nat and Arn each a cup. "What are you two arguing about?"

Arn shot a look at Nat then he took Sarah's arm. "Let's go into the front cabin. I've got something to ask you!"

"We can't. Will and Jenny are in there."

Arn heard Nat force a cough. He looked at Nat. "Oh knock it off. We are going up top-side." He headed for the door, pulling Sarah along in back of him.

After they disappeared Ellen started laughing. "Man, you sure got him going. Sarah knows what's happening, and is excited about it. Don't worry, she is going to act surprised."

Nat chuckled. "Well, he made it so damn obvious from the start. I think they will be a nice couple. They really care about each other."

"That's true." Ellen got a serious look. "Nat?"

"Yes?'

"Have you ever thought about who could do the marrying, if you wanted to get married?"

Nat thought for a minute about what she had asked. "No---I hadn't thought about the possibility of that ever happening. One thing is, I don't know if I could ever do it. Another thing is that I'm starting to get up in my years. Right now things are too unstable for me to consider it. By the time things do get stable, if they ever do, I'll be too old for anyone to want to be with me.

Just then Arn and Sarah came back into the cabin. They came and stood in front of Nat. Arn looked at him. "Well?"

"Well what?"

"You gonna do it?"

"Do what?"

"Oh shit! You know what! Are you gonna marry us?"

"If you insist. But let's wait until we drop anchor. I'm sure Lisa would like to be in on this too."

The rest of the trip went well, except for the semi-rough waters, and they arrived late in the afternoon. As they pulled into the waters in back of the Dungeness Spit, the surrounding area seemed to have a deathly silence about it.

After all the boats had been lashed together, and the anchors dropped, Nat got Arn and Sarah together. While the others watched, Arn and Sarah became man and wife. Congratulations were made by all and it was a joyous occasion.

A few hours of daylight were left, so Nat sent Jim out with a small party to look the immediate area over for possible mutants.

Nat called Arn down to the cabin. "Arn, I want you to search among our people for a doctor, a teacher, and an engineer. If you find any, send them to see me."

"I'll do it right now."

About ten minutes after Arn left, there was a knock on the door. "Come in!"

A man in his late thirties came in. "My name is Howard, and I understand you're looking for a teacher."

"I am. Please sit down. There are several children in our group. When we start building our town, we are going to have to have a school for them, and give them an education."

"I agree, sir."

"That is going to be your job. It is going to be up to you to get a school built and to set up an educational system for these kids and the ones that follow. Do you think you can do it?"

"I give you my word that I'll do the best I can."

"Thank you."

"Thank you. I'll help you anyway I can." They shook hands and Howard left.

He had no sooner left when two more men came by. "Arn said you were looking for an engineer. Is that true?"

"Yes it is."

"Well, I'm a structural engineer, and this man with me worked for me, and is as good as being a fully fledged engineer."

"What are your names?"

"This here is Charlie, and I'm Bill."

"Okay, I want you to find an architect if possible, if not, you two design a school, medical clinic, a central supply building, and some basic designs for some houses. We also have to build a dam for electricity. Do you think you can do it?"

Bill thought for a minute. "It's a pretty big order, but we'll give it our best shot."

Nat thanked them and they left. He then got out his maps of the Olympic Mountains to look for a good site to build a town. After giving it much thought, he decided that the best area would be on the east side of Mount Olympus in the Elwa Valley.

Ellen came in just as Nat was pouring a cup of coffee. She looked pale as a ghost, as she sat down. "What's the matter?" Nat inquired. "You don't look well."

She looked up at Nat, and tears began to stream down her cheeks, then she put her head down and covered her face with her hands, and started sobbing uncontrollably. She was sobbing so hard, that her whole body was shaking. Nat sat down beside her and put his arms around her. She laid her head on his chest. "Oh Nat! It was horrible!" She sobbed.

CHAPTER 6

Nat waited until her crying settled down. "Would you tell me what happened?"

"One of the women had a premature baby, and it looked horrible." She said in a strained voice then started sobbing again.

Nat picked her up and took her to the forward cabin and laid her on a bunk. "Now you stay here and try to pull yourself together. I'll be back very shortly." He turned and went up topside.

As Nat came out on deck he saw Lisa standing by the railing just staring off into the distance. Walking over to her he saw tears flowing down her cheeks. "You were there also?"

She nodded. "Yes."

"Can you tell me about it?"

"I'll try. Ellen and I were on the boat next to theirs when a man stuck his head out and said his wife was starting to have a baby. It was so---so---deformed."

"Where is the baby now?" Nat queried.

"I don't know. The doctor took it."

"Doctor?"

"Yes. He showed up almost immediately after it was born."

"How about the mother?"

"She went into hysterics when she saw the baby and the doctor gave her a sedative. Ellen and I left right away and came back here."

As he started to leave to find the other boat, she painfully called out to him. "Nat? What's going to happen?"

"What do you mean?"

"Is this going to be everyone's fate? Will there ever be normal babies born? Will we die out, and the mutants survive?"

Nat took Lisa into his arms and held her while he tried to think of the right words to say to help her troubled mind. "What you experienced is bound to happen again, and we have to learn to accept it. It won't be easy, and we will never be able to totally accept it. There will always be sorrow. We feared that this might happen, and now our fears have been realized. But, I don't believe for one second that we aren't going to have normal babies born and mankind, such as us, shall live on and build another society. We <u>have</u> to survive, and we <u>will</u>."

Nothing more was said as they held onto each other. After several minutes, Nat asked her which boat it happened on, and she told him.

"You had better go down below and stay with Ellen. She could use some support right now also."

As Lisa went below, Nat headed for the other boat. On the way Arn stopped him. "Hey! Where are you going in such a big hurry?"

"We have a problem that I think I should look into." Nat answered with concern.

"What's the problem?"

"We've had a birth on one of the boats, and I understand that the baby is pretty badly deformed."

"I'm coming with you." Arn said, and they both proceeded on to the other boat.

As they came on board, a man come out and stopped them from going in. He stuck his hand out. "Hello! You haven't met me yet, but I know that you're Nat, and the young fellow with you is Arn."

Nat shook his hand. "That's right. Then you must be the doctor."

"I am. Alan. Alan Senyek. Medical Doctor."

"How are the mother and baby?"

"Mother is sleeping. Baby is dead."

"Dead?"

"Yes stillborn luckily."

"I understand that it was badly deformed. May I take a look at it?"

"'Fraid not. I immediately put it into a sack with weights and put it overboard, and I think that for all concerned, nothing about this should be publicized. As far as anyone is concerned it was a premature stillborn baby, and should be left at that."

Nat stood silent for a moment, and then spoke. "I suppose you're right. There are other women with us that are expecting, and we don't need to scare them prematurely." He then looked at Arn. "Do you agree?"

"Yes, most definitely."

"Doctor, would you come over to my boat where we can talk for a spell?"

"I would be most honored."

After checking on Ellen and Lisa, Nat and the doctor sat down to talk.

"Well, doctor, tell me a little bit about yourself."

"If you would like. I was born in Tacoma, grew up in Seattle, went to the University of Washington, studied medicine there and back east at a major clinic. Finally settled down in Bellingham."

"Where were you when the bombs were dropped?"

"Hiking in the mountains up in British Columbia. In fact I saw them hit off in the distance. I knew right away what happened. As luck would have it, I was close to a cave. I didn't think I had much of a chance, but I crawled into it anyway. I had a couple off weeks supply of food, so I stayed put. When it started raining a few days later, I figured I just might have a chance. The rains were good hard ones, so I knew the air would get purged enough to breathe safely."

"What did you do when you first ventured out into the open?"

"For the first couple of weeks I didn't see any people anywhere. That is living people. When I did find living people, I was horrified. They needed medical attention, and bad. I found some doctor's offices and pharmacies and gathered up what I could. The more people I treated, the more I became intrigued with the effects of radiation."

"I found just about every type of radiation sickness possible. It didn't take long before I put them into two different categories, those that had been mutated beyond help and those that seemed normal. The ones that were mutated shied away from anyone that looked normal, and stayed in dark places. The mutated only came out at night to forage for food. They could not stand light of any intensity so the food they ate was not cooked. At first they just killed the normal people as if they resented them. Somewhere along the line they became cannibalistic. In the beginning they only ate animals, but that ended once they tasted human flesh. I've never tasted it myself, but I read somewhere that it almost has a sweet taste to it."

"For the first couple of months I was able to get close to some of them and tried to treat them, but they were beyond any treatment I knew of. Their skin had become super sensitive to sunlight and water. When water got onto their skin it seemed to act like acid and melt the tissues. It created a terribly foul odor also. The sunlight created an instant sunburn. Their eyes changed too. The eyelids shrunk back and the eyeballs protruded somewhat. Any type of light will blind them, except a very dim one, such as the noon, or fire. Because of this change in their eye structure, they can see in the dark as well as you or I can see in the light."

"Do you think that through reproduction, they will eventually return to normal sometime in the future Doctor?"

"No! Before you ask me why, I'll tell you. What we have witnessed is an evolutionary change in humans brought on by radiation. The genes have been altered permanently in almost all the cases of mutation. Before this holocaust scientists were making many discoveries in DNA and RNA, but no one could have predicted what the effects of massive doses of radiation would do to the structure of man."

"I predict that somewhere down the road they will start forming into groups and fight each other, and prey on each other when they can't find any normal people to eat. When this happens, we will be caught in the middle. This idea of yours about building a town is a long shot, but it's the only chance the normal people have of existing."

"Another thing I might point out is that if by some chance one of them does have a normal baby, they will undoubtedly kill it. They have already accepted the way they are, and a normal baby would be a freak to them."

"How normal are the normal people?" Nat asked.

"Not everyone is as normal as we would wish them to be. A good portion of us are very normal, but there are quite a few that suffer from some form of radiation sickness. That woman that had the baby also has other disorders with some of her vital organs. I don't expect her to live too much longer, because there is no way of treating her. There are more than a dozen people in our group that are suffering from untreatable radiation sickness, and sadly, all of the women that are pregnant at this time fall into that category."

The doctor continued. "Another sad fact is that a lot of our men have probably become impotent because of the radiation and will not be able to produce offspring. In fact the number of men able to is relatively small. So, to put it plain and simple, we will be producing far fewer babies than people we are losing to start with."

Nat had a grim look on his face as he spoke. "You draw a very disheartening picture Doctor. I realize that the odds are not on our side. But, we have to try. No---we have to succeed at building a new society. Don't you agree?"

"There is absolutely no doubt in my mind about the importance of a new society, and a better one I hope."

"Well, Alan, I'm glad we have you in our group. When we build our town, I'll see to it that you get a small clinic built as soon as possible. In the mean time, just keep up the good work."

"I'm getting pretty low on medical supplies, but I'll do what I can."

"Tomorrow we will be going into Port Angles. Maybe you can restock a little there. I'm sure the pharmacies and doctor's offices will have some things we can use. Also there is a hospital there."

"I sure hope so. I've found that so far those places have been pretty well ransacked, but I'll make do with what I get."

As the doctor started to leave, he stopped and turned around. "By the way Nat. I've been keeping notes on all the cases I've treated. If you ever get time, you are welcome to look at them"

"I would be very interested in doing that some time. Thank you."

Shortly after the doctor left, Jim came in. "Well Nat, I looked the area over for a few miles around us, and I don't like it one bit."

"What did you find?"

"Soon after we landed we came across a pickup truck by a house. Upon examining it we discovered it had a cellar. Since the pickup was in working order and looked as if it had been driven lately, we assumed that some mutants were probably holed up in the cellar. After setting the house on fire, five of them came running out of the cellar, they was easy to shoot because they couldn't see so good in the sunlight."

"As we drove around we burned out a couple more small groups, I tell ya Nat, this area has an awful lot of those mutants around here."

Nat thought for a minute. "Any idea as to how many?"

"Probably a few thousand at least."

"How many of us would you say there are?"

"Oh---about one hundred and sixty-five. Give or take a couple."

"That means the odds are not exactly in our favor I'd say."

"No shit!" Jim retorted.

Tomorrow we will see what we can do to change the odds."

"What have you got in mind?"

"When we get into Port Angeles, most of the people can start looking for things that we need, and a group of us can spend our time looking for, and destroying mutants. I think it's high time for them to become aware of the fact that they are being hunted too."

"Good! Well, I got to get going back to my boat and get something to eat. I'm starved. See you in the morning."

"Good night."

Nat went forward where Lisa and Ellen were. Lisa, will you go find Arn and tell him I want to talk to him?"

"Sure, I'll be back with him in a few minutes."

After Lisa went out, Ellen looked at Nat?"

"I'll let you know when Arn gets here. How are you feeling?"

"I'm okay now. Sorry I fell apart."

"No need to apologize. I understand."

A few minutes later Arn came in followed by Sarah and Lisa. "What's the problem?" Arn asked. "Lisa said for me to get my ass down here, 'cause you wanted to talk to me."

"Everybody sit down and I'll tell you." After they sat down, he continued. "Jim went ashore with a small party as you know. He said that the area is heavily populated with mutants, probably a few thousand"

They all looked at each other and Arn spoke up. "I sure hope they don't find out that we are here."

"I'm afraid they will find us. Jim said they killed several of the mutants, so I'm sure they will be looking for us as soon as it gets dark."

"Do you think we should leave before it gets dark then?" Ellen asked.

"No, because it will start getting dark in less than an hour. If we were to try to leave right now it would be pure stupidity. It would take us almost an hour to unleash all the boats pull anchor and get out of here. Several of these boats do not have running lights and would get separated from the rest. Also, if the ones with running lights had them on, it would just be advertising they were there. Don't forget, the mutants are also out there with boats. I think our chances are better by staying right where we're at for tonight."

"Now Arn, I want you to go around to the boats on the outside and make sure that they be on sharp alert tonight. Tell them I expect an attack to-night. In fact tell them to post double guards. Remind them to make sure all guns are fully loaded."

"Oh, by the way," Arn interjected, "I came across a guy earlier that had a couple of bazookas."

"Good! Tell him to keep them handy. Another thing for them to keep handy is flare pistols. Any questions?"

Sarah spoke up. "Yes. Are we still going to go into Port Angeles?"

"Yes we are. In fact, when we get there, a group is going to look for the mutants and kill as many as possible. While they are doing that, the rest will be looking for things that will be needed."

Ellen spoke with hate in her voice. "I want to kill those goddamn mu-tants!"

"Me too!" Stated Lisa.

"Alright. In fact I'll let you two head up the group."

Arn started to chuckle, and Ellen looked him square in the eye. "What's so funny?"

"Nothing! I was just thinking that a good name for your group would be 'The Assassins'.

"You call it what you want!" She snapped. "But I want revenge for what those bastards have done!"

"Alright! Alright!" Nat said. "Arn, get going and tell the people what's up."

As soon as Arn was gone Ellen turned to Nat. "I don't think he realizes how much I hate those goddamn mutants."

"Actually, I think he does. He may not have suffered the loss of a loved one because of them as we have, but he has become very close to us, and he knows we have suffered deeply because of them."

Lisa spoke up. "Nat's right Ellen. Arn has become so close to us he is just like part of us. We all think very highly of Arn, and if anything happened to him it would hurt us just as deeply as if he were one of our own family."

Ellen went over and gave Lisa a hug. "Your right. He is kind of like a brother, and you and Sarah are like sisters."

Sarah had been setting there not saying anything. She then got up and went over and hugged Lisa and Ellen. "I feel that way too."

Lisa started for the door. "Let's go start forming 'The assassins'." She was laughing as she went out the door. Sarah was right behind her.

As they were heading out the door Nat called Ellen back. "You forgot to mention what part of the family I am." He said with a smirk.

She looked at him with a mischievous smile. "To be honest with you. I wish you were my husband. But, for right now, you are many things to all of us. A brother, a father, a leader, and our hero." She turned and headed for the door. Just as she got to the door, she stopped and turned around. "And to me a lover." She then blew him a kiss and went out the door.

Nat smiled, poured himself a cup of coffee, and then sat down to think about what she had said.

Nat stood watch until midnight, and then Arn took over to stand watch until four o'clock.

Everyone was having a hard time sleeping because of the anticipation of expected attack. Sarah had gone with Arn, and Will and Jenny were in the forward cabin. Nat got his pipe out, lit it, then propped his pillow up and leaned back to try and relax.

The silence was broken by Ellen. "I almost wish they would attack and end this suspense"

"Me too!" Lisa agreed.

"And if you don't get any sleep, you're not going to be able to fight as good as you can." Nat added.

"What about you?" Ellen asked.

"I'm working on it."

"How can you be, with a pipe in your mouth?"

"It helps me to relax."

Lisa got up. "Would anybody like me to put some coffee on? Since it's quite evident that none of us are going to get to sleep until daylight."

Nat swung himself out of bed. "Might as well."

After the coffee had been poured, they sat there, each with their own thoughts. Nat was thinking about their defenses. Ellen was wondering about the future, and Lisa was thinking about the past.

Nat looked at his watch. "Two thirty." He mumbled out loud.

Lisa looked at him. "Maybe they won't attack."

He shook his head. "Oh, they will. Of that I am sure."

They finally turned their talk to things that had happened since they had joined together. Over an hour had gone by when the first shot rang out. The air was filled with the sound of battle.

Everybody headed for the deck. As they came topside they got behind whatever they could. The mutants were raining bullets down on them. Nat crawled over to Arn. "Go up on the bridge and aim that spot light up on the hill!" Then he yelled for anybody else that had a spot light to do the same.

Nat heard somebody yell that the mutants were on the spit also, and had the group in a cross-fire. The spit was only about thirty yards away from the boats on that side. He hollered at Ellen. "Work your way over to Jim's boat. He has some dynamite on board. Tell him to find someone with a good throwing arm, and have them toss some sticks of dynamite at the spit. Lisa! Go tell that guy with the bazookas to send one over to the spit side."

The spot lights seemed to help for a little bit, but they were starting to shoot them out. "Start shooting the flares up there!" Nat yelled. All of the sudden flares started lighting up the hill side. Nat could pick out mutants in their glow, so he started aiming at them instead of just shooting and hoping he hit one. Jenny was loading guns for Nat, Sarah, and Will. Nat reached back for another gun and it wasn't there. He quickly looked back and saw Jenny holding her arm, and blood seeping through her fingers. "Get inside and find something to wrap that!" Just then he heard

Sarah yell, and he looked over towards her. She was laying face down on the deck. Nat started to move towards her, but just then Arn came around the corner and saw her. Arn got to her in a flash and rolled her over. Nat could see blood on her chest. Just then a bullet hit right next to Nat. He started loading his guns as Arn pulled Sarah inside.

Nat got his guns loaded and started shooting again. Lisa appeared at his side. "That guy with the bazooka is good. He's killing a lot of them. It seems like they are firing less shots."

"It seems like it. How about reloading for Will and myself?"

"Okay. Where's Jenny?"

"She got hit in the arm."

Lisa started reloading as Arn came out and started shooting. Nat looked over at him, but he didn't look back.

About a half hour later the shooting had slowed down to sporadic shots. That went on for a short time, and then all shooting stopped.

Lisa started to go inside. "I'll check on Jenny."

Nat grabbed her arm. "Just a minute!"

"Why?"

He tried to think of something to say just as Arn came over. "Nat, I gotta go find the doctor for Sarah."

Lisa looked at Arn. "Sarah?"

"Yeah. She got shot."

"How bad is she Arn?"

"The bullet hit her in the chest just below the right shoulder, and the bullet is still in her."

Before he could say another word Lisa had bolted for the door and disappeared inside.

"Well, you had better get going." Nat said. "Just remember that the doctor is probably trying to take care of a lot of people right now. Just tell him about it, and I'm sure he will get here as soon as he can."

"I know. I'll be back as quick as I can!"

Nat went inside to see if he could be if any help. Bending over Sarah, he lifted the cotton wadding. "How do you feel?"

"I hurt so bad! Nat?"

"What?"

"Will I die?"

"No, but you lost a lot of blood. Arn went to get the doctor. You just try to relax and take it as easy as possible."

Lisa pulled Nat aside. "Ellen should have been back by now. "I'm worried."

"So am I. Maybe I better go look for her."

"No, I'll go. You better stay here in case somebody has to find you. They will look here first."

"I guess you're right. Look over at Jim's boat. That's where I sent her."

As she left, Nat went to pour himself a cup of coffee. "Well, son-of-a-bitch! If that doesn't beat all!"

"What's-a-matter?" Will asked.

"Those dirty bastards shot a hole through my coffee pot!"

"What are you going to do about it?" Jenny asked.

"Oh, I have another one here someplace." He started looking into the storage compartments. "Those women can sure hide things."

A few minutes later Ellen burst in and hurried over to Sarah. "I just heard about you getting hit. How ya doing?"

"I hurt really bad, but Nat said that I'm going to be alright."

Lisa had come in right behind Ellen, and was now just standing there watching Nat, but not saying anything. Ellen stood up. I need a cup of coffee." She walked over and picked up the coffee pot. "Nat?"

He was down on his hands and knees looking in a compartment under one of the bunks, and didn't even look up. "What?"

"There is a hole in the coffee pot."

He stopped looking, and sat on the floor, then looked up at her holding the damaged coffee pot. "Yeah, I know. That just goes to show you that they have absolutely no respect, for anything. To go and shoot up a man's coffee pot is about the lowest thing that anyone can do to somebody."

Everyone just looked at him. Then they all started laughing. Just then Arn came in. "What's so funny?"

Then he saw Nat sitting on the floor. "What's the matter with you? You look upset. Why are you sitting on the floor?"

"I'm trying to find the other coffee pot."

"Oh! Is that what you're looking for?" Lisa asked with a laugh. "It's right up here in this cupboard."

"I looked there."

"Must not have looked too hard." She then reached up and brought out the coffee pot. "I'll put some on right away."

Nat got up and looked at Arn. "Did you find the doctor?"

"Sure did. He gave me this morphine to give to her, and he would get here as soon as he can." He gave the morphine to Nat. "Will you do it?"

"Sure." He took the morphine and injected it into Sarah. "This will help you until the doctor gets here." He then turned back to Arn. "Did he give you any idea about how long it might be?"

"He told me that it might be quite awhile."

Nat turned to Ellen. "Heat me some water, and get me some clean towels."

Arn looked at him. "What are you going to do?"

"I'm going to make an attempt at getting that bullet out before that wound starts closing up to tight. Get me the first aid kit, and open it up while I wash my hands"

After he set up the first aid kit he headed toward the door. "I'm going outside. I don't want to watch. Then he stepped outside.

Nat washed his hands then opened a package that contained a pair of rubber gloves and put them on. "Lisa, will you take that long piece of stainless steel and wash it with that alcohol for me?"

She cleaned it and handed it to him.

Now undo her blouse and slip it over her shoulder." He waited until she had finished slipping it over the shoulder. "Pull her bra strap down over her arm, then remove the cotton pad and clean as much blood from around the wound as you can."

After she had finished doing as she was instructed, he stuck the rod down into the wound. Sarah started to move, so he had Ellen come over and hold her as still as she could.

He felt the end of the rod touch the bullet, and pulled it out. "It's in there pretty deep. Take those long locking pinchers and boil them, the wash them with alcohol. Oh, and do the same with the scalpel."

CHAPTER 7

As soon as the instruments were sterile, Nat continued with the task of removing the bullet. Lisa kept the blood sopped up as he cut the bullet hole a little larger. He then inserted the pinchers, grasped the bullet and removed it.

"A bronze tip! Good! It looks like there are no fragments missing. Now, let's pull the wound closed as tight as we can and tape it, then you can put a dressing over it. When you're finished, tape her arm across her midsection so she doesn't move it. That will limit the muscle movement and give it a chance to start healing."

He took the bullet outside and gave it to Arn. "Here it is. She will be fine now. Weak, but alright. It won't take too long for her to get her strength back tho'."

Arn looked at the bullet, then at Nat. "Thank you. I'll admit that I wasn't too sure whether you could get it out."

"Neither was I, but not knowing how long before the doctor would be here, I had to try. If the doctor had taken to long then the wound would have started to close up, and he would have had to cut it out. She is out right now, but why don't you go in there and be with her when she comes to."

"Yeah, I think I better. Thanks again Nat."

They both went inside, and Will approach Arn. "Since the forward compartment is set up with a double bunk, why don't you and I move Sarah in there? That way you two can be together."

"Thanks Will."

The two of them moved her into the forward compartment, and Will came back out. "I don't know about anybody else, but I'm about to fall asleep standing up. I'm hitting the sack."

"I second that." Mumbled Ellen as she crawled into a bunk.

Not another word was spoken as everyone else followed suit. Nat was awakened by someone shaking him gently. As he rolled over, he saw it was Lisa. "What's the matter? What time is it?"

"It's almost noon, and Jim is topside. He wants to talk to you."

"Okay. Is there any hot coffee?"

"Just finished making some."

"Will you pour me a cup and one for Jim too?"

"I already did. Here."

He took both cups and went up topside. Jim's hand was bandaged up. "You get hit in the hand?"

"Kinda. My spot light stuck last night, and just as I reached up to try and turn it by hand, a bullet hit it. It peppered my hand with glass. The cuts are not too bad tho'. I hear that Sarah got hit. How is she?"

"She will be alright. She got hit in the shoulder. The doctor was so busy last night I went ahead and removed the bullet myself."

"That's what I heard. I ran into the doctor, and he said that by the time he got here, you had already taken care of it. He also said that you did a damn good job."

"I must have been sleeping pretty hard, because I didn't even hear him come in. Have you had a chance to survey the damage yet?"

"Somewhat. It's pretty bad, Nat."

"Fill me in as much as you can."

"At least 37 dead and I don't know how many wounded yet. Hank is going to each boat right now getting an exact count. Two boats sank from bullet holes, and the others are pretty well bullet riddled."

"Sounds bad."

"It is! We can't afford to lose any more people."

"I know. I'm going below to do some thinking. Let me know what Hank comes up with on the count."

Nat went below and first checked on Sarah and Jenny, then sat down to think.

After a while, Hank showed up. He poured a cup of coffee and sat down, then looked at Nat. "How are you doing?"

"Okay I guess. Can you give me a run down on the results of last night?"

"Two boats sank, thirty-eight dead, and forty-two wounded. The wounds range from slight wounds to three that might not make it."

"Can you break it down into men, women, and children?"

"Men, twenty-four dead. Women, nine dead, and children, five dead, and one of them was just two years old."

"Alright, I think I got a pretty good picture. You want to tell Jim to come on back over here. I want to talk to him."

"Okay."

A short time later Jim showed up. He got a cup of coffee and sat down. "What's up?"

As Arn came out and sat down, Nat explained what he had decided. "I want everybody to consolidate onto as few boats as possible, but don't overload. If a boat sleeps eight, then only put eight on that boat. Pick the best boats we have. Also I want the fastest boat available, but it's not for sleeping on. Whatever boats are left, sink them."

"We are going to go past Pot Angeles, and look for a cove to hole up in until the wounded are well enough to make the trip into the mountains."

"Jim, I want you to take a couple of good men, and the fast boat, and stop in Port Angeles. There are two things I want you to do. One is, to sink any boats you see there. Two, scrounge around and find enough stainless steel to cover the fast boat from the water line up. Make sure you get a couple extra pieces about six feet square that can be used like mirrors."

"It's already getting late in the day, so go ahead and get the fast boat and get into Port Angeles. When you leave, just head west along the shoreline until you find us."

Jim got up to leave. "I'm on my way."

"Arn, you go start organizing the other boats. If someone has a hand pump, get it and pump the fuel out of the boats we are leaving. I'm going to go ahead and start out. As you get each boat ready, send it on its way. You come on the last boat to pull out. Make sure you sink the boats that are left behind. Any questions?"

"No. I'll go tell Sarah I'll see her later, and get going."

About fifteen minutes later, Nat pulled out. As they rounded the end of the spit, he had Ellen take over the controls. "We will stop at Port Angeles and fuel up. We should have enough time to do it before the next boat gets that far. I'm going below to look at the maps, and see if they give me any clue as to a good cove to hole up in."

A short time later Nat came back up topside. "My maps are not detailed enough, so I guess we will have to just look for one. I'll take over now."

"Jim passed us a while back. It looks like he will beat us into Port Angeles."

Nat looked up ahead. "That must be him way up there."

As they were pulling into the dock, they noticed that the boat sinking was under way. Lisa and Ellen tied up the boat as Nat went to see about getting a pump for the fuel.

The man sinking the boats came over. "Hi Nat! I got a pretty good start. This axe works great on most of them, but some of the one with thicker hulls, I have to knock out the plug. There are a few that we will have to drop a stick of dynamite in. This is almost fun."

"Is that right? Well, you had better get on with your fun, because there isn't a lot of time. Where are Jim and the other guy?"

"They went looking for stainless steel. Well, I'll get back to work. See ya later."

When Nat finish they cast off and as they rounded the end of the spit they were just ahead of the first boat.

A cove that would fit their needs finally showed up about an hour before sunset. Nat started placing the boats together as they pulled into the cove, with the bigger boat on the outside. At just about sundown, Jim arrived, and told them that three more boats were pulling up the rear, and should be here very shortly.

Upon getting the last boat into place, Nat told Jim to find the doctor and come over to his boat, so they could start making plans for the safety of the group. He then picked six people to pull guard duty for the night.

They were just getting ready to eat when the doctor and Jim arrived. "You got here just in time for supper. Canned ham and lima beans, and Lisa did a damn good job at making them. Grab a bowl and have some."

"Don't mind if I do." Jim said. Want some Doc?"

"Sure, why not? I haven't eaten today, because I've been too busy tending to the wounded. But, before I start, let me go in and check on Sarah."

A few minutes later he came back out and sat down with a bowl of food, "Nat, I would like to compliment you on the job you did removing that bullet. You should have been a doctor. I changed the dressing while I was in there, and Jenny's should be changed also, which brings me to a situation that is disturbing. My supplies are almost completely gone."

"That's one of the things we are going to talk about after supper. But first, let's enjoy this delicious meal before it gets cold."

The doctor finished his quickly, and then turned to Lisa. "This is the finest meal I've had since before the war. Do you think I could get a second helping?"

"Thank you, doctor. Give me your bowl, and I'll get it for you."

After dinner Nat laid out what he had in mind. "Tomorrow, Lisa and Ellen are going to go into Port Angeles to seek out and kill as many mutants as possible. They are going to take a few people along to help them. Doctor, I want you to go with them and see what kind of medical supplies you can scrounge up. Don't take any unnecessary chances like snoop around in any place that might be dark enough for the mutants to be living."

"Jim, Arn, and I," he continued, "are going to do some modifying on the fast boat. How much of the stainless steel did you get Jim?"

"Not a whole hell of a lot. I ran out of time. Although I did get some spotted, but it will take a little work to get it loose. It's in a restaurant."

"Did you get the boats sank?" Nat inquired.

"Pretty good! We didn't get all of them, but we got all the ones that looked like they were being used."

"Instead of you working on the fast boat, why don't you take another boat in, and finish off the boats, then see about getting the stainless steel?"

"Okay. I'll take an extra man along too."

"Arn, tomorrow I want you to help me remove a few good spot lights from some of the other boats. We are going to mount them on the fast boat. Oh, and Jim, while you're in there, see if you can find any extra batteries."

"What have you got planned?"

"We are going to make the fast boat into a chase boat. If a mutant's boat comes by, we will chase it down and get them before they have a chance to tell others that we are here."

Jim stood up to leave. "Well, I guess I better get a good night's sleep. I didn't get much last night. If you think of anything else, let me know in the morning before we leave. Good night, and thanks for the splendid meal."

The doctor also bid a good night and left after complimenting Lisa again on the meal. After they left Ellen spoke up. "The doctor ate like he hadn't had a meal in weeks. Did you see how fast he put that food down?"

"Who cooks for him?" Lisa asked.

"Nobody in particular." Nat answered. "He eats with whoever he's with at meal time, and if he's not with anybody, he fixes his own, and I think he probably does a lot of fixing his own."

"That's too bad." Ellen said. "We should invite him over for supper once in a while."

"It's okay with me, if it's okay with everyone else." Nat said.

"It's fine with me." Lisa said. "Besides, I find him a very nice man."

All of the others agreed.

That night the weather turned bad and it rained for the next three days and nights. They took advantage of the bad weather and got the chase boat finished. The sides were covered with stainless steel and they mounted six spot lights top facing forward and six more facing to the back, with mirror like stainless steel in back of them.

Nat also sent a party ashore to check the houses in the area for anything they could use, and then burn the houses. He also had them fall trees across any roads that might lead down towards the cove they were hiding in.

The next two months went fairly smooth for the group. Just about every day a small party went into Port Angeles to scrounge for useful items, while another group searched the area for mutants.

Finally the day came when the doctor felt that all the wounded, that hadn't completely healed, were well enough for the journey into the mountains. Excitement was running high the morning that Nat made the announcement.

Somebody yelled from the group,. When are we leaving Nat?"

"As soon as everybody gets ready!" He yelled back with a smile.

It took about an hour for everybody to get ready to ship out. All the boats were running wide open, like a race was on to see who could get to Port Angeles first.

As soon as everyone had gathered on the dock at Port Angeles, Nat gave them instructions on what to do. "All of those that are able spread out and find as much working transportation as you can, and then meet down by that restaurant and motel on the water front. I'll tell you what to do then."

Ken came over. "I noticed when we came around the spit that a helicopter was sitting out there at the coast Guard station,. As soon as I find a car or something, I'm going out there to see if it still works. If it does, and there is fuel out there, I can fly it."

Nat looked at him and grinned. "That's a damn good idea Ken If it works, we can fly up the Elwa Valley and spot a good place to build our town. Get going!"

An hour and a half later everybody met down on the waterfront. They had found all types of transportation from small cars to a semi truck. Nat got up on the back of a pickup truck as everybody gathered around. As they quieted down Nat spoke. "Our raiding parties have pretty well eliminated the mutants in this area, but still take caution at all times.

"Howard, since you're the teacher, I want you to go to the schools and the college and try to get as much as you can for doing your job. Make sure you take a pickup to put the things in. Also you might pick two people to go with you. Now get going. We have to find what we need for generating electricity for a dam. Does anyone know what to look for?"

Jim spoke up. "I do! I use to work at building dams."

"Okay, get going and see if you can find what we need. Doctor, you scout around and find what medical equipment you well need to build a small clinic. When you get everything located, I will assign a crew to help you load it on that semi truck."

"The rest of you look for building supplies, like tools, nails paint supplies etc. Also, always be on the lookout for canned food that might still be good. Oh, and before I forget, meet at six o'clock on the road going west towards Forks. I'll be there on the road, so just drive until you see me. Is there anybody here can run a bulldozer?"

Two men stepped forward and stated that they could.

"I want you two men to find us a good one and a way to haul it up the valley as far as we can. We will need it to cut a road up the valley from where the current road ends. Now, let's get going."

Nat heard a loud noise from the spit at that time, and turned around. The helicopter was lifting off and then heading towards them. Ken flew low over them and pointed up on the hill."

"There is a play field up that way. He must want us to meet him up there." Lisa informed him.

"Well, we better head up there." He jumped into the pickup he had been standing on, and Lisa and Ellen jumped in with him.

Ken had already landed when they arrived at the play field and was waiting for them. "It took a little tinkering because it had sat so long, but I got it alright. I also checked the fuel supply at the landing pad, and there is plenty of it to last for awhile."

"Sounds like a dream." Nat said. "I got a map of the area with me, so let's fly up the valley right now, and pick out a spot."

"Okay, hop in, and we are on our way."

They all got in and started the flight up the Elwa valley. The clouds were surrounding the mountain tops, so it seemed as if they were flying up a tunnel. It took them about forty-five minutes to fly the length of the valley. Nat then had Ken turn around and fly back down at a lower altitude. Nat finally decided on a spot that had been a ranger station. On his map it was named Elkhorn. Just up the river was a stream called Lost River, which could be dammed up for a reservoir and a power dam. "Okay, Ken, take me down and drop me off on the highway west of Port Angeles."

They found a large parking lot alongside the highway, and Ken landed the helicopter there. As Nat got out, he told him to fly Ellen and Lisa back into town so they could join the others in searching for things that were needed.

About an hour later, Nat looked down the road and saw a big truck with a lowboy on the back, and on the lowboy was a big bulldozer. As it pulled up to a stop by Nat, the two that he had told to find it got out of the truck. "Is this what you ordered?" One asked.

Nat looked it over. "I reckon' it is. That's a D-9 isn't it?"

The other man spoke up. "Shor' is! It will rip a road through them woods pretty easy."

"I think you're right." Nat agreed. "Now take it up the Elwa to the end of the road, and start building a road from there up the valley." He got the map out. Right here is where we are going. It used to be a summer ranger station."

The man that had been riding turned to the other man. "You go ahead and start out Pete. I'm going to scout around to find a fuel truck and fuel for the 'dozer, then I'll catch up to you." As the truck headed down the road he turned to Nat. "Have you checked any of the vehicles around here to see if any of them run?"

"No I haven't. I've just been setting here by the road in case somebody should show up early."

"Okay. I'll check them and get busy looking for a fuel truck." He said as he left.

As people started showing up, Nat checked things over. They had done a good job at getting useful items. By the time most of them had arrived, he had come to the conclusion that their town was going to be built pretty fast.

While he was standing talking to a group of people, some one hollered. "Look up the road! Somebody is coming this way." Everybody looked in that direction, and what they saw, was an old school bus slowly making its way towards them. It came to a stop about a hundred yards from them, and just sat there. When nobody got out, Nat told the others to stay put, as he started walking towards the bus.

The bus started moving again, and met Nat half way, then stopped again. As Nat walked up on the driver's side, the window opened and a harsh looking man stock his head out and looked Nat in the eye. Nat just looked right back into the man's eyes. After a couple of minutes passed the man spoke to Nat. "You friend or foe?"

"Well, that depends on you. But, speaking for the others with me, and myself, I hope its friend."

The man looked down the road at the others, then back at Nat. a smile came across his face as he stuck his hand down to Nat. "My name is Ron, and you don't know how happy we are meeting you folks."

Nat took his hand and shook it. "Nat is my name. How many in your party?"

"Ten is all that is left out of the forty-two that we started out with."

"May I come aboard?"

"Please do!"

Nat walked around to the other side of the bus, and climbed inside. As he looked around he saw that there were seven women, a boy that was about fourteen years old, and one other man besides Ron. Turning back to Ron he asked. "Where did you start out from?"

"Southwest Washington, around the Southbend area. You wouldn't happen to have a doctor in your group would you?"

"As a matter of fact we do. What's the problem?"

"That woman in the back has been shot in the leg, and it's getting pretty bad. It happened three days ago."

"Well, drive on down to the others, and we will have the doctor take a look at her."

Ron drove the bus down to the others, and Nat got off and asked Arn where the doctor was.

"I don't know if he has got here yet. I'll go see if he is here."

"If he isn't here yet, drive down by the hospital and get him up here right away. He should be there getting equipment."

Nat then boarded the bus again, and Ellen joined him. "Ron, this is Ellen." They greeted each other, and then Nat told Ellen to check on the woman that was hurt. He then asked Ron to tell him about his party.

Ron had a hopeless expression on his face as he told his story. "Not too long after the holocaust, me and a few survivors got together and decided to seek out others for survival reasons. A lot of the people we met wanted to go it alone. After about three months, we numbered forty-two strong.

At first, we were pretty well left alone but after a while we found out that we had to protect ourselves from the so-called loners. It was as if they resented us banding together. They tried to rob from us and at times kill us for what we had, such as food and weapons."

"It wasn't too long before we started to be attacked at night. In fact, most of the attacks have been at night ever since. Well, we decided that we should go on the road rather than be sitting ducks in one spot. There was a school nearby, so we took three buses and hit the road, working our way north."

"We crisscrossed back and forth from the ocean to the interior as we came north. Most of the people we came across seemed to be on the hostile side. Although down by Chehalis we found a fairly large group numbering about eighty. By this time our numbers were down to thirty-one. They asked us if we wanted to join them, but we could see they were having a hard time of it. One thing was, we felt that they were too vulnerable to attack. Also, their food supplies were not all that great. After taking a vote, we decided to look for a safer refuge. We also had learned by this time that we were fighting two elements. Renegades by day, and cannibalistic mutations by night."

"Seven of our group- decided to stay there and the rest of us moved on. One night, just south of Olympia we got hit pretty hard and lost another eight people. The next day we all consolidated onto one bus and headed back towards the coast"

"Just north of Hoquiam we came across four men and a woman. As we started to get off the bus they started shooting at us. They killed three of our party and wounded one seriously before we were able to kill them. The one they wounded died the next day."

Three days ago we had broke down outside of Forks, and while we were working on the bus, two men attacked us and killed two more, and wounded the woman in back of the bus. We were able to kill one man for sure, and I know the other was badly wounded, even tho' he got away."

"Well, as soon as we got the bus going, we got out of there. This bus has broken down two times since then. It's on its last legs. We were hoping to find another one when we got here."

"I'm sure you can find one around here someplace, if you look where the schools are. But, before you go looking, let me make you a proposal."

"What might that be?"

"The people you see here have banded together, and are going to build a town up in the mountains. We feel that it is out best hope for building a future for mankind." Nat went on and told him about all their plans for the town and why they had picked that area to build.

Just then the doctor showed up and came on the bus. "What's up Nat?"

"There is a woman in the back of the bus that has been shot pretty bad, and needs immediate attention."

Okay. I'll see what I can do."

Ron looked at Nat. "I sure hope he can help her. All of us have grown pretty close to one another."

"I know what you mean. He's a damn good doctor, and if anything can be done, he's the one that can do it."

"About your proposal, I'll talk it over with the others. I think I know what their answer will be though. On my part, I think it's the best, and probably the only logical plan there is."

"You talk to them, and then let me know. Right now I have to go check on things so we can get moving. Talk to you after a bit." Nat then went to join the others.

As Nat was looking everything over, a fuel truck pulled up by him. The driver rolled down the window and hollered, "I'm going ahead and try to catch up with Pete!"

Nat waved him on, and he started out for the Elwa to catch up with the other truck.

Shortly after that, Nat started sending the other vehicles up the road. Just then Ron showed up at his side. "Looks like we are going to throw in with your group. It will be nice to settle down in one spot."

"Glad to hear it. Just turn your bus around and follow the others."

Ron headed back to the bus, and Arn showed up. "What's going on with the bus people:"

"They are going to join us. I want you to get in back of them and follow them. That bus could break down before they get up in the mountains. If it does, make arrangements to transfer them to other vehicles with the stuff they want to keep."

By the time everyone had gotten to the spot where the new road was being built, it was getting dark. Nat sat up guards for the night as everyone was setting up temporary campsites. He then found Ellen, Lisa, Arn, Sarah, Will, and Jenny and helped them to set up camp for the night.

Ellen poured Nat a cup of coffee and sat down beside him. "That woman on the bus had an infection pretty bad. The doctor cleaned it up and gave her some antibiotics. He said that there is a slim chance that she might lose the leg though."

Well, let's hope not,"

"Those people on the bus sure are a bunch of nice people."

Lisa came over to where they were sitting. "We have a little extra food tonight. How about me going-over and fetching the doctor for supper?"

"Sure!" Nat said. "But, if you don't watch out, you're going to spoil him. This makes three times in a week."

"So? We happen to enjoy his company. And besides that, you sure seem to get into some pretty heavy discussions with him yourself."

After supper Nat and the doctor sat down by the fire, as Nat lit up his pipe. Nat stared into the fire as he spoke. "I haven't had too many opportunities lately to just set by a fire and enjoy my pipe." The doctor didn't answer, so he went on. "It's been one hell of a fight so far, but I really think we're gonna make it. We still have a long way ahead of us. In just a few days now I hope we are able to start the building process."

Alan still didn't speak. After a few minutes of silence Nat looked at the doctor. "You're sure quiet. What's going through your mind?"

The doctor took in a deep breath and slowly let it out before speaking. "Well, for starters," he chuckled, "I was just thinking how nice it was to have a meal fixed for me. You know Nat? I think I should be thinking about getting me a woman to take care of me. If it wasn't for all these good folks looking out for me, I probably would starve to death. And did you ever notice how my clothes are always patched up when I get a tear in them: It seems some lady always insists on doing my sewing and fussing over me. Now, don't get me wrong, but I always just thought they were being kind-hearted. But the more I think about it, maybe it's something else."

Nat leaned back and started laughing. "Doc, from what I hear around here, you are exactly right. Right now we have more women than men and those women, or at least some of them have had their eyes on you for some time now."

Just then Ellen walked up to them. "Glory be! That's the first time in a long time I've seen you laugh. What brought that on?"

"Just man talk."

She walked around in back of Nat and started to massage his shoulders. "You two must have been talking about women then, so I won't ask any-more."

"Where's Lisa?" Nat asked.

"She and Sarah went for a walk. They said they wouldn't be gone long.,"

After about ten minutes Lisa showed up. She looked over at Ellen mas-saging Nat's shoulders. "I'll bet the doctor could use a little of that treat-ment too. Right Doc?"

"Well, I sure wouldn't turn it down."

As she stepped behind the doctor Lisa stated. "What you need is to find a good woman to do this for you all the time."

Nat and the doctor just looked at each other but neither spoke a word.

After visiting for a while the doctor got up to leave. "I guess I had better go check on my patients before I turn in for the night. Good night and thank you for a splendid evening."

Lisa sat down where the doctor had been seated, and looked at the other two and just smiled.

Nat narrowed his eyes and spoke. "Would you mind telling us what that smile means?"

CHAPTER 8

"Oh. ---Just some good news for a change,"

"Well?" Asked Nat.

She looked into the fire. "Maybe I shouldn't be the one to tell you."

"Oh come on!" Ellen said as she walked over to Lisa. "You brought this up. Now spit it out before I take you down and sit on you until you tell us!"

Lisa laughed. "You better watch out, or you might turn out to be the one getting sat on."

Ellen reached for Lisa and then the wrestling match was on. Lisa being the quicker one kept slipping out of Ellen's grasp. This went on for a good ten minutes before Lisa finally got Ellen down and was sitting on her.

Nat, in the mean time was just sitting there, smoking his pipe and enjoying the fun.

Suddenly Ellen quit struggling and looked up at Lisa. "Okay! You won this one. I give."

Lisa just smiled then stated. "Sarah thinks she's pregnant." Then she stood up and watched Ellen's expression.

At first Ellen just lay there with a shocked look on her face, then she jumped up and ran over to Nat grabbing him and knocking his pipe out of his hand, which he had just finished picking up after having dropped it when Lisa had spoken. "Nat! Did you hear? Sarah thinks she's gonna have a baby! Isn't that beautiful? Did you hear?"

He leaned over and picked up his pipe. "damn! I lost the tobacco out of it!"

She grabbed his pipe out of his hand. "Are you ignoring me?"

Nat looked up at her and smiled. You make that awfully hard to do."

"Well then, say something!"

"I can't think of anything to say."

"You could say you're happy or something like that!"

"Actually, I'm over whelmed with joy. I think Arn will make a good father, and I hope it's a boy."

Ellen turned to Lisa. "I'll bet Arn is on cloud nine right now. I'm surprised that he didn't come running to tell us the good news."

"He couldn't. Sarah hasn't told him yet."

"Why not?"

"She is going to wait until after she talks to the doctor. Remember what I said? She thinks she's pregnant. So let's not say anything until she knows for sure."

Nat looked at Lisa. "Did she tell you that you could tell us about it?"

"She told me I could tell you if I wanted to, but if I did, to ask you to not say anything to anybody else. Tomorrow she is going to talk to the doctor. She turned to go. I'm going over to Will and Jenny's to visit for awhile, then over to Arn and Sarah's. And by the way, Jenny definitely is going to have a baby."

Nat just about dropped his pipe again. "I'll be damned! I better make a point of going over tomorrow and congratulate them. But right now I think I'll turn in for the night." He turned and went into his tent.

He had no more than laid down when Ellen came in and laid down beside him. "Nat? I'm so filled with joy that I want to share it with you."

Pulling her to him, he started caressing her and kissing her. Before long they were undressed and enjoying the pleasures of sexual passion.

The next day brought clear skies and sunshine over the beautiful Elwa Valley. As Nat came out of his tent, he looked up at the sky. An eagle was winging its way up the valley. He thought to himself as he watched the magnificent bird. 'We are going that direction too. Like you, I hope we find what we are looking for. I shall make you our symbol of hope.'

He walked towards the fire, and Ellen met him half way with a cup of coffee. She kissed him on the cheek. "Good morning. What was you just looking at?"

"That eagle flying up the valley. Kind of like a symbol of hope. Taking a sip of coffee he sat down by the fire.

Lisa kissed him on the cheek and gave him a plate with steak and eggs on it. "Venison steak and duck eggs. I'll bet you didn't know it, but the whole camp had a hard time sleeping because of you"

"Me? Why me?"

"I've never heard you snore that loud. I think everybody could hear you."

Ellen laughed. "She's not kidding. I think even the ground shook."

He looked at her. "That wasn't from me snoring. Now let me eat this fantastic breakfast before it gets too cold to enjoy."

Arn showed up just as they finished eating. "Man! What a night! I thought we had a mad bear in camp last night, so I grabbed my gun and went looking. But it just turned out to be you snoring."

"I told you so!" Lisa said.

"Ah shit! Maybe I did snore a little loud last night, but I think you guys are trying to make it worse than it was. Besides that, I didn't hear it and I had a damn good night's sleep. So there! Where's Sarah?"

"She said she felt a little sick this morning, so she went over to see the doctor. Well, I gotta get going. I'm going up to the head of the new road and ride on the bulldozer for awhile. Pete said he would teach me how to run that thing. See ya later."

After spending a couple of hours going around camp checking on things and talking to various people Nat went up the road to watch the bulldozer for awhile. When he got there, Arn was busy trying to drive the big machine with Pete sitting beside him shaking his head and coaching Arn. As they backed up to make another pass, Arn saw Nat and waved with a big smile on his face. He waved back, and then took out his pipe and lit it.

Just then, Sarah came up and waved for Arn to come over to her. Pete stopped the bulldozer and idled it down as Arn jumped off. He ran over to Sarah as Nat watched. She said something to him and then he threw his arms around her and picked her up then started to do a dance while he held her. All of the sudden he put her down and started running towards Nat. About halfway his foot caught on a root and he made a complete flip, landing on his back. In an instant he was back up running again. He was running at such speed that he almost knocked Nat over when he grabbed him by the shoulders. Nat's pipe went flying over the bank. Arn started yelling. "I'm a father! I'm a father! Did you hear me? I'm a father!"

Nat grabbed his arms. "Yes! I heard you! Did Sarah have a baby?"

"Not yet! But she is going to. Isn't this great?"

"I think it's fantastic."

"I gotta go tell Lisa and Ellen!"

"Just-a-minute there knot head!"

"What?"

"I think you should let Sarah do that. But it wouldn't hurt for you to go along with her."

"Alright,. I promise to let her tell them."

Sarah then joined them. "Isn't it fantastic Nat?"

"It sure is! Congratulations to both of you. Now get down to camp and tell the others."

As they headed down towards camp, Nat went over the bank to retrieve his pipe. "This is getting to be a damn habit!" He growled out loud.

"What's getting to be a habit?"

Nat turned around and seen Pete standing there looking down at him. "Picking up my pipe! That's what!"

"Well, quit dropping it."

He picked up his pipe and started back up. "I didn't drop it! Damn! Now I have to refill it!"

"What's all the excitement about with Arn?"

"Sarah is going to have a baby."

"Hey! That's great! What does that make you then?"

"Huh?"

"Well, you have been like a father to them two, so does that make you a grandfather?"

Nat was silent for a moment as he put some tobacco into his pipe, then he looked Pete right in the eye. "You know, I kind of like that idea. We'll just have to see what happens."

"Congratulations Grandpa!"

Nat punched Pete on the shoulder. "Thanks! Now get back to work. We've got to get a town started so the kid has a place to grow up."

"Alright." He laughed as he turned to go back to work. "I'll try to give you a mile today!"

Back in camp, Lisa and Ellen were hanging around the tent waiting for the official word from Sarah. Lisa looked up and saw them coming. "Here they come!"

"I see them. Isn't it neat! Just look at that proud look on Arn's face."

Before they even got close to Lisa and Ellen, Arn shouted. "Hey! We got something to tell you!"

"You promised me you would let me do the telling!" Sarah said in a stern voice.

"I will! I will!"

Sarah walked over and took the two women by the hand,. "I'm almost two months along."

"That's wonderful!" Ellen cried, and threw her arms around her. She then went over to Arn and gave him a big hug and kissed him on the cheek. "Congratulations Papa!"

Lisa gave Sarah a hug and started crying. "I'm so happy for the two of you". Then turning to Arn she kissed him on the cheek. "Now you take good care of her, and don't let her do any heavy work or you'll have Ellen and I to answer to!"

Arn grinned. "Yes Ma'am!"

It took them a few weeks to reach their destination, but everything went well. Every fourth day they moved their camp up to where the bulldozer was working. Parties went into town and kept gathering things for their new town. Game was plentiful, so Nat went out every other day with a couple of men and brought back fresh meat to feed everyone. The women always canned some of the meat for use during the winter. Arn finally learned how to drive the bulldozer pretty good and gave Pete a rest every other day.

When they reached the town site, Nat and a few of the men marked out where different things were to be built, and everybody pitched in to get the job done. Once the bulldozing was finished for the town, it was taken up to where the dam was to be built and work got under way there with Jim's supervision.

The men were split up into separate working parties. One group worked on getting a building built for the doctor, and others went to work building houses, another worked on the dam. Each day six people were picked to go into town to tear down buildings and bring lumber back. Every other day, three were sent out to hunt game for their food. Most of the women worked right alongside of the men while others handled the food end. All children that were old enough pitched in and did whatever they were able to do.

Within a week the town had started to grow. Nat seemed to be everywhere helping everybody. It only took three weeks to get the first house built. That evening, after supper, everybody took a tour through the house. It had been plumbed and wired just waiting for the water and electricity to be hooked up to it. After looking the house over, Nat stood on the porch and called everyone over.

"This is one fine building. The first of many. The medical facility will be finished in a few more days, and then a building for our food supplies will be started. As far as having electric power, Jim says we should have it within a month and a half. By that time we will have several building ready for it, a crew has been putting in water pipes from the river, and they tell me that this house will have running water by next week."

"I want to thank all of you for your hard effort, and I also want to say that we are one hell-of-a-team. I'm proud of each and every one of you. We are on our way now, and I know for sure that we will make it."

"But, before we go any farther I think we should decide on a name for our town. Then, let's get down to the business of deciding who gets to be the first to move into this house and becomes our first permanent resident."

Jim jumped up on the porch. "Hell Nat! As far as the first resident goes, that's already been decided by these good folks. I've talked to nearly everybody, and they feel like I do that you should be the one to move into the house. Also, since you have led us here and been the one that made all this happen, I'm going to suggest that we call this town Nathanville after you." He turned towards the crowd. "How do you all feel about that?"

Cheers welled up out of the crowd as everyone was in agreement. Nat held up his hands for the crowd to quiet down. As soon as they were quiet he spoke. "I thank all of you for your graciousness, but let me make another suggestion for a name. When we first started up this valley, I saw an eagle. I watched it every day, and I still see it every day. It has a nest over yonder hillside. I've considered it a kind of symbol of hope. Now, my suggestion is that we call this Eagletown."

The crowd roared with agreement. Jim turned back to Nat and laughed. "I always knew you were smarter than me. Eagletown it is! Easer to say too."

Nat raised his hand to quiet the crowd. "Now as far as the house goes, I'm going to decline the offer,." He bent over and picked up a basket. "In this basket I have placed the names of all the married couples. Ron? How about you coming up here and drawing a name to see who gets the house?"

Ron came up on the porch. "Gee! Now I kinda wish I was married to get in on this."

Nat laughed. "If you got somebody in mind, let me know now, and I'll fix it so you can."

He laughed as he reached into the basket. "Not yet, but I'm working on it." Upon pulling out a piece of paper, he handed it to Nat.

Everybody was dead silent waiting for Nat to read the name. He looked at the name, then looked up and smiled. "Hank and Alice!" The crowd whooped and hollered cheers for them.

Jim leaned over and asked in a low voice. "When did they get married?"

"Didn't you know? About two weeks ago I did the honors."

"Well if that doesn't beat all! The son-of-bitch didn't say a word! I better go congratulate them."

Just then Hank and Alice came up on the porch. Jim grabbed his hand and started shaking it. "Congratulations, although I ought to kick your ass."

"Why would you want to do that?"

"For not telling me about you and Alice tying the knot."

"Shit Jim, we been together all along. So we decided to go ahead and make it official. What's wrong with that?"

"Not a damn thing! I think it's great! Is it too late to kiss the bride?"

Alice laughed. "If you didn't, I'd be mighty disappointed,"

Jim gave her a kiss then stood back and looked at both of them. "Damn! This is great!" Then he slapped Hank on the back. "You two had better get your stuff moved in before dark. I'll help you. Let's go!   "

Nat stepped down off the porch and walked down by the river. After arriving at the edge he looked around and saw no one, so he pulled out his pipe and carefully put some tobacco in it then lit it. As he drew the smoke deep down into his lung he let his mind slip into deep thought. He was so deep in thought that he didn't even hear Ellen and Lisa walk up in back of him.

Standing with a hand in each pocket, he held his pipe between his teeth. One came up on each side of him, and they each grabbed an arm. "Gotch ya!" Ellen yelled. Neither one of them was ready for Nat's reaction. His reflexes acted automatically by both hands coming out and the palm of each hand caught them in the middle of their backs pushing them forward. Both women landed in the water. Along with his pipe.

He realized instantly what had happened. "Oh shit!" Reaching out with both hands, he helped them back out of the water. "Now see what you made me do?"

Ellen pushed her hair out of her eyes,. "Man! Have you got good reflexes?"

Lisa looked over at her. "The next time you get any bright ideas like sneaking up on him, you do it alone."

"Well, I didn't expect him to throw us in the water."

"Okay! Okay! Now who is going to go back into the water to retrieve my pipe?"

"Let Ellen. It was her idea to sneak up on you!"

Ellen didn't say anything. She just shrugged her shoulders and waded back into the water and retrieved his pipe.

He took the pipe and let the water drip out of the stem. "Can't smoke a wet pipe, so I guess I'll have to quit smoking till it dries out. Probably washed all the flavor out of it."

Ellen really felt bad then. "I'm sorry Nat! Really I am. The next time I get to go into town, I'll try to find you another one, I promise."

"Make it one of those fancy ones. I've never had one of those fancy pipes." He then swatted her on the butt.

"Ouch! I said I was sorry!"

"You would be a lot more sorry if I had of landed in the water." Nat retorted as he laughed.

Lisa grabbed Ellen's arm. "Come on! Let's get back to our tent and get some dry clothes on. Coming Nat?"

He looked up in the sky. "I'll be along shortly. See there! That's our eagle making its way back to its nest."

The women stopped to look. "Oh look!" Cried Lisa. "It's got a fish in its talons!"

"Isn't that beautiful!" Stated Ellen.

They turned and left as Nat stood there watched the eagle. It landed on a dead tree near its nest and started eating its catch. Nat spoke out loud towards the eagle. "You're strong, and a good symbol of survival and hope, just like these people who have became your neighbors. As you flyover each day watch us as we grow and become stronger. This is Eagletown, and you're its guardian. From the looks of your nest, you've lived here for quite awhile. For these good folks, it's a new beginning."

As Nat turned to go, the eagle let out a loud screech that reverberated throughout the valley.

The nest morning while Nat sat at the fire drinking a cup of coffee, the doctor came over and sat down without saying anything. Lisa poured him a cup of coffee. "You look troubled." She said.

"I am!" He said solemnly. "I would like to talk to Nat alone if I can."

"Of course. I'll get Ellen and we will go for a walk. How much time do you need?"

Alan thought for a second. "About a half hour."

"Okay." She left to get Ellen.

As soon as they were alone Alan looked at Nat. His voice was strained as he spoke. "We had two more births last night."

Nat looked over at the doctor. He knew the answer before he asked the question. "What did they look like?"

He hesitated before he answered. "Terrible! Do you want me to try to describe them?"

"No. How are the mothers doing?"

They will be okay. I have them under sedation for right now. Both were premature. One was stillborn."

"And the other?"

Alan looked into the fire as tears started cascading down his cheeks. He put his face into his hands and he sobbed as he spoke. "Never in my life have I even considered doing what I did. I was torn between professionalism and humanitarianism. The child was so… so… grotesque and deformed!" He paused then continued. "I took it back to my tent and gave it an injection which ended its life." He looked up at Nat. "Now I don't know if I did the right thing or not. It probably wouldn't have lived for long. But I felt that if it lived only shortly it would be harder on the mother to let it go."

Nat stood up, walked over to the doctor and put his hand on his shoulder. "Alan, sometimes, as we both well know, we have to make a life or death decision. It's not an easy thing for anyone to do. You are an exceptional doctor, that's why this is so difficult for you. Your life is dedicated to saving lives, not taking them. I, and all the others, admire you for that. We all have faith and trust in whatever decision you make, and we support you all the way. It would be very difficult for the child, and mother, had that child been allowed to live. It's easier for a mother to lose a child at birth than a week or a year later. A woman's love for her child grows as the child grows. As cruel as it seems, you did the right thing. That baby may have only lived for a short time. Think of the consequences if it had. We could discuss the ifs, from now until forever, and never have the answers,. In some matters we do not need to know the answers." Nat paused for a minute. "Where are the babies now?"

Alan took out a handkerchief and wiped his eyes. "I wrapped them in blankets. They are in my tent."

"We better go bury them right away."

Nothing more was said as they took the bodies out into the woods and buried them. Upon arriving back at camp the doctor went to tend to the two women who had the babies. Before parting, Alan took a hold of Nat's arm. "Thank you."

"That's alright. You don't have to thank me." He turned to leave, then stopped and looked back at the doctor. "If you feel up to it, why don't you come over for supper tonight?"

"We'll see how I feel then." He stated as he slowly walked away towards the center of camp.

After supper the doctor, and Nat, walked down by the river and sat down on the bank of the river. Neither one spoke for a long time. Nat took out his pipe, filled it, and then lit it. He took a draw of the smoke in, let it out, and then looked down at the pipe. It just didn't taste right. He took another draw, and it tasted even worse. After tapping out the tobacco on a rock, he slipped the pipe back into his pocket.

"Alan, I got something on my mind that's bothering me quite a bit."

The doctor didn't answer.

"It's about Sarah and Jenny."

Alan knew what he was going to ask him. He also knew that he was going to have to choose his words with caution.

Nat continued. "We've had three births so far. One on the boat, and now two here. All three have been born mutated. Besides Sarah and Jenny, we have one other that's pregnant,. That other woman, Doris is her name, is due next month. What's your prognosis on the next three?"

Alan let out a sigh, and then spoke. First, let me remind you that on the boat I told you that Doris had radiation sickness. Not as severe as the two who had babies last night. That could be why she is able to carry her baby this long. Frankly I'm surprised that she didn't miscarry. To be totally truthful, I expect hers to be mutated. If this turns out to be the case, I hope it's stillborn. If it's mutated and born alive, please have mercy on me for what I have to do!" He paused or a minute, then with a broken voice continued. "Nat, I feel a deep guilt for what I did last night."

Nat opened his mouth to speak, but the doctor held up his hand to stop him. "Let me finish please. One part of me tells me I did the right thing, but still somewhere down inside of me is the guilt. Guilt for taking an infant into my hands, alive, knowing that it did not ask to be brought into the world in that grotesque form, and then destroying that life with my knowledge that's suppose to save lives. It's a terrible thing to be placed into a position where you have to make a decision on who lives or dies."

"I have been fighting a mental battle within myself all day. What gives me the right to decide on who lives and who dies? All my life I have been against the so-called mercy killing idea. Perhaps it's because I had never been face-to-face with that situation before. I became a doctor because I felt compassion for the sick. My mind was compelled to put out the possibility of having to take a life without hesitation, but last night I did that very thing. What really bothers me is the fact that I didn't hesitate. The question then becomes. Should I have used reasoning before I acted? The humane side of me says I did the right thing."

"Like I said before, I have been fighting a mental battle all day. My final diagnosis of the situation is this. I can be both humane and professional. Last night I did what had to be done. Had I stopped to reason out whether to let the child live or to do what I did, the results would still have been the same. Like you asked me this morning. What kind of life would that child had if it had been allowed to live? The answer to that if, is very logical. There would have been much more grief and pain than there was from the impact of the discovery of its physical condition. The mother and father of the child think that it was stillborn. Only you and I know the truth.

"I still feel a deep guilt for taking that life, although I know now that I did the right thing. If I'm faced with that situation again, I'll take the same course of action and learn to live with the guilt feeling."

They both sat quietly for several minutes with Nat digesting what the doctor said, and the doctor hoping that Nat understood what he was saying. Finally Nat asked the question that he did not want to ask, but knew for his own peace of mind he had to. "If Sarah and Jenny's babies are mutated, and born alive, would you terminate their lives also?"

"Yes Nat. I'm afraid so."

"Thank you for your honesty, and straight forwardness. If that's what comes about I do not want to know if they are born alive. I will not ask you one way or another."

Alan stood up and reached out his hand to Nat. Nat stood up as they shook hands. Alan spoke with admiration. "You are the best friend any one could ask for. It's easy to see why you are a leader of men. Every person that comes in contact with you draws strength from you. If they are confused and don't know the way, you have a special something about you that makes them find the way. We all wanted this town, but we didn't know it until you brought us all together. I honestly do not think that it would have happened without you. No other person in the world could have brought this group together and made it work as you have done. I deeply admire you, as I'm sure every man, woman, and child here does."

Nat was at a loss for words to say at first, and then he spoke humbly. "Thank you for the kind words, but please don't put me on a throne. I'm not a king, nor a leader of men. I only lead and show the way when I feel that I can, or am asked to. If I'm asked to, and don't feel I can, then I'll decline, but if no one else will, then I feel it's my duty to try."

The doctor turned to go. "I must go check on my patients. Bye."

Nat sat back down to be alone for awhile.

CHAPTER 9

A couple of days later Nat went out in the morning hunting by himself, as he choose to be alone so he could get into a deep thought without any interruption. His direction took him upwards, and he found a rock out-cropping which afforded him a panoramic view of the valley. The sky was clear and the suns warmth was felt strongly, so he stripped down to his waist to enjoy the sun's rays.

Taking advantage of his solitude he let his mind slip back to the past. Closing his eyes he thought about when he first met his wife. His job as an investigator for the Department of Natural Resources had taken him back to Washington D. C. to give a report to a senate committee. After a grueling three hours of answering questions, from what he felt was stupid senators who didn't even know about woods and wonders of nature, he had walked to a nearby restaurant for lunch. It was cafeteria style, so after filling his tray to make up for the breakfast he had missed and a little extra for lunch, he managed to get a table by himself. He had just taken a couple of bites of food when he heard a soft gentle voice.

"Would you mind if I shared the table with you?"

Looking up towards the voice he became totally speechless. The voice was coming from the most beautiful woman he had ever seen in his life. Her black hair cascaded down over her shoulders resting against the red jersey knit dress she was wearing. Nat opened his mouth to speak, but nothing came out.

She smiled and waited for a few seconds, then asked. "Does that mean I may join you?"

Somehow he managed to nod his head yes. As she sat down he kept staring.

Sitting down, she spread a napkin across her lap, then put both elbows on the table and cradled her chin with both hands. With a twinkle in her eyes she reprimanded him. "It's not very nice to stare. Especially with your mouth open."

He quickly closed his mouth and looked down, turning a dark red. I'm deeply sorry ma'am."

"What did I do to cause that sort of reaction anyway?"

Nat stammered a little. "It's---It's because your beauty awed me."

She blushed a little. "Well, I must admit that I've never had a man react that way before."

They quickly became comfortable with each other, and she was a totally captivated audience as he told her about his job and his experiences in the wilds.

Time slipped by so quick that he didn't have time to find out anything about her. She looked at her watch. "Oh dear! I must get back to work! Thank you for a very enjoyable lunch." As she got up to leave, Nat jumped to his feet.

"I forgot to ask you your name!"

She smiled and presented her hand. "Nancy. What is yours?"

Nathan Sargent, but people call me Nat."

"Well Nat, I'll look for you in here tomorrow then, and you can tell me more about your very interesting job. Bye for now."

"Bye!" He sat down again. Looking down at his tray, he realized he hadn't even eaten yet.

The next day the session went right through lunchtime. Nat was having a hard time concentrating on the questions because all he could think about was Nancy, and how he might not get to see her again. This was Friday, and his last day to appear at the hearings.

His flight back to Seattle left Sunday evening, and for the entire flight he was filled with sadness because he didn't get to see her again before he left.

It took him a couple of weeks to convince himself that it was just a chance meeting, and that he should just forget about it. Then about a month later he was up in the mountains on a field expedition when the supply plane flew over and dropped him fresh supplies.

As he opened the drop, a letter dropped out. Picking it up he noticed it was special delivery from the U. S. Supreme Court. He gathered everything up and went back to his campsite. After pouring himself a cup of coffee, he opened the letter. It was written in longhand. Quickly he looked at the signature which read Nancy Coleton. His heart leaped with joy. The letter told him that she worked for the U. S. Supreme Court as a secretary and that she had checked on the hearings and found out why she had not seen him. She then inquired how to get in contact with him by writing to the Department of Natural Resources. Nancy also went on to say she was going to spend two weeks in Bellingham visiting an aunt she hadn't seen in a couple of years, then gave the aunt's name and address, and dates she would be there.

He calculated quickly. That's next month, only three weeks from now. If he hurried, he could wrap this trip up by then. He wasn't that far from Bellingham, and he had to go back through there on his way to Olympia.

In two and a half weeks, Nat was packing up his field notes and gear. It was a Sunday so he decided to take time going through Bellingham and locate that address so he could drive right to it when Nancy got there.

The house was at the end of a cul-de-sac off a street in the suburbs. Without thinking he pulled up in the driveway and stopped to look at the house. It was a typical middle class rambler and the yard was very well landscaped and in excellent trim. While he was admiring the yard, a car pulled up in back of his.

A lady in her fifties got out of the car and walked up to his window. As he rolled down the window the lady stepped back and looked at the identification on the car door, then looked at him. Kinda early aren't you?"

"Huh?"

"Nancy won't be here until Tuesday night."

"You know who I am?"

"I think so. I'll bet you're that young man she told me all about in her letters. I think she said you name is Knot."

"Nat."

"Oh yes. Nat. Well get out of the car and come on in."

"Oh, I couldn't do that. You see I just came down out of the mountains, and I haven't even had a shower."

She got astern look on her face. "Knot! Before my husband died, he worked for a paving outfit, and he came into the house looking a lot worse than you do now. So don't you fret over how you look. Just get out of the car and come into the house."

"Uh—that's Nat.,"

But she had already stared walking towards the house. He shrugged his shoulders and got out of the car. When he got into the house he looked around and saw that it was spotless, which really made him feel embarrassed.

She saw his uneasiness. "Come out into the kitchen and sit down. The chairs are vinyl so you can't do them any harm. What would you like to drink? I have coffee, tea, juice, or would you rather have a cold beer?"

"Uh---coffee if it's not too much trouble."

"No trouble at all." She quickly put on a pot of coffee. "Just have a seat there at the table. You must be quite a man. Nancy has never given any man a second thought in her life. But according to her letters, and I've had two of them, she s completely hooked on you. She said you belong in the city like a moose belongs in the middle of down town New York City. Just from the looks of you, I'd say she is right. Does you work keep you out of the city much Knot?"

"Uh---yes ma'am. It's Nat."

"Oh yes! Well anyway, she's always wanted to learn about the outdoors, but her father was nothing but a city slicker. When he looked at the countryside, all he could think about was how many houses or shopping malls could be built there. Given a chanced the fool would level the whole county and build houses and shopping malls. Why my sister ever married him I'll never know."

"Now Nancy, she is different. When she went to the zoo, she would start crying because she thought it was sad for the animals to be caged up. To her they should be turned loose where they belong. One thing for sure, and that is, you'll never get her to go to a zoo anymore."

One time a chipmunk came around their house. Nancy started feeding it and it was a pet to her. Then that old fool of a father of hers set a trap and killed it. I don't think she ever forgave him for that. I don't blame her either. I thought that was the cruelest thing he ever did."

The coffee finished brewing and she poured him a cup. "Do you take anything in it Knot?"

"Uh---no. Just black. It's Nat."

"Oh yes! I can see why Nancy flipped over you. You got good upbringing. Not like those aristocrats back east. Nancy says all they think about is drugs, booze, sex, and fancy parties." She looked him in the eye. "Do you drink?"

"Well---to be honest ma'am. I have been known to take a drink once in a while."

"Nothing wrong with having one every once in a while. I do that myself. I'm not supposed to know it, but Nancy likes to have a glass of wine every now and then, but I suppose you already know that. Did you meet her at one of those fancy parties back there? She never told me how you met."

"Oh no! We shared a table in a restaurant."

Just then the telephone rang and she went to answer it. After a few minutes she came back and sat down. "That was nosey Matilda next door. She saw your car in the driveway. I swear. Curiosity is the only thing that keeps that woman alive. She also wanted me to take her down to the store. Probably so she can question me about you."

Nat stood up. "Well, I really have to get going. It will take me a couple of days to get my notes in order so I can take some time off."

"Are you going to take Nancy camping?"

"I will if she wants to go."

"Oh she will. She says she's coming out here to visit me, but I'm no fool. She's coming out here to see you. But don't feel bad. Just seeing that girl happy is what I care about."

She walked out to the car with Nat so she could move hers out of the way. As he got into his car, she waved goodbye. "See you in a couple of days Knot!"

"Uh---that's---never mind."

It wound up taking him three and a half days to get his notes organized and submitted, but they gave him time off until Nancy had to go back home. He looked at the clock as he picked up his briefcase to leave. Just past noon, he had time to get a haircut and beard trim. He went straight home from the barber shop, and jumped into the shower.

As soon as he came out of the shower he called information in Bellingham. "Dorthey Williston, please?" He gave the address and wrote the number down. He hesitated before calling, trying to decide what he should say. Finally he decided to just play it by ear. She had gotten in Tuesday night and he hadn't had time to call her as he had been working overtime to get his work, finished. Quickly he picked up the phone and dialed the number.

It took a few seconds for the call to click through, and then it rang twice. The voice on the other end took him by surprise. "Hello! Dorthey's hen house! Dorthey clucking!"

Nat hesitated for a moment. "May I speak to Nancy please?"

"That you Knot?"

"Uh---yes it is." (Why fight it he thought?)

"She is right here. Been sitting by this phone ever since she got here. Even took it to bed with her last night!"

He heard Nancy in the background. "Aunt Dorthey! You're going to scare him off!"

Nat chuckled as he waited for her to get on the phone.

"Nat?"

"I think so. Your aunt has me wondering tho'. I'm afraid she might think my last name is Head, and that's what scares me."

She quickly apologized for her aunt. "I'm sorry she keeps calling you that. I'll try to get her to get it right. Where are you?"

"I'm at home right now. I live just north of Olympia. Can I take you to dinner this evening?"

"I'd love it!" She cupped her hand over the phone. "I think we should ask aunt Dorthey to go along also."

Nat laughed. "What ever you say."

"What time should I be ready?"

He thought for a minute about the distance. "It's a long drive, so make it about seven o'clock. Is that alright?"

"I'll be ready. Please drive carefully. I'll see you when you get here. Bye!"

"Bye!" Hanging up the phone he felt a happiness that he had never known in his life. He hurried into the bedroom closet to find his suit.

Taking it out he realized that the only time he had worn it was to the Governor's Ball four years ago. Good thing he had the foresight to cover it with plastic.

Just as he was ready to leave, there was a knock on the door. Opening it, he saw his friend Jerry from work standing there. "Hi Jer'. I'm just leaving. What's up?"

Jerry stepped inside. "I hate to tell you this Nat, but we just got a special assignment in, and the boss wants you to go out and do the study on it right away. Might take you three weeks. It's a touchy on. That's why he wants you to go."

At first Nat was stunned. Then he felt the anger rising in him. "Bull shit! I'll quit my job before I'll do it!"

Jerry threw up his hands. "Just kidding! Calm down!"

"That's the rottenest, sneakiest, and I might add, the shittiest joke you ever pulled, and you're a rotten son-of-a-bitch!"

He looked at Nat's suit. "Wow! That's the first time I've ever seen you dressed like that! I'm used to seeing you in the department's uniform all the time. You sure look strange."

"I feel it too! Well listen Jer', I got to get going. Sorry I can't talk."

Jerry walked out to the car with him, and then laughed. "You might impress her with the suit, but I'm not too sure about the land rover. You should have at least washed it."

"Nat looked at it. "Oh shit! I forgot all about that. No time to do it now. Maybe she will understand. I hope!"

"Why not go rent a car?"

"No time for that either!"

He jumped into the land rover. "Talk to you later!"

As he got into Bellingham he remembered he hadn't bought any flowers. Looking at his watch he saw that there was still a little time. He was watching for a flower shop when he spied a pet shop. Quickly he pulled over in front of it, and went inside.

"Can I help you?" Asked the man behind the counter?

"Would you by any chance have any chipmunks for sale?"

"Got one mean one left. Half price."

"I'll take it!" Nat pulled out his wallet and paid for it.

As he went out the door the man warned him. "Don't reach into the cage or he will take your finger off."

Nat arrived at the house fifteen minutes early. Holding the cage behind him, he reached to knock on the door, but it opened before he had a chance to strike it. Nance stood there wearing a tight fitting black dress with a red scarf tied around her neck and wearing red high heeled shoes. Again he stared.

Nancy laughed. "You're staring again!"

"Oh! I'm sorry. Here!" He held the cage out to her. "Oh, Nat! It's so cute! Thank you!" She then set the cage down and put her arms around him and kissed him full on the lips.

He felt his heart miss a beat and his knees getting weak. "May I sit down?"

As he sat in a chair, Dorthey came in carrying him a cup of coffee. She took one look at him. "That suit looks terrible on you. It's not you!"

"Aunt Dorthey!!!" Nancy shrieked. "That's rude! He looks very nice!"

"Well, it just ain't him! She then headed back for the kitchen.

Nancy was beet red from embarrassment. "I'm terribly sorry Nat."

He stood up. "Don't be. She is right. I don't even feel like me in this suit. Don't be upset with her, she tells it like she sees it, and I like that. She's a pretty neat lady. I also know that you're a very special lady."

He walked over to her. "And I also know that I'm crazy about you." Putting his hands on each side of her head, he bent down and kissed her on the lips.

She blushed as she looked into his eyes. At that moment she realized that she loved him with all her heart. She then kissed him back. "Nat?"

"Yes?"

"Would you take the chipmunk with you the next time you go out into the woods and set it free?"

He put his arms around her and held her tight. "We'll do it together. Tomorrow."

She pulled herself out of his arms. "Right now we better feed it. Aunt Dorthey!?"

"What dear?" She asked from the kitchen.

"Do we have anything we can feed the chipmunk?"

Dorthey came out of the kitchen carrying a small sack. Got just the thing here. Sunflower seeds! Those little nutcrackers love 'em."

Nancy took the sack and then took a few out.

As she started to open the cage, Nat warned her. "Careful! The guy at the pet shop said it was mean and would bite."

She knelt down by the cage which was sitting on the coffee table. It is so frightened. Look its shaking all over."

As she talked to the chipmunk she opened its cage and slowly put her hand in putting some seeds right in front of it. Leaving her hand there, she kept talking, then slowly picked up a seed and held it right in front of its mouth. It let out a little chirp, then reached its tiny paws out and took the seed. As it held the seed and broke open the shell, Nancy took one finger and started petting it. She kept petting it as it finished that seed. Pulling her hand back a little she turned it palm up. The chipmunk picked up another seed, then jumped up on her hand and sat there while it ate it. As it jumped down to get another seed, she withdrew her hand and closed the cage. "All it needed was love."

Nat was amazed. It took him longer than that to gain an animal's confidence. "Ahem." He cleared his throat. "I think we have a dinner date, and I'm a little hungry."

"I'll go get my coat." She headed down the hall.

He turned to Dorthey. "Are you coming with us Mrs. Williston?"

"Not on your life! This nights for love." She winked at him. "No curfews around here, so stay out as late as you want."

Nancy came back and handed her coat to Nat. "Aunt Dorthey told me earlier that she won't be going. There is a special on television she doesn't want to miss."

He looked over at Dorthey, and she just smiled and winked at him. Smiling, he winked back.

They went to a restaurant that featured seafood and he ordered fried oysters, while she had the salmon steak. This time he made a point of talking a little less, and eating more. It was almost eleven when they returned to the house, and she asked him to come in for a while.

He put his arm around her as they sat down on the couch. The only light that was lit, was a little light on the television set. Neither spoke, and after a few minutes she laid her head on his shoulder and fell to sleep. Nat suddenly felt very tired, so he closed his eyes.

Suddenly he felt a tapping on his arm. Opening his eyes he saw Dorthey standing there in her robe. She motioned for him to pick up Nancy and follow her. Gently picking her up, he followed Dorthey down the hall. She held a door open and pointed inside. Once inside he saw a large bed with the covers turned down. As he laid her down on the bed, Dorthey took Nancy's shoes off then pulled the covers up over her.

Dorthey pulled Nat's head down and whispered into his ear. "You lay down on the other side. It's too late for you to drive back to Olympia."

He protested. "I can sleep on the couch."

I won't hear of such a thing! It's a back breaker to lay down on. Go ahead and sleep in here. You're both adults." She then winked at him and went out closing the door behind her.

He stood there for a minute, and then walked over to the other side of the bed. Stripping down to just his pants, he laid the clothes on a chair. As he pulled cover down it dawned on him how wrinkled his pants would get from sleeping in them, so he took them off, folded them and slid them under the bed. Upon lying down he felt drained.

Nancy rolled over towards him. He felt her hand on his shoulder as she spoke. "Thank you for a beautiful evening." She then got out of bed, and he could hear the rustle of clothing as she undressed. Nat kept his back to her as she slid back into bed. Her naked breasts felt hot against his back as she kissed him on the cheek. "Good night Nat." Then laying down she slipped her arm under his and rested it against is chest while she snuggled up against his back.

He could tell by her breathing that she went right to sleep. The heat from her body, the scent of her perfume, and her steady breathing put him into a deep sleep feeling good all over.

Nat was dreaming about Nancy when he felt a hand gently shaking him. The shaking stopped, so he opened one eye, and then both eyes were wide open. Nancy was standing there holding a small tray with a cup of coffee on it, wearing a long flowing pink robe. He could tell she wore nothing under it as the top part was open showing just enough of the gentle curve, and smooth skin of her breasts to be extremely sensual. Her right foot was forward enough for the robe to slip to each side baring her beautifully shaped naked leg, nearly to her thigh. He stared.

"You're staring again."

"I'm sorry." He felt the flush in his face as he forced himself to look away.

She sat the tray on the nightstand then bent over and kissed him on the cheek. "It's nearly ten o'clock, and you promised me you would take me out to the woods to free the chipmunk."

He sat straight up in bed. "Oh shit! I've never slept this late before!"

She sat down behind him, then laying her cheek against his back, reached around under his arms and gently ran her hands over his bare chest. "It did you good to get a decent night's sleep." She purred.

He felt himself getting an erection. "I had better get dressed." She didn't move. "Well?"

"Well what?" She inquired.

"Aren't you going to leave while I get dressed?"

"No."

He reached down and groped under the bed for his pants.

Nancy chuckled. "I laid them over on the chair."

He started blushing. "Oh well." Getting up he hurried over to the chair and grabbed his pants. As he pulled them up he hoped she hadn't noticed the bulge in his shorts. Slipping into his shoes, and pulling his shirt on, he turned around. "I have to go out to the car and get some different clothes if we are going out to the woods. You better hurry up and get dressed."

After getting the clothes from the car, he headed down the hall. The bathroom door was closed, so he thought Nancy had gone in there to get dressed. Upon entering the bedroom he discovered he was wrong. She was standing at the foot of the bed in only her bra and panties, holding a shirt on one hand and a pair of pants in the other. "Will this be okay to wear?"

Nat blushed and stammered. "Oh---sure. Uh---yeah, that will be fine." He looked back at the bathroom door.

She laughed. "You can change in here silly."

Blushing, he quickly changed his clothes, and then started for the door.

"You forgot something Nat."

He turned around."Huh?" She had her pants and shirt on so he felt a little more at ease.

Walking over to him she handed him his cup of coffee. "It's getting cold. You better hurry up and drink it. There's more in the kitchen."

As he left the bedroom he noticed that the bathroom door was still closed, which struck him as being strange, as it had been open when he went out to the car.

When he entered the kitchen, he saw Dorthey sitting at the table playing solitaire while she smiled and hummed a tune. He poured a fresh cup of coffee, then walked over and stood behind Dorthey. She kept on humming and smiling. Nat bent over and kissed her on the cheek. "I don't believe I've met a craftier lady in my life."

Dorthey went right-on humming only a little louder. As he sat down she quit humming, scooped up the cards and looked at him. "Have you asked her to go camping yet?"

"Well, no. Not yet."

"What's taking you so long? She will only be here for another week and a half."

He threw up his hands and laughed. "Okay! Okay! I'll ask her this afternoon if she wants to leave tomorrow and comeback in a week."

"Nine days"

"She might not even want to stay a week."

"Ask her."

A couple minutes later Nancy came into the kitchen. He decided not to wait to ask her. Walking over to her he asked. "How would you like to spend---nine days out in the woods?"

She threw her arms around him. "Can we really?"

"That's what I'm asking you."

"Oh yes! Yes! Yes!"

He looked over at Dorthey. She was looking at him with an "I told you so!" smile on her face.

"I've always wanted to go camping! I've even dreamed about it, but I've never even had the chance to go even over night. Don't we need a tent, sleeping bags, pots and pans, dishes silverware, and all kinds of things?"

"Hold it right there! That land rover I'm driving out there is always ready to go. I keep everything that's needed for camping right in the back. All we have to get is some food and fill up the water jugs."

He looked down at her feet. Also pick up some hiking boots for you. I always carry an extra sleeping bag in case one gets wet, and I have two packs. We better get you some different clothes too those are alright for a day in the woods, but they would never do on a nine day trip. If we get down town and get what we need, we can still get out there before dark and set up camp."

As she ran to get her coat, Nat gulped down his coffee, and looked at Dorthey. "Once she gets out there, she might want to come back early."

Not on your life! This is her dream come true. She would spend the rest of her life out there if she could. Mark my words! She's a determined gal, and she wants to learn the ways of nature more than anything else in the world. A lot of her spare time has been reading about nature." She looked at him with a knowing look. And Knot, you're the man that can teach her, and give her what she wants and needs."

Just then Nancy came back. "I'm ready! Let's go! She went over to her aunt. "Aunt Dorthey, isn't this fantastic?"

"Yes dear, it is. Now get going!"

As they left, a tear came to Dorthey's eye. She knew this was going to be the turning point in Nancy's life, and she was overwhelmed with happiness for her.

The nine days seemed to go by rapidly for them. Every day they went on hikes, with Nat trying to keep up with all of her questions about nature and nature's way. In the evening, by the campfire he talked about the land he had purchased up in British Columbia that had a small hidden cove. He explained that his folks were both killed in an auto accident, and he had inherited a large sum of money so he didn't really need to work. His plans were to someday quit his job and move to Canada and spend the rest of his life on his land, only coming in to civilization to get supplies once a year.

By the ninth day, they had decided to get married. She went back to Washington D. C. and gave them a two week notice, then at the end of the two weeks came back west.

They had a simple marriage out in the woods with only the preacher, Dorthey, and Nat's friend Jerry present.

She went out on all of his expeditions with him and worked right along side of him. In the evenings by lantern, she would organize and rewrite his field notes for him. After two years, he quit his job and they went to live on their land in Canada, building everything from scratch.

Nat was startled back into the present by a rock falling behind him from somewhere up above. Grabbing his rifle he rolled to one side, stopping on his stomach, with the gun pointed up the rugged mountain side. Slowly he checked the entire area, but saw noting. The ground rose over a hump about a hundred yards up ahead of him. Silently but quickly he worked his way up, stopping every once in awhile to listen for the slightest noise. Just as he neared the top, he heard more rocks rolling on the other side. Stepping behind a huge rock he crouched down, and waited, keeping his rifle ready for action.

Chapter 10

He didn't move for nearly fifteen minutes, and then he looked up at the sky. By the position of the sun he knew it was mid-afternoon. Glancing down at his watch he saw it was a little after three-thirty. Nat was used to sitting patiently while watching animals in the wild. With a death-like silence he waited for something to happen. Then he heard a noise again, but it seemed farther away. Slowly he crept out from behind the rock, and worked his way over the top. Stopping suddenly he stood straight up and laughed. Over across the draw was a small herd of mountain goats. His presents startled them and they promptly bound up and away over the next rise out of sight.

After retrieving his shirt he headed back towards camp. Not too far from camp he spotted a big buck. He brought his gun up and took aim. Just as he started to squeeze the trigger, he heard a shot and saw the buck drop. Staying where he was he waited. Within a minute Lisa sprang out of the woods on his left and hurried over to the deer. Quickly she cut its throat, and then she castrated it and cut the scent pads off its hind legs. Nat continued to watch as she cut it open and removed the guts. Separating the heart and liver, she stuffed them back into the chest cavity, and then tied the front and hind legs on each side together. Using another piece of cord she wrapped it around the midsection to keep the inter cavity closed. She laid down next to the deer and slipped her arms through the deer's legs, then rolled over onto her stomach with the deer coming onto her back. Struggling she stood up with the buck hanging on her back like a pack. Grabbing her rifle she headed for camp.

"Nat hurrying to catch up with her stepped on a dead branch making a loud crack in the stillness. Lisa spun around promptly, pointing her rifle right at him. He threw up his hands. Don't shoot! I give up!"

"Nat! You almost made me shoot you!"

Well, I was just getting ready to holler when I stepped on that damn branch."

"You're usually not that careless."

"I was hurrying to catch up with you to help you carry that magnificent catch back to camp." He took the deer from her and slung it over his shoulder "What brings you out here? You never went hunting by yourself before."

"You had been gone so long, that I became concerned, so I was tracking you when I saw the buck. Since I wasn't too far from camp, I decided to shoot it, and take it back in, then start out again looking for you."

"Thank you for your concern, but you should know by now that when I go into the woods, I'm going into my natural environment and I'm perfectly at home and safe."

"Well, I still worry about you."

That evening after a late supper, Nat was sitting by the fire having afresh cup of coffee. As he settled back, he reached into his pocket out of habit, took out his pipe, and went to fill it with tobacco. Catching himself, he turned it around in his hand looking at it. At that instant Ellen reached around from in back of him, grabbed the pipe and threw it into the fire. "Hey! What did you do that for?"

"You said the flavor was washed out."

"Well---."

"Well? Have you been smoking it?"

"No, but---,"

"Then why keep it?"

"I guess just out of habit. I'm used to always having it handy. I'm going to be lost without it."

"Well don't despair. Close your eyes."

He closed his eyes, and felt her put something in his pocket.

"Okay!"

Opening his eyes, he reached into his pocket and pulled out a beautiful pipe. It had silver inlay and carvings on it. All he could do as keep turning it over and over in his hand looking at it.

"Well?" She asked. "How do you like it?"

He suddenly felt mischievous. Getting a dissatisfied look on his face he answered her. "It's ugly!"

"No it isn't!"

"Sure it is! Just look at it! They carved all over it!"

She couldn't' believe what she was hearing. "But you said that you wanted a fancy pipe!"

"I said fancy not cut up."

"Just what do you call fancy then?"

"Oh---one with silver inlay and carvings all over the bowl part of it. Deep cherry red with a black plastic mouth piece."

She knew she had been had. "Well, if you don't like that one we'll just throw it in the fire also." She grabbed the pipe from him.

"Hey! Wait a minute!" He jumped up to try to get the pipe back.

Bolting as he grabbed for her, she took off running for the woods. Nat had the advantage with his longer legs, and soon caught her. Throwing his arms around her from the back he picked her up as she struggled. "Give me that back!

"You said it was ugly!"

"I was just kidding! Are you gonna give it to me?"

She quit struggling and smiled. "Are you talking about the pipe or something else?"

Setting her down, he turned her around. "Give me the pipe and then I'll give you something else."

With a sly smile she handed the pipe over. "You are going to give it to me out here in the woods?"

"Sure." He bent down and kissed her, then turned around and headed back towards the fire.

"Is that all?"

Nat laughed. "Yep!"

"You rat!"

The next month brought the completion of the doctor's clinic, more houses, running water, and hot weather to ripen the berries, while most of the women toiled to get them canned. Some of the fields down by Sequim had wheat in them, so a crew was sent down there to harvest it, so it could be ground into flour. With the flour and by using some old wood cook stoves they had found, the women were able to make bread. Some cattle had been rounded up so they were also able to have fresh milk and cream.

Spirits were running high with things so bountiful. Daily the aroma of fresh bread and pies drifted through the little town by the river. Then, tragedy struck without warning.

After checking through camp for any needs, Nat went over to the dam site to see how it was doing. He saw Charlie coming across the dam. "Morning Charlie!"

"Morning Nat! How does it look?"

"Damn good! Looks like you're almost ready to go."

"Just about. The water level needs to be a little bit higher. Expect that to be up there sometime during the night. We still got a couple more days work on the spillway tho'."

"Where is Jim?"

"Down in that first hole hooking up the first unit."

"Thanks!" He went over to where Charlie had indicated, and descended down the ladder.

Jim looked up as Nat was coming down. "Man! Am I glad to see somebody? I could sure use an extra hand on this."

"Just tell me what you want, and I'll be glad to help."

"Grab that wire there, the black one, and hold the end over so I can get the damn thing hooked. I've been fighting this damn thing for a good ten minutes. It's near impossible to hold the tension of that wire and this one here at the same time, and then try to fasten them down." It only took a minute with the two of them working together. "Thanks!"

Nat stepped back and looked around the concrete walled room. "This is one hell-of-a nice job. It's a miracle how fast you men got this built."

Jim laughed. "It's easy when you don't have any inspectors looking over your shoulder trying to tell you how to do it. Another good thing is that we all worked together. No unions to tell you that your job is such-and-such so you can't be over there helping that other man do his job, because you're not getting paid for that. I never did like unions, because as far as

I'm concerned, all they did was slow down the job and cause the cost of living to go up, with all their strikes for higher wages. The poor bastard that got the raise wound up losing his wages while on stride, and then had to pay a bigger price for the product later. He still lost in the end. Not to mention the poor and elderly who really got the shaft."

Nat nodded in agreement. "I kind of like our system here. We look out for and help each other. I hope as our group grows, it grows in the right direction. We need a society and system that is based on that principal."

"Yeah! And I think it can be done too."

"When do you think we will have electricity?"

"If all goes well, by noon tomorrow."

"That's music to my ears! Sure a lot of concrete here."

Jim smiled. "Sure is! I'm glad we were able to get that concrete plant working in town. We've kept those trucks rolling almost constantly. I was talking to Ken yesterday, and he said that the daily search for mutants has really paid off. He doesn't think there is a one of them between Forks and Port Townsend and that includes Neah Bay."

"I hope not." Nat continued looking around. "From the looks of things, this is a pretty solid structure"

"You know, that Charlie is a whiz on stress points. Bill drew up the basic design, but Charlie seems to be a natural when it comes to bulk structures. I'll bet he could design and build a dam to hold back the biggest river in the world."

"Bill said he was good. Well, I guess I'll get going. Need any more help before I leave?"

"No, I got it made now. Thanks."

Nat went back to his campsite and put the coffee pot on the still hot coals of the campfire.

Just as he sat down, Lisa came up. "I'll put on a fresh pot if you will put some more wood on the fire It's just about lunch time so I thought I would get it started before you got back."

Nat looked at his watch. "I guess it is that late. Time sure has a way of slipping by on a person. Since you mentioned food, I do feel a little bit hungry."

"Been going around checking everything again?"

"As usual, and helping whenever I can."

"Is everything going well?"

"Better than well. These people are fantastic. Jim tells me that we should have electricity by noon tomorrow. I just can't get over how fast they built that dam. Best damn crew ever put together."

Lisa smiled to herself as she thought. 'He is sure proud of these people.' She put the coffee pot on the grate over the fire. "I'll have some soup for you in about a half hour. Do you want some fresh bread with it?"

"No, just the soup. Where is Ellen?"

"She's helping on the food storage today."

"You two gals are quite the workers. It seems like every day you're doing something different. You're either working with the food, or driving nails. I know you have been in town helping tear down buildings, and gone out on the searches for mutants. Jim tells me you both have helped on the dam at one time or another, not to mention, I saw you helping put in the water lines from the river.

Come to think of it, I don't think there is one project around here that you two haven't had your fingers into."

She laughed. "Give me a couple of minutes, and ill think of something."

"The two of you even helped the doctor deliver Doris' baby last week."

Lisa was silent for a moment as she recalled that incident. "That was sad."

"It sure was. Too bad it had to be stillborn. That was our first normal baby."

"At least it gives us some hope." She replied.

"That it does."

As Lisa was cleaning up after lunch, Ellen came running up crying. She threw her arms around Nat. "Sarah had a miscarriage!"

"Where is she?"

"Down at the clinic."

Lisa was gone like a flash, running towards the clinic. Nat pried Ellen loose. "We better get down there!"

As they entered the clinic, Lisa was on one side of Sarah and the doctor was on the other side. Nast walked over next to the doctor and took Sarah's hand. "How are you feeling?"

"Very weak. I'm sorry Nat." She started crying.

"It couldn't be helped."

"But I've let Arn down and everybody else too."

The doctor gave her an injection. "I'm giving you a sedative. Now try to rest."

She looked at Nat. "I think Arn blames me. He just walked out of here without saying anything." The sedative took over very quickly and she slipped off to sleep.

Nat looked over at Lisa. "Do you know where he went?"

She was crying. "No I don't."

The doctor spoke up. "I think he went in the direction of the river."

"I'll check down there. Ellen, you and Lisa stay here for now."

He found Arn sitting on a log down by the river's edge. Sitting down next to Arn he spoke first. "Arn, I want to talk to you."

"Leave me alone! I don't want to talk to nobody!"

"Well, I'm going to say what I have to say, and then I'll leave."

"Arn glared at him. "Didn't you hear me? I said I don't want to talk!"

Nat continued. "What has happened to Sarah has happened to thousands of other women, and it will more than likely happen in the future to others. Sarah did not ask for this to happen, and neither did anybody else. I know you hurt inside. We all hurt inside, but right now Sarah hurts more than anybody. She thinks she let you down. She thinks she let everybody down. But the worst hurt for her right now is that she thinks that you blame her, and that you are going to reject her. Right now she needs your strength more than anything else in the world. When you walked out of that clinic, you took her strength, and her will to go on in life with you."

Nat stood up to leave.

Tears started to plunge down Arn's cheeks. He tried to wipe them away with his shirt sleeve. "I'm not blaming her!"

Nat turned back toward him. "Then why did you leave?"

"Because I felt myself falling apart. I didn't want her to see me crying."

Nat was silent for a moment. "Sometimes we cry because of happiness, but most of the time we cry because of pain. When the pain is inside our hearts, we cry because we care." He remembered his wife's death. "Believe me, I have cried from that pain inside. Now go to Sarah, and tell her how much you love her. And if you cry, she will know that it's because you care."

Arn slowly stood up and started walking towards the clinic. Nat spoke to him before he had gotten ten feet. "And tell her you want to try again."

Arn stopped for a second, and then continued on.

Nat then went into the woods and wept.

Nat didn't return to camp until several hours after dark. Quietly he crept into his tent and laid down on top of his sleeping bag. After dosing off for a few minutes, he woke up feeling the presents of someone else in the tent. Rolling over onto his back he could make out the form of someone on their knees beside his sleeping bag. He lay there on his back not saying anything.

"Are you awake?" Lisa asked in a whisper.

"Yes."

She didn't say any more for a few minutes, then spoke with sadness in her voice. "I'm sorry." Reaching down she stroked his cheek. "I know you think of Arn and Sarah as if they are your own children."

Nat raised his hand to her face. As he touched her cheek, he felt the tears flowing downward. Slipping his hand around in back of her head, he pulled her down to him.

Lying down next to him she kissed him with passion, and then laid her head on his chest. Soon they both drifted off to sleep.

They were awakened by Ellen's voice from outside the tent. "Coffee is done, and I just about have breakfast ready."

Nat woke up quickly as he realized Lisa was still in his arms.

Raising her head off his chest, she kissed him on the lips. "Thank you." Standing up, she looked down at him with compassion, and then turned and went outside.

He lay there for a few minutes with an uneasy feeling. Keeping his eyes cast down on the ground, Nat walked over and sat by the fire,

Ellen brought him a cup of coffee, kissed him on the cheek. "Good morning sleepy head." As he looked up at her, she smiled, then, turning around went back to finish preparing breakfast.

After breakfast Nat went down to the clinic. Inside the outer room he found Arn asleep in a chair, so quietly he went into the room where Sarah was, closing the door behind him.

She looked at him and the tears started to come to her eyes. "I'm sorry Nat."

He walked over to her and brushed a tear from her cheek. Bending over he kissed her on the forehead. It was just an unfortunate occurrence. Don't blame yourself for what happened. Nobody else is blaming you, so let's pick up the pieces and continue on." He handed her a tissue. Now wipe away those tears, and try to give me a smile."

She took the tissue, then after wiping her eyes, looked up at Nat. Then, with a weak smile she reached up and pulling his head down, gave him a kiss on the forehead. "You are the kindest person in the whole world"

Just then the door opened. Turning around, Nat saw the doctor come in with a cup of coffee in his hand. "I saw you come in. Would you like a cup of hot coffee?" He asked, holding the cup out to Nat.

"I think I will"

The doctor walked over to Sarah. "How are you feeling right now?"

"Much better. When can I go home?"

He checked her pulse, and then examined her eyes. "Whenever you want to, but take it slow for a while."

"Well then, if you two gentlemen will step out of the room, I'll get dressed right now,"

The doctor laughed. "Just don't forget to take that character sleeping in my outer room with you."

She was laughing as they left the room.

As they came out, Arn stood up. "How is she Doctor?"

"Fine! In fact she's getting dressed right now to go home."

"Oh boy! Arn said as he headed for her room.

The doctor grabbed his arm. "Hold on for just a minute young man. Keep in mind that she has to go slow and take it easy for a few days she lost a lot of blood."

"That means you do the cooking yourself." Nat laughed.

Arn looked at Nat. "I can't cook."

"I know! I've seen it when you've tried. Maybe Ellen or Lisa will come over and help."

"Gee! I hope so."

Arn then went into Sarah's room. Almost immediately he stuck his head back out. How long do I have to wait before I can try again doc?"

Ther doctor looked at Nat and winked. Then turning towards Arn said. "Oh---about a year."

"A year!!!"

Nat and the doctor broke out laughing.

Arn failed to see the humor. "Are you serious Doc?"

"Give her a month if you can make it."

"Thanks!" He said blushing, and closed the door.

Realizing that this was the day they were going to get electricity, Nat went over to the dam. There already was a small crowd gathered on one end. Everyone gave Nat their condolences for what had happened to Sarah. Thanking them, he turned to Bill. "I don't see Jim."

"He's over there in the transformer building."

Nat went over and entered. Charlie and Jim were busy going over everything. "Hello!" Nat called.

"Hello!" Jim answered without looking up. "Sorry about what happened yesterday."

"Me too." Added Charlie.

Thank you." He looked around. "How much longer?"

"Just as soon as I'm finished here I'm going to let Bill know, and then Pete is going to open the valve to start the turbine. After I check things down here, we can then throw the switch." He looked at Nat. "Then presto! We got electricity, I hope."

Charlie looked at Jim. "We will."

It took nearly two hours before everything was checked and rechecked. Nearly everybody had shown up for the big event finally Jim announced to the crowd. We're ready to throw the switches!"

"Then let's do it!" Somebody yelled from the crowd and cheers of agreement followed from the rest.

Jim raised his hands. "Just a minute! This is a big event! A lot of you people helped build this important structure, and I'm proud of you. The only problem left is who gets to throw the switches?" Everyone standing around Jim turned and looked at him without saying a word. "What's wrong? Did I say something wrong?"

Nat smiled at him. "No."

"Then what's the------?" It then dawned on him what they was trying to tell him. "Me?"

"You got it!" Pete said.

"Well shit! Times a wastin'!" He said as he headed for the switches, and the crowd applauded him.

Jim threw the switches, and as the flood lights over the dam came on, a roar from the crowd filled the air. There were tears of joy as everybody shook hands, hugged each other, and expressed their feelings.

As Jim came back out, everybody crowded around him. The men slapped him on the back and shook his hand, and the women took turns kissing him.

It was well nigh to an hour before most of the people had straggled back towards the town. The only ones left at the dam were Nat, Jim, Bill, Pete, Charlie, and Hank. "You guys wait right there!" Jim voiced as he headed for a clump of brush. He searched through the brush for a minute, and then returned with a bottle of whiskey. "Been saving this bottle of hooch just for this day! Are you guys going to help me drink it, or do I have to do it myself?

Pete laughed. "Just pop that top!"

He opened the bottle and offered it to Bill. "Take a swig."

"Hell no! This dam is your baby! You take the first tip of the bottle!"

Everyone laughed as Jim tipped the bottle up and took a healthy swig. Wiping his mouth on his sleeve he let out a bellow. "Damn! That tastes like the purest nectar in the world!" The bottle was then passed around until it was empty.

Chapter 11

By the time the rainy season set in, most everybody had a house, and those that didn't, shared with somebody else. Nat, Lisa, and Ellen shared a two bedroom house. Each of the women had a bedroom and Nat slept on a couch in the living room.

The doctor came over one evening a week for dinner, and the other evenings were split up at different women's houses. On one particular evening, Nat and the doctor were sitting in the living room having coffee right after supper. They sat there in silence for a few minutes, and then the doctor looked over at Nat. "I feel like a lamb being led to the slaughter." He chuckled.

"Why is that?"

"Seven women, all fussing and fuming over me. Every evening I'm invited to supper at one or the others. Why, I haven't had to fix myself supper for over two months now. And to top that off, they even bring me lunch down to the clinic every day. The funny thing is they all seem to have a set schedule worked out. No fights or arguments either. They all get along great. One of them even stops by some mornings and makes me eat a breakfast."

Nat laughed. "What's so bad about all that?"

"Nothing. I feel like a king." Alan then got serious. "Each one of them would make a fine wife, and one of these days I'm going to have to decide on which one I would take for that noble position in my life. Quite frankly it's a tough decision. Whichever one I pick is going to cause the others to be hurt.

"I understand what you're saying, and I don't have an answer for you." Just then Lisa brought the coffee pot in to fill their cups. "Why not get a woman's point of view on this?"

"What's that?" Asked Lisa.

Alan blushed. "That's alright. I'll work it out somehow."

She looked at him. "Why Alan! You're blushing!"

Nat chuckled. "He's gotten into a predicament, and he is not sure how to handle it."

"Well, it can't be that bad."

"I have to admit," said Nat, "It could turn out to be a messy situation."

"What is it?" She queried.

"It seems there are several women all trying to win his heart, and he doesn't want to hurt any of their feelings. The plain and simple fact is that when he has to decide on one, he is not sure what to do."

She gave it some though, and then going over to Alan she put her hand on his cheek and kissed him on the other. "It's very simple! When you make the decision, your heart will make it for you. As far as hurting the others feelings, don't let that enter into your making that decision. I happen to know all the women involved in what's going on. They have discussed this very subject. Since there is a shortage of men around here, they are simply letting you know that they are available. They are not competing for you in any way. If you should choose one of them, or someone else, they all would be very happy for you and the one you picked. I will tell you this. As soon as you show your affection to one, the others will step aside. Then you can court that one if you wish, without any complications." She kissed him on the cheek again, picked up the coffee pot and went out into the kitchen.

There was a long silence before Nat spoke. "Well there you have it, plain and simple."

Alan was amazed. "And all this time I thought they were competing."

Nat laughed. "Never underestimate the power, no, the logic of women."

"How can you underestimate what you don't have the foggiest idea about?"

Nat roared and then slapped his knee. "Well, I don't know about you, but I'm not going to drive myself insane trying to figure out something that can't be even part way figured out."

The winter turned out to be an extremely harsh one, with a lot of snow, and freezing temperatures. Most of the people just stayed home, only venturing out to go to the supply building to get provisions, or to visit with the others.

Late one evening in January, shortly after Nat had gone to sleep there came a frantic pounding on the door. Leaping to his feet, Nat hurried to the door and jerked it open. "What the hell?"

The doctor was standing there with tears streaming down his cheek. "It's a boy!" He yelled with joy. "Jenny had a beautiful healthy baby boy!"

Tears sprang to Nat's eyes as Lisa and Ellen came running from their bedrooms in robes.

"Come in! Come in!" Nat told the doctor.

Both women kissed Nat, and then as the doctor closed the door and turned around they kissed him.

Lisa asked the doctor. "Is she at the clinic?"

"Yeah! Sally, that helps me once in a while, is taking care of things!"

"I'm going down there!"

"Me too!" Said Ellen, and they both headed for the door.

Coming to his senses Nat scolded them. "You two put some clothes on! It's snowing and cold as hell out there!"

They didn't even listen as they bolted out the door. Not thirty seconds elapsed when they heard a scream. Nat ran to the door and went out on the porch just in time to see Lisa helping Ellen up out of the snow, and then they took off going as fast as they could with the winds whipping their robes up flashing their pantied backsides as they went.

Nat came back in, slamming the door behind him. "Of all the dumb stupid---ah never mind!" He looked at the doctor. Alan, this is one of the happiest occasions experienced in many a years."

"It's the most wonderful birth I have ever delivered."

Nat went to the closet and rummaged around in his pack, then brought out a bottle of bourbon. "This calls for a drink. Been saving this for a special occasion, and I can't think of a more special one. Would you have a drink with me?"

"I've never had a drink in my life, but right now I think I will join you in celebration."

Getting two glasses from the kitchen, Nat poured them a half of glass of bourbon.

Watching Nat down his all at once, the doctor shook his head, and then took a big swallow. Instantly he started coughing and choking. As soon as he got over the coughing he remembered what he had heard them say in the movies. "Damn! That's good stuff!"

Nat looked at him and laughed. "The first swallow is always the hardest." Then pouring himself another half glass, tossed it down.

The doctor managed to get the rest of his down, and then sat his glass down. "Kinda makes you feel warm all over!"

Nat poured him another half glass. "Sure does!"

Just then they heard the town bell they had mounted in the center of their little settlement.

Alan laughed. "I'll bet that's Will waking everybody up to make the announcement." Then he tossed his drink down just like Nat.

Lisa and Ellen came back to the house a couple hours later. As they came through the door cold and shaking, they saw Nat passed out, face down, in the chair with his feet hanging over one side and his head over the other while he still clutched the empty bottle. The doctor was sitting on the floor in the corner passed out with a smile on his face.

"How could they do this?" Ellen shrieked.

Lisa shook her head as she looked around. "It probably wasn't hard. Nat isn't much of a drinker, and Alan doesn't drink. Come on! Help me get the doctor off the floor. He can sleep in my bed."

"What about Nat?"

She looked at him and thought a minute. "He can sleep where he's at, and I'll sleep on the couch."

"Serves him right, since it's no doubt that he was the instigator!" Ellen retorted as she bent down to help Lisa get the doctor up off the floor.

Nat came to a couple hours later having to go to the bathroom. Slipping as he got up off the chair, he fell on the floor, and then picked himself up. "Oh shit!" He stated as he held his head and staggered to the bathroom.

The lights were out so he didn't see Lisa lying on the couch. Flopping himself down he heard an "Oomph!" He jumped back up. "What the hell!?"

Lisa got up and turned the light on. There was fire in her eyes as she scolded Nat. "Getting yourself drunk is one thing, but getting the doctor drunk is another thing!"

"I didn't twist his arm."

"Maybe you didn't twist his arm, but if you hadn't offered it to him he wouldn't have drank!"

"Oh---that would have been rude to drink in front of a man and not offer him some."

"He has never drank in his life!"

"He has now."

"Oh Nat! How could you?"

It then dawned on Nat that she was standing there not realizing that her robe was wide open. All she had on under the robe was a pair of panties and her breasts were fully exposed. "Damn! You are sure a beautiful woman!"

She looked down to where his eyes were looking then blushing she quickly pulled her robe closed and tied the sash. "We put Alan in my bed, so I'm sleeping on the couch. Your sleeping bag is in the closet. You can sleep on the floor." She then lay down on the couch and turned her back to him.

The next morning as he came into the kitchen and sat down, neither Ellen nor Lisa spoke to him. Ellen sat a cup of coffee down in front of him, and then returned to helping Lisa finish breakfast. As they sat down to eat, Nat asked."Where is the doctor?"

"He is still sleeping." Lisa said in a cold voice.

"I better get him up so he can get down to the clinic."

Ellen glared at him. "You leave him be. Let him sleep it off if he can. I've already been down to the clinic, and everything is just fine."

Breakfast was finished in silence with Nat realizing he was in a lot of hot water. As soon as he finished, he headed for the clinic. Jenny was holding the baby as Will stood beside the bed.

"Good morning! How is the little tyke doing?"

"Just great! Answered Jenny.

Nat walked over and looked down at the baby. "Finest looking baby I ever seen!"

Just then Sally came in. "Good morning Nat." She stated in a cold voice.

Nat looked at her. "Do you have anything around here for a headache?"

She let out a very audible "Humph!" Then went to get him something for his hangover.

"Ellen was down this morning," Will said, "and she told us that you got the doctor drunk last night."

"Ah---I didn't get him drunk. We were both celebrating, and we both got a little bit feeling good."

Will laughed. "We heard you both passed out."

"The doctor passed out, and I fell to sleep."

"Draped over a chair sideways?"

He realized Ellen must have told them everything. "That just happened to be where I was at when I fell to sleep."

Will and Jenny were laughing when Sally brought Nat some pills and a glass of water. She turned to Jenny. "I'll be back in after your company leaves." Then giving Nat an angry look went out the door.

He looked after her. "Damn! You would think I beat the doctor up or something, with everybody mad at me."

Jenny laughed. "We're not mad at you Nat. Oh! Guess what?"

"What?"

"Guess what we named the baby?"

"William! After Will?"

"Well, sort of." Will said. "But its Nathan William."

"Why not William Nathan?

Jenny reached out and took Will's hand and they both looked at Nat. She spoke with respect. "Because we both kind of look up to you as a father."

Nat looked down and fidgeted with the leather tie strings on his shirt as he felt humble and proud. "I don't know what exactly to say, except thank you."

"And also," Will added, "we want him to think of you as his grandfather."

He was filled with pride as he answered. "You both make me feel very honored,"

Jenny reached up and pulled Nat's head down to her and kissed him on the cheek. "Do you want to hold your grandson?"

Taking the baby into his arms, he was filled with pride as he looked down at the child. "Hello little Nat!" The baby's eyes were open and seemed to be staring at Nat. Looking at Will and Jenny he asked with pride. "Do you think he knows I'm his grandpa?"

With a tear in her eye, Jenny answered him. "I'm sure he does."

He handed the baby back to Jenny. "You better go back to mama. She's probably gentler than I am."

"I doubt that!" Jenny laughed as she took the baby.

Just then the outer door opened and Nat heard sally. "Good morning doctor."

Then he heard Alan mumble. "Good morning Sally."

As Nat came out of the room he saw the doctor, who was standing there in wrinkled clothes, bloodshot eyes, messed up hair, and pale. "You okay Doc?"

Alan managed a weak smile. "I think so."

Just then Sally dropped something on the floor and the doctor grabbed his head. Nat laughed. "Good thing the bell ringing was done last night instead of this morning."

"Don't even suggest such a thing!"

Sally brought him something for his headache. "Thank you Sally." Then he headed for his office with Nat following him.

Nat closed the door behind him. "Boy I sure caught hell for last night.,"

Alan sat down behind his desk and looked up at Nat. "I thought maybe you did from what they said to me when I got up."

"They didn't get on your case did they?"

"Not exactly,. They apologized for you getting me drunk, and then told me you had been informed as to how they felt about it."

"That all?"

"Well---no."

"What else?"

"I told them I had gotten myself drunk, and that they shouldn't blame you for it."

"And?"

The doctor put his hands up to his head. "Do you have to talk so loud?"

"Sorry! I didn't know I was. What else?"

"They still blamed you, and said I didn't have to stick up for you."

"Anything else?"

"Well---yes."

"What?"

"Brace yourself ol' pal, because they said they wasn't through with you yet."

"What's that suppose to mean?"

"It means that when they get finished with you, you're going to know they didn't like what you did."

"Oh shit!"

"You're welcome to stay down here for a couple of days if you want. Maybe they will cool off then."

"Thanks for the offer, but I'll go home. I just don't know why they got so upset. In fact, they are downright pissed."

There was a knock at the door. "Would you see who it is Nat?"

He opened the door, and Sally came in with a distraught look on her face. "Doctor! Something has to be done about the visitors!"

The doctor looked at her. "You don't have to yell. What seems to be the problem?"

She threw up her hands. "The waiting room is full! They have all came to see the baby! Why, some of them even have toys!"

"Please stop yelling. I'll be out in a minute to see what I can do." On her way out she slammed the door, and the doctor grabbed his head. "She just can't know what it's like to have a hangover." Mumbled Alan.

The waiting room was nearly full as the doctor and Nat came out. Just then the outer door flew open, and in burst Jim carrying a stuffed animal almost as big as he was. Alan's mouth dropped open as he gaped. Walking over to him, he confronted the barrel-chested man. "My god! What is that for?"

Jim roared. "The little feller needs something to sleep with"

The doctor grabbed his head as the pain pulsated. "I don't believe this is happening."

"What's a matter Doc?" You got a headache?" Jim bellowed with concern.

"Yes. And it's getting worse!"

"Oh---that's bad!" Jim said in a loud voice, and then yelled over at Sally. "The doc's got a bad headache! You better get him something for it!"

Trying to keep his composure, Alan remarked. "She has already given me something."

"Well, I sure hope it starts helping you! You really look a mess!"

Under his breath, the doctor mumbled as he turned back to the crowd. "If you would stop yelling, it would help." He raised his hands to get everybody's attention. As soon as they quieted down, the doctor paused a minute to relish the quiet. Then, with throbbing head he spoke. "Now I know all of you wonderful folks are here to express your joy to the parents, and to see their magnificent son."He paused a few seconds. "But, too much company can be very tiring for both baby and mother. He looked at Jim and the huge stuffed animal. Not to mention how annoying it can be. So, what I'm going to have Sally do is give each one of you a slip of paper with a time on it. Whatever time is written down for you is the time you will be allowed to visit."

Jim protested. "But I carried this over here trying to keep the snow off of it. If I have to make another trip it might get soaked."

The doctor closed his eyes and shook his head, then looking Jim in the eye informed him. "You can leave it here in the waiting room until it's your time to visit."

"Well don't anybody go telling the little feller that it's out here! I want to surprise him."

Walking past Sally on his way to his office, he spoke in a low voice. "You better put Jim off as long as you can. I don't think Will and Jenny are quite ready for that monstrosity he's got with him."

Nat was heading for the outer door when Jim yelled at him. "Hey Nat! Where ya going"

"For a short walk"

"Wait up! I'll go with you!"

Nat was waiting outside as Jim came out holding a slip of paper and shaking his head. "What's the matter Jim?"

"Ah---I don't get to visit until tomorrow afternoon." As they walked Jim continued. "I can hardly wait to see that little feller." He paused for a minute. "I sure hope I can get the kid to call me Uncle Jim. When he starts talking that is." Jim added quickly.

"I'm sure it will come easy for him." Nat laughed,

"I wonder what they named him."

"Nathan William!"

Jim stopped in his tracks. "After you!?"

Nat smiled with pride. "Yep!"

Jim slapped Nat on the back. "That's great! Congratulations!"

The slap on his back reminded him of his hangover as a pain shot through his head. "Oh shit!" He moaned as he put his hand up to his head.

You got a headache too?"

"Yeah." And that slap didn't help it any.

"I'm sorry! You should have had Sally give you something for it!"

"She did."

"Oh! Okay."

Remembering the stuffed animal Nat asked him. Where did you get that thing you brought into the office?"

Awhile back I went into town to find some cable, and this house had a big shed out back. I figured that I might find some in the shed. Well, I didn't, so I went into the house to look around. Walking into one of the bedrooms, I spied it sitting there on the bed, so thinking about Will and Jenny's upcoming baby, I smuggled it into camp. Kept it hid pretty good too. Nobody even knew I had it except Silent Sam. Since he can't talk, there was no need to worry about him telling nobody."

After walking for a while longer they went separate ways, with Jim going-over to the dam to check on things as was his daily habit, and Nat going back to the house.

As he entered the house, Lisa was puttering around in the kitchen, but he didn't see Ellen. "Where's Ellen?"

"Over at Arn and Sarah's." She answered with icicles in her voice.

He went into the living room and sat on the couch. "Is there any coffee made?" He asked in a voice that could be heard out in the kitchen. A few seconds later she brought him a cup of coffee, then handing it to him turned around and headed for the kitchen without saying a word. "So I'm going to get the silent treatment am I?"

She spun around with fire in her eyes. "You better be glad it's the silent one instead of a verbal one!" The silent treatment didn't last long. Within two minutes she was back. "Nat? How could you be so cruel I've never known you to be cruel to anyone. Alan has become such a dear friend of ours. He's never taken a drink in his life, and then you get him drunk and leave him sitting on the floor." Tears were trickling down her cheeks. And today he has to feel terrible from a hangover. I just know he is suffering because of what you did. You didn't have to bring that bottle out while he was still here. He respects you as a very close friend and since you did bring out that bottle, you could have stopped him from taking a drink. He listens to you. I just don't understand what possessed you to get him drunk. For your sake, I hope he still respects you, because if he doesn't, you have lost a very close friend. There is nothing wrong with having a drink to celebrate. You had a drink when the dam opened, but you didn't get drunk, let alone get somebody else drunk. You knew Alan didn't ever drink."

He looked up at her. "Are you finished?"

"For now, but when Ellen gets back, I imagine she will have a lot more to say to you."

"Well, for starters, I do not feel for one second that I did anything cruel, nor even unjust for that matter. Did it ever occur to you that Alan had been under a lot of pressure and feeling a lot of sorrow due to the fact that the first four babies born were lost? That man has been through a lot of mental strain because of it. Then to top that off, Sarah had her miscarriage. That bothered the good doctor considerably. It bothered all of us. It tore me up inside, and you know just how much it did tear me up. But, I didn't get drunk to drown my sorrow, not that that thought didn't cross my mind. The doctor and I got drunk celebrating a joyous occasion. We both feared that Will and Jenny's baby might be born mutated, but it turned out to be a normal and healthy child. We did not plan to get drunk, it just happened. Alan is old enough to make his own decisions on whether or not to take a drink. Like I told you, I did not twist his arm. Yes, I offered him a drink. That I won't lie about. By getting drunk we released our tensions. I am sorry he got drunk and passed out. I'm sorry I got drunk and passed out, but I am not sorry we had a drink and celebrated the biggest and most joyous event our little town has ever experienced or will ever experience on that magnitude again. That being the first birth of a normal healthy child. If it had been Arn and Sarah's, the same thing probably would have happened. This is our hopes and dreams come true."

Nat vaguely remembered how they had been laughing about something, but he couldn't remember what, and Alan had backed into the corner to keep from falling down. Himself having turned and ran into the chair, falling across it, and that was the last thing he could remember.

He continued. "As far as leaving the doctor on the floor, well, the last thing I remember was him standing in the corner laughing about something that was probably said. That's when I passed out. If he had passed out before me and landed on the floor, you know damn good and well, I would not have left him there."

"And another thing! I did not know before last night that he had never taken a drink. If I had known, I would not have dug out that bottle. I feel sorry for the way Alan is suffering today, that's a fact, but I do not feel ashamed about last night. So---to end this little explanation I shall. You and Ellen can be pissed off if you want, but it won't change what happened last night!"

Lisa hung her head down feeling ashamed,. "I'm sorry Nat. I guess I just didn't stop to think." She had tears in her eyes. "I suppose you're pretty mad at me right now, and you have every right to be. I acted stupid and immature." Raising her head she looked at him. "Will you please forgive me?"

He reached up and took her hand, then pulled her down beside him. "I already have." He said with a gentle smile. Remembering her standing exposed with her robe open the night before he commented. "You really are a beautiful woman."

"Do you really think so?"

"Yes." He said in a soft voice, and then he pulled her to him. Their mouths parted and their tongues met. Bringing his hand around to her front he tenderly cupped her breast kneading it gently as he felt the heat building in his loins.

She reached up and removing his hand pulled away. "No Nat. Ellen might walk in."

Nat looked deep into Lisa's eyes. All of the sudden he felt a strange sensation racing through his body as he realized that her eyes held the same compassion as Nancy's had.

Lisa's mind was reeling as her heart beat rapidly. She wanted to tell him how much she loved him, how much she needed him, and how badly she wanted him. Opening her mouth she started to tell him these things, but the words just wouldn't' come out. Quickly she stood up and went into the kitchen to hide her tears.

Nat wondered what she was going to say. Probably apologize for her actions again. But then he remembered that feeling that went through his body as he looked into her eyes. Why did he think of Nancy at that moment? Nat tried to rationalize.

The more he thought about it the more he realized that in a lot of ways Lisa was like Nancy. She had the same type of beauty and gracefulness. Lisa new and understood the ways of nature. Nancy felt bad every time Nat had to kill an animal for food, even tho' she knew it had to be done for their own survival. Lisa had no qualms about killing an animal for food, because she knew it was part of nature's ways, and she accepted that.

Nat caught himself. This is stupid comparing the two women. Besides that, Ellen has been kind of sweet on me from the beginning. Lisa must know that because she was worried about Ellen walking in on them. Well, he thought, I just won't let it happen again.

At the same time Lisa was in the kitchen doing her own thinking. I wish I could tell him how I feel, but he would probably think I was silly. Besides, Ellen loves him very much. I know they have had sex more than just once. She has never tried to hide her feelings about him. He must have similar feelings towards her. They make a nice couple. Also she and Ellen are very dear friends, and she wouldn't want to do anything to ruin that.

What had happened in the other room can't be allowed to happen again. I just won't let it happen again.

Nat rose, grabbed his coat, and headed for the door. "I'm going over to the dam to talk to Jim!" He hollered out to Lisa as he went outside.

What neither one realized, was that two people that belonged together let a true and perfect relationship slip out of their hands that even Ellen would have accepted without any remorse or ill feelings.

CHAPTER 12

As Nat arrived at the dam, Jim was standing on top looking down at the ice covered reservoir. Walking up alongside of Jim, Nat commented, "Lot of ice in there."

"That there is! A lot of pressure too!"

"Well, spring isn't too far off. It will melt then."

"That's what worries me."

"What? The ice melting?"

Jim looked up at the hills. "Not this ice, but what's up there! If we get a fast run off, it could mean big trouble."

Won't the spillway handle it?"

"Maybe. Maybe not. That's something we won't know until it happens,"

"Well, let's hope for a slow melt."

"Even if we get our slow melt this spring, there is still the next spring, and the next spring, and so on. Sooner or later we will get the fast melt. When that happens, and only then will the dam prove itself."

"Are you worried about how good the dam is?"

"That dam has limitations just like me and you. Now the ideal situation when you build a structure like this is to build its limitations way beyond what's needed. When we built this dam we tried to anticipate what the necessary limitations were, and then built it better, but". Jim shrugged his shoulders, "it was all guess work. None of us had been here before, so we couldn't really anticipate what a fast run off could produce. We didn't have a geologist to dig through the dirt to give us any clues or anything like that, so we guessed."

They stood in silence for a short time, and then Nat headed back into town.

Before winter was out, Sarah couldn't conceal the fact that she was very much pregnant. The only ones that knew about the occurrence besides Arn were the doctor, Lisa, and Ellen. It was Sarah's choice to keep her condition from anyone else, do to what had happened to her first pregnancy, and the disappointment that had resulted from the miscarriage.

Nat was coming back from the food storage building when he decided to see if Arn was home. He had a few ideas to discuss with Arn. Approaching the house he realized that he hadn't been to visit them for over a month. Lisa and Ellen had gone over quite often, and Arn had come over to talk to him a few times, but Sarah hadn't been with him. Arn just said she was busy, but she sent her love.

Arn answered the door. "Hello Nat! Come on in." As Nat entered, Arn gestured to a chair. "Have a seat. What brings you by?"

"I have some ideas that have been kicking around in my head, and so I thought maybe I would mention them to you."

"Okay, but let me get you a cup of coffee first."

Just then, Sarah came out of the kitchen carrying two cups of coffee. "Hi Nat! I heard you come in so I poured you a cup of coffee. How have you been? It's been a while since I've seen that kind and gentle face of yours."

But Nat couldn't answer. He was staring at the swell in Sarah's midsection that showed she was with child. Suddenly he leaped to his feet and throwing his arms around her he gave her a big hug, causing her to spill the coffee she was holding. "Why didn't you tell me?" He then stood back with his hands on her waist and looked at her.

She lowered her head as she spoke. "Lisa and Ellen told me how hard you took it when I had the miscarriage. I didn't want you to get your hopes up again just to be let down and hurt again. Believe me, I wanted to tell you, but I didn't want to let you down again if I lost this one. After talking to the doctor yesterday, I was going to tell you this evening."

Arn felt guilty. "I wanted to tell you, but Sarah absolutely forbid it."

"That's true." She said. "And so did Lisa and Ellen, but I wouldn't let them."

Nat kissed her on the cheek. "You had your own reasons, and I accept that. You said that you saw the doctor yesterday. What did he say?"

Smiling she responded to his question. "I have an excellent chance of carrying this one all the way."

"How far along are you?"

"Five months."

He looked over at Arn. "Didn't waste any time, did you?"

Arn blushed slightly as he chuckled, "You told me to try again."

Nat laughed slapping Arn on the back. "Damned if I didn't! I'll take that cup of coffee now!"

"As soon as I refill the cups." Sarah said with a lilt in her voice.

Nat realized he had caused the coffee to get spilled. "Oh shit! I'm sorry."

"That's okay." She laughed. "I'll clean it up."

As she left for the kitchen, Arn looked at Nat. "What were those ideas you wanted to talk about?"

"Well, the time is going to come when this new society, so to speak, is going to have to set up a form of government."

"What's wrong with what we have?"

"Not a thing for right now, but we have to look to the future. As we grow in numbers, we will have to have guide lines to go by."

"Do you have something in mind?"

"Well, sort of. The Inca system."

"The what system?"

"Inca! The Indians of Peru."

"Oh yeah! Wasn't they the ones that the Spanish conquered or something?"

"That's right. They had a social system that endured for many years."

"But they still got whipped."

"Only because of their lack of understanding of the world outside of their civilization."

"I don't understand."

"The Spanish brought many things that they had never seen or heard about, such as shinny armor, horses, weapons that made loud noises, and fair skinned men with beards. The Spaniards literally intimidated them into submission."

"Anyway," Nat continued, "their social system is something to be looked at. They had a ruling family for one thing. But I'm against ruling families, because they always seem to become tyrants, demanding more from the people to satisfy their own greed. The good thing about the Inca nation was that everyone was cared for. They had large storage areas for food. When a person reached a certain age they retired. The sick and elderly were always taken care of. As a person reached an age where they were able to work, they were put to work. Some people built roads and bridges, others did the farming, while still others did the building of homes and other structures. All of this was watched over and kept in order by the ruling family."

"It sounds pretty good to me." Remarked Arn. "But what do you replace the ruling family with?"

"A council chosen by the people."

"How many would be on that council?"

"Five council members. Under this leading council we would have departments such as transportation, education, defense, law enforcement, and so on. Now to start with, the people pick the five members for the council and heads of each department. Each year the people only pick one person to serve at the level of department head, at the same time one of the five council members steps down. The new council member comes from the department level."

"How do you pick which department head moves up to the council?" Sarah asked, having came back and joined them.

"When the departments have been established, by the people, they are arranged into a certain order. Each department head serves at the head of a department for one year. At the end of a year that person moves to another department for a year, and so on, until that person has served at the head of each department. After they have served as head of every department they automatically become the one to move up to the council, which that person serves on for five years then steps down. If the people wish to elect that person back into a department level they can, but they must work their way back up to the council."

"When the first five are picked, do they stay for five years?" Arn asked.

"No. Each one is given a number. The numbers are then placed into a container, and then someone draws the number out. Say a person has the number three and it is the first number drawn, then that person serves for three years. Second number two years, and so on. For the first few years the council members will not have served on all the departments. But as the years go by that will correct that situation."

"I like it!" Stated Sarah.

"Me too! Agreed Arn. "Let's call a town meeting and present it!"

"Okay. Call it for noon in three days. You go down this afternoon and ring the bell and announce it. Make sure everybody get notified. We don't want to leave anyone out."

Nat was happy, but he wanted to be by himself for awhile. Coming into the house he only found Lisa in the kitchen. "Would you pack me some food? I'm going camping."

"But its still winter!" She exclaimed with a surprised look on her face.

"That doesn't matter. I've camped in the winter before. I just want to be alone for a bit is all. I might be gone until day after tomorrow. Where is Ellen?"

"She went down to get some supplies. I expect her back any minute. Was there something you needed her for? If so, I'll go hurry her up."

"No. I was just going to have her help me round up my camping gear."

"It's all stored in my closet except your sleeping bag and pack which is in the hall closet."

Lisa carefully laid out some jerky, bread, coffee grounds, and a small package of butter. She then remembered that his camping coffee pot was up in the cupboard.

Just as she sat the coffee pot on the table Nat hollered from the bedroom. "I found everything except the coffee pot!"

"It's setting here on the table. I had it out here in the cupboard."

He was carefully putting everything in the pack when Ellen came in. What are you doing?" She asked with a shocked voice.

"Going camping!"

"Oh no you're not!"

He turned around and looked at her. "Says who?"

Lisa moved to the doorway going into the living room and leaned against the doorway to watch.

"Says me! That's who! It's below freezing out there and everything is covered with snow!"

"Number one, I'll be sleeping in a tent. Number two, I'll be dressed warm! Number three, I'll go camping any damn time I feel like it!"

Lisa smiled to herself. You would think they were married, arguing like that.

Ellen strutted right up to Nat. "I don't want you to go camping in this weather."

"Well, I want to go!"

"How long do you plan on being gone?"

"I might be back tomorrow."

"That's crazy to go camping in this weather for one night!"

Nat looked over at Lisa. "Do you think I'm crazy?"

"I'm not going to answer that!" Then she looked at Ellen. "You're not going to talk him out of it."

Ellen glared at Nat, and then dumped the sacks of supplies she had been holding on the couch and headed for her bedroom. "You have to be the most stubborn man in the world!" She declared on the way.

Nat just shrugged his shoulders and finished packing, and then putting on his heavy fur coat he asked Lisa. "Do you know where my snowshoes are?"

"Out on the porch." She then reached up on the wall and took down his rifle. Handing him the rifle she opened the door for him. "Please be careful."

"Thank you. I will! Promise!"

After hiking about for nearly four hours, Nat found a good spot to set up camp. For that night, and the next two nights, he thought about many things including the upcoming meeting, and Sarah's pregnancy.

Mostly his thoughts were about his home back up in Canada or more to the fact whether he should return home or stay around Eagletown.

Mostly his thoughts were about his home back up in Canada or more to the fact whether he should return home or stay around Eagletown.

If he returned home it would not be the same without his wife there to share in all the happiness that the short valley and cove produced. The valley ran quickly into a canyon which rose rapidly into the mountains. They used to hike up the mountains every once in awhile to just sit and look at the views which were displayed before them in all of nature's beauty At times if the weather was right, they would camp for a couple of days so they could watch the sunsets,.

Going home would mean that some change would have to be made. Especially in the area of security. For someone to come by land would be impossible if they didn't know the trail. Also the nearest road inland was many miles away. To land on the beach was out of the question also. They were lined with cliffs either way you went from the cove. What it came down to, was that the only way to enter was by water through the opening in the cliff that the stream had cut thorough eons of time before.

Securing the gap into the cove would be the only major problem to overcome. If he used small poles that wouldn't support the weight of a person and lashed them loosely, it would prevent anyone from trying to walk on them to loosen them. Also he could put large spikes through them to prevent a boat from trying to skim over them at high speed. Once the float was in place, he would be relatively safe.

On the other side of the coin is Eagletown. He did feel that it was part of him. The town had been his concept. Even the name and location was his brainstorm, but the people had built it, so really it was their town. The people! Now, there was the finest group of people ever assembled into one group. It was kind of like one big happy family.

There is Alan, a doctor so dedicated to his work that if you hadn't seen it, you would refuse to believe it. He may be a small man, but he sure was big in his heart and actions. The woman that captures his heart is going to be one lucky lady.

Arn, young, ambitious, and always trying to learn how to do new things. Somewhat like Nat when he was a young man. Always listening and thinking when others are talking. Not quite as tall as Nat, who towers over others at six feet three, but still managed to attain a solid six feet, which seemed to contrast with Sarah's five feet seven. They really cared for each other also. Arn also had a sense of fairness about him that was unusual for a young buck like him. It's true that Nat worried about them as if they were his own kids.

Will and Jenny also fell into that class. They had come right out and told Nat that they looked up to him as their father, and even named their child after him. Will was a damn good worker too, always getting in there and taking on more than his share of the load. Jim had commented on that fact several times.

But when it came to getting the job done, Jim led the pace. He seemed to have a way about him that when he jumped in there and started working, you did too. Nat had heard him praise someone for their work, even if it wasn't as good as another's. When Nat complemented him on doing that, Jim had looked at him and said. "I'll always praise a person for doing the best they can. They may not be as good as the next person but that doesn't enter into it. The fact that they're doing <u>their</u> best is what counts." Even though Jim was a short, stocky, robust man, he had a gentleness that was unmatched. Once, while they were building the road, Jim noticed a bird's nest in a bush with eggs in it. Since the road was being built right next to it, Jim stood guard over it to make sure it didn't get destroyed by accident.

Another time, he spotted a baby bird that had fallen from its nest. Then with hands that looked like they would break an egg just trying to pick it up, he gently picked up the little bird, and holding it in one hand, climbed the tree using only the other hand and placed it back into its nest.

Another person that stood out in Nat's mind was Silent Sam. You always seemed to feel safer when Sam was around, probably because he seemed to be watching over everybody with his shotgun that was never out of arms reach. When he had gone hunting with Nat, he amazed Nat by the way he could move his tall, lanky frame through the brush without making a noise. Even though he couldn't talk because of his mouth being so mis-shappened, he was defiantly one of the favorites around town. He always stepped aside for the women, and if they were carrying a load, he would always take part of it and carry it for them, putting off where ever he was going. Not being able to talk, didn't keep him from setting with the others when they were just gathered around having a discussion. If someone asked him if he agreed or disagreed on a certain point, his eyes would show their delight at being included in the discussion. Nat would always make a point of asking Sam whether he agreed or not to what he was saying. Sometimes Sam would disagree with Nat, and that would bring about a series of yes or no questions out of Nat as he tried to pin it down Sam as to what exactly he disagreed with. You could tell Sam loved this, when it happened.

Nat's thought turned to Lisa and Ellen. They were defiantly two different types of women. Lisa was quiet and reserved in her actions, while Ellen was open and forward. When they were walking, Lisa moved gracefully, almost sensually and Ellen walked with a sort of springy movement. They both fussed and fumed over him, although it seemed that lately Ellen did more than Lisa. He had never had sex with Lisa, even though he had come close. Ellen on the other hand had filled his need for sex quite well. In fact, she had came right out and told him her bedroom door was always open.

Well, Nat decided, if I go back to Canada, I'll ask Ellen to go with me. Besides, he thought, I think Lisa is interested in Alan.

On the third morning, Nat came awake with a start. Quickly he reached for his rifle, and then lay there listening for what could have awakened him. It was just after daybreak, and he realized this was the day of the meeting. Just then he heard a rustle of branches and a heavy thud. Nat smiled as he recognized the sound. The spring thaw was coming. Putting his boots on, then stepping outside he looked up at the sky. Crystal clear and the sun would give more warmth when it peeked over the mountains. With happiness in his heart, Nat packed his things and headed back towards town. By the time he reached town the sun was up and water was dripping from the eaves of the building.

Entering the house, Nat saw Jim standing talking to Ellen. Both turned towards him as he closed the door. Ellen ran to him and threw her arms around him and kissed him. "Oh Nat! I was getting so worried!"

"She sure was!" Jim remarked. "She was trying to get me to go looking for you."

"But you said you were only going to be gone for one day!" Ellen stated.

"Well, if you hadn't gotten your feathers all ruffled up, and flew into the bedroom, I might have told you not to expect me until this morning!"

"I'm sorry I got upset Nat."

"Besides that, I told Lisa when I would be back."

Lisa looked at him. "You told me you would be back yesterday."

"Well maybe I did. But you weren't worried were you?"

"No."

Ellen turned around and looked at Lisa. "No!?" Is that why you cleaned the house three times this morning, trying to keep busy so you wouldn't show how worried you were?"

"Well, maybe I was a little bit concerned."

"A little bit? I bet you said at least a half dozen times, 'I wonder why Nat isn't back.'"

"Alright! Alright!" Nat had heard enough. "We have a meeting to go to in about an hour, and I want to get cleaned up a little before I go."

Jim headed for the door. "I better get going. See you all at the meeting."

"Okay Jim." Nat answered. "See you there."

The meeting was held in the food storage building, as it was the only structure large enough to hold everyone. Arn stood up and got everyone to quiet down. "This is an important meeting folks, so let's get under way. Now you all know what it's about already so I'll let Nat explain it to you."

After he had detailed his proposal, several people voiced their agreements. Ron then took the floor. "We like your plan Nat, so what's our first step?"

"I suggest we pick a committee of ten persons to meet and decide on what departments will be needed. After they have done this, we all meet again. At that time we will vote on ther proposals. Now, when you came in you were each given a piece of paper and a pencil. What I want you to do is write the names of ten people you would like to be on the committee. Put your own name on it if you want to. But before we start, let me ask if there is anyone who defiantly does not want to be on that committee?"

Several people chose not to be asked, including the doctor and Lisa. Nat turned to Lisa. "Why don't you want to be on it?"

"Because I'm just not any good when it comes to politics. So I'll let someone else who is more knowledgeable do it."

"Well at least you're honest about it. "Facing back to the crowd Nat got their attention again. "Now that we know who not to put down, let's get on with it. The ten people with the most votes are it."

When all the votes were counted, there weren't any surprises. Nat's name had been the first on every list. The others included Jim, Arn, Pete, Ron, Ellen, Bill, Howard, Ken, with Hank completing the lineup. It was then agreed that the committee would meet in one week at Jim's house, and then have another town meeting to present their suggestions for the different departments.

The meeting of the committee went well with them picking eight departments: Defense and War, Transportation, Law enforcement, Utilities and Construction, Agriculture and Supplies, Education, Medical and Health, and Distribution of Food and Supplies.

As each person entered the town meeting they were handed a piece of paper with the departments listed with two boxers, one labeled yes and the other no.

Nat quieted everyone down as soon as all were present. "If you folks will look at the piece of paper you received as you came in, you will notice that eight departments are listed. This is the order that each department head will work through starting with the department for the distribution of food and Supplies. When that person has headed each department up to and including the Department of Defense and War, they will automatically step up to the council and serve on it for five years."

"Now, what we are going to do is have each of you mark yes if you agree to the committee's choice of departments. If you don't agree, mark no. If you wish another department added, mark no, and write your suggestion on the bottom of the paper, then sign your name so we can call on you to give your reasons for creating that department. "Let's vote now."

The voting went quickly, and as the votes came forward, the committee checked for any no votes. All votes went into the yes pile except one, which Pete put in the no pile.

Nat picked up the piece of paper with the no vote and read the suggestion. He then looked up at the crowd. "We have one no vote with a suggestion for a new department."

The crowd quickly got quiet. "The only problem," Nat continued, "is that the person forgot to sign it. That person suggested we add a department for Human Production."

The silence was broken by Sarah. "Arn! You didn't?"

A snicker went through the crowd as they all looked at Arn. Nat spoke up quickly. Folks, it seems Arn is the one who forgot to sign his name, and since he is the one that suggested it, I think it's a good idea that right here and now we accept his suggestion and appoint him the head of that department with the stipulation that he only gets one assistant, namely Sarah. Now Arn, you are officially the head of that department with Sarah as you only assistant. You have everyone's permission to conduct your department in your own home. Preferably in the bedroom."

The crowd yelled their approval and applauded. Everyone laughed as Arn turned beet red, and Nat could see Sarah giving Arn a good scolding.

It was decided that the people would vote on the Council of Five in three months. Anyone choosing not to be considered was to put their name on a list just inside the entrance to the food storage building.

Lisa was the first person to put her name on the list. A few days later, Nat added his name. The next day Jim asked him why he put his name on the list.

"Well Jim, I did that for two reasons. First is, that everybody looks to me for the answers. This way they will get used to depending on their own peers. I do not want any position for at least one year. Second, there is still the possibility I may return to Canada. Lately my thoughts have been weighing whether I should stay in Eagletown or go back to my home. My decision will be made within a year, one way or the other."

Jim looked at him with a concerned look. "Speaking for myself, and the others, I'm sure, we would hope for you to decide to stay here. If you should decide to return to your home, each and every heart here will go with you and wish you well. It's true we do look to you for our leadership, and I realize that we have to learn how to lead ourselves. You have given us the tools to do it, and by damn, I know we can."

CHAPTER 13

Two weeks later the rains came. Heavy rains continued for a week causing a fast melt and heavy runoff from the mountains. Jim was spending all his time at the dam, only going home to grab a nap.

Right after breakfast, Nat heard a knock at the door. Opening it he saw Phill standing on the porch completely drenched. "Come on in and dry out a spell."

"Thanks, but I have to get home and put on some dry clothes then get back to the dam. Jim wants you to come up to the dam."

"Did he say why?"

"The water is coming up fast, and he wants you to come up and see the problem."

"Okay. I'll get my boots on and head up there."

As Nat closed the door, Ellen and Lisa came out of the kitchen. "What's going on?" Asked Ellen.

"Waters on the rise at the dam. Jim wants me to get up there right now."

"Do you want us to come along?"

Nat thought for a second. "No, I would rather you two brew up some coffee and fill all the thermos bottles and bring them up there."

As Nat approached the dam he saw Jim standing out on the dam with Silent Sam, Pete, and Charlie. Walking out on the dam, he saw that the water was only a foot from breaking over the top of the dam. They all greeted Nat as he joined them.

Leaning on the hand rail, Nat looked down at the water as Jim spoke. "Been raising two inches an hour. In about six hours it's going to shoot over the top."

"How about the turbine rooms?"

"We built water tight entrances to those."

"Is the dam going to hold?"

"It's good and solid, but the area between the dam and spillway is in danger of washing out along with this end of the dam. Once the water goes over the top, it's going to start eroding the ground on both ends of the dam."

They stood there not speaking for awhile, and then walked back off the dam just as Lisa and Ellen showed up with hot coffee for them.

Jim took his coffee, and then turned back to look at the dam as Lisa asked. "Is the water going to get any higher?"

"I'm afraid so." Jim answered with a slow nod.

"What are we going to do?"

"If we had any sacks we could fill them with that sand and gravel over there and make a barricade on this end and build a wall between the other end and the spillway. The only trouble is, we don't have any sacks, and I don't know where we could get them either." He kept watching the dam.

Phill then returned after donning dry clothes. "Jim, how about if we fire up the dozer and push dirt up on this end?"

"Well it might slow it down on this end for a spell, but it would be loose dirt and wash away pretty fast. There is no way we could get the dozer over to the other side tho', so the area over there would wash out anyway."

Lisa went over and talked to Sam about something, and they quickly started back towards town.

"I wonder where they are headed?" Ellen said to Nat.

He looked after them as they went out of sight. "I haven't the slightest idea."

After a few minutes, Jim turned to Pete. "Go get the dozer." Then he turned to the others. "We can't just stand here. Might as well try to save this end anyway."

An hour later, Pete still hadn't shown up with the bulldozer, and Jim's concern for the dam was starting to show a man desperate for a solution to the problem. Nat walked over to Jim. "I wonder what's taking Pete so long?

"I was wondering the same damn thing!" He turned to Phill. "Go see what the holdup is with Pete!"

As Phill left, a few other people showed up wondering what could be done. Jim explained the situation to them.

It took Phill a half hour to get back to Jim. "Pete said that since the dozer had been setting so long, he is having a hard time getting it started, but expected to have it going in a few minutes, and be here within a half hour."

"Shit!" Hollered Jim. "I sure hope so! Times running out pretty damn fast!"

A few minutes later, they heard the town bell faintly over the roar of the water cascading over the dam.

Nat looked at Jim. "I wonder what in hell is wrong now!"

"Beats me! Whatever it is they will send somebody up to tell us."

Jim and Nat went up to the switch shack, as they called it, to get out of the rain. Just before they entered, Jim looked up at the sky. "Rains have slowed down. Looks like they might stop for awhile. If they would at least slack off for a few days, it sure would help."

Ten minutes later Ellen came running in. "Pete is coming!"

"Good!" Jim roared. "We better get out there!"

As Pete neared the dam they heard a horn blowing and everyone looked up to see Silent Sam's red pickup coming slowly around the corner into view. It wasn't the truck that surprised them. It was what was following. The whole town was running along in back of Sam with some of them carrying shovels and picks.

They just stood there watching as the truck came up to them and stopped. Lisa jumped out and ran up to Jim. "The back of the truck is full of gunny sacks, and even some money bags from a bank. We are all ready to start work. Just tell us what to do.

"First form a line from the sand and gravel pit to the other side of the dam. Some can fill the sacks, while somebody else wires them shut. Then pass them along to the other end of the line. As the sacks arrive put them in a pile. I'll need ten people to go over there and start building a wall about ten feet wide and six feet tall all the way from the spillway to the end of the dam, then across the end of the dam."

Ten people including the doctor and Lisa headed for the other side while the others formed a line. The kids started holding sacks and others filled them. As soon as a sack was filled, somebody grabbed it, twisted the top and held it while another wired it shut. The sack was immediately passed along the line to the workers at the other end. They were filling and tying so fast that as soon as a person passed a sack along, they just had time to turn and take another sack.

Nat looked up just as Sarah arrived,. "What in the hell are you doing up here?"

"I want to help!"

"You can't help in your condition!"

"There must be something I can do!"

"Yeah there is! Get your backside back to town and round up a bunch of coffee pots and coffee grounds, then go over to Jenny's and you two start making coffee and filling thermos jugs. Jenny is more than likely at home with the baby. Take Sam's truck with you, and when you get the jugs filled, bring them up here with lots of cups. Now get going!"

As she left, Nat said out loud more to himself than anybody in particular. "Crazy kid!" He noticed that Phill, who was beside him, was laughing. "What's so funny?"

"She forgot to say something to you!"

"What?"

"Yes father!"

Nat realized then that he had spoken to her as if she was his daughter. "Well, I guess I do think of her as my own kid. Arn too, for that matter. Come to think about it, I guess Will and Jenny are kinda like my own kids too in a way."

"You ever have any of your own?" Phill inquired.

"No."

"I had a daughter. She and the wife were in Vancouver when it happened."

"Sorry to hear that."

"Well, at least they went quick."

"How did you come to join up with Jim and the others?"

"We lived darn near on the west coast of Vancouver Island. Alice was a neighbor that lived up the road a piece. She was a recent widow. Only had been married a year and a half. He met a logging truck on a corner. Killed outright. Well anyway, Hank lived a little farther on up the road, so we kind of got together. There was me, Alice, Hank and his wife and two kids. Supplies got a little short so we went on the move to survive. We saw Jim and Sam walking down a road, so we stopped and got to talking, and then we just all stuck together after that. Met other along the way also. We had a pretty good sized group at one time, but then we started losing them from attacks by the mutants and renegades. We might not have made it if you hadn't come along."

Nearly four hours later, the word came down the line that the water was starting to run over the top of the dam. Jim looked over to the other side. Seeing that they had a good pile of bags piled up for the crew to keep them busy for a little bit, he started channeling every other bag to the end closest to them. He also noticed that given another hour they would be finished over there.

About forty-five minutes later the word came down that footing was getting hard to hold on the dam due to the force of the water. Jim gave the order. Everybody back on this side. We've done the best we can over there." All the ones on the dam that had been passing sacks worked their way back. Nobody seemed to notice that the ten on the other side kept working to get finished, as they had enough filled bags to do it.

A little while later Jim looked over across the dam. "What in the hell are they doing over there?"

"Looks like they are just finishing up!" Somebody said.

"That water is damn near a foot deep going over the dam! They can't wade through that!" Jim bellowed.

"What are we going to do?" Hank asked.

"Get me that rope up in the shack! Quick!"

As soon as he got the rope he tied one end around his chest and holding on to the railing started working his way across the dam. Nat and Phill fed the rope out as he went. Everybody could see that Jim was fighting the force of the water all the way. Upon reaching the other side, Jim signaled for more rope. He then tied the crew together on the rope at about three foot intervals. Lisa was the last one in line as they started back. As Nat and Phill kept the slack out of the rope, Jim and the others inched their way across the dam.

Then it happened a little after they had passed the half way mark. Somebody lost their footing and went down pulling the others loose from the railing one by one. Jim, realizing instantly what was happening, crawled over to the other side of the railing and braced himself like a piece of steel with a piece of rope tied to it. Having braced himself just as the last one went down, he felt the rope around him come tight like a burning fire as it dug into his body. The last three in line were hanging over the dam fighting for air to keep from drowning.

Nat heard Ellen scream. "Oh god! Do something!" But he was already moving to get another rope. Quickly he tied it around him and started out towards the others, staying on the upstream side of the guard rail.

Terror was in everyone's face as they stood watching this terrible event going on. Sarah had shown up with fresh coffee as Nat was working his way out to the others. She grabbed Arn by the arm. "What happened?"

"They lost their footing coming back across the dam!" He answered with an alarmed voice.

"Is there someone hanging over the side of the dam?" She asked with horror in her voice.

"Three people are! One of them is Lisa!"

Sarah turned white. "Oh no!" Then buried her face in Arn's chest, not being able to watch.

As Nat reached them, Jim had managed to pull the first two back to the railing, one of them being the doctor. Lisa was still over the edge, as Nat reached for the rope to take it from Jim. Grabbing the rope he noticed that Jim's knuckles were white from the grip he had on the rope. Agony was in Jim's face while fear was in the doctor's face.

Upon pulling the third person to the railing, Nat saw Lisa appear from over the edge. At first, fear gripped him because she didn't seem to be moving. Then his heart leaped with joy as he seen her lift her head to take another breath of air. Nat pulled the fourth person to the rail, then the fifth realizing that it was Will.

Will grabbed the rail with one arm and then reached back with his other hand to help Nat pull on the rope.

Nat hollered above the roar of the water. "Just hang on to the rail! I'll get the others!"

After getting the sixth one to the railing it seemed easier to pull the others up with less weight. As he pulled Lisa up to her feet, she threw her arms around him and started crying. Tightly, Nat held on to Lisa with one arm, and holding the railing with the other, he motioned with his head for the others to follow as he started edging his way towards the end of the dam.

The struggle seemed to last forever. As they neared the end of the dam, Nat felt Lisa's arms losing their grip. What's wrong?"

"I'm losing the strength in my arms. They feel numb."

"I'll hold you! Don't worry, we only got a couple more feet!"

A six foot wall of sand bags was across the end of the dam. When they reached it, Lisa couldn't lift her arms up for someone to grab to pull her up. Nat, wrapping a leg around one of the railing post, grabbed the front of Lisa's jacket with his left hand, then brought his right hand up between her legs and lifted her up to Ken and Hank who reached down and grabbed her. They couldn't pull Lisa all the way up because the rope was attached to the next person. Nat took out his hunting knife and cut the rope. Quickly they pulled her up, passing her to waiting arms in back of them.

One by one, Nat helped he others up to awaiting arms, as he cut the rope behind each one. Jim and Nat were each pulled up by the ropes that were attached to them. Exhausted, Nat sat down on the sandbags, happy that all were rescued.

"You all right?" Arn asked as he knelt down beside him.

"Yeah. Just a little worn out."

"You're a hero, saving all those people!"

Slowly shaking his head, he looked at Arn. "No, I didn't save those people. I helped save those people. The real hero is Jim. If he hadn't did what he did, they all would have gone over the dam and drown before we could have pulled them out."

"I guess you're right."

"How are the others?"

"They're on their way down to the clinic. The doctor wants to check them over. Jim didn't go down tho'. He is over there lying down."

Nat looked over to where Arn indicated. Jim was lying on his back with Hank and Charlie kneeling beside him. Wearily he got to his feet and walked over to them. Bending down he could see that Jim was in pain. "You better go down to the clinic and have the doctor take a look at you Jim"

"I'll be alright. Just let me lay here for a few minutes, and then I gotta check the barrier."

"Listen you bull-headed son-of-a-bitch! I'm not blind! You're hurting bad! I can tell! So don't give me any of that gotta check things bull shit! You're going to the clinic whether you want to or not! If you can't walk, then we will carry you! You hear me!?"

"The dam----"

"The dam is fine! We have saved it! Can you stand up?"

Jim tried to get up, but couldn't make it. "Still too weak I guess."

Nat stood up and looked around. "Any vehicles up here?"

"No. They used what was here to take the others down to the clinic." Arn informed him.

"Well, hot foot it down there and bring one up here so we can get this bull ox down to the clinic. Charlie! I'm putting you in charge here. Keep your eye on things. Pick a couple people to stay here with you. If there are any problems that come up, send one of them down to get me." Nat then took his coat off and laid it over Jim. "It's a little wet, but it should help you keep warm."

Jim had tears in his eyes. "Thanks for helping saved those people."

Nat patted him on the shoulder. "That's all right. Take it easy now, and no more talking."

The heavy rains had turned into a light sprinkle by the time Nat had gone home, changed clothes, and gotten down to the clinic. Sally was just going into a room when he entered. "Sally! What room is Jim planted in?"

Although Sally had a lot of respect for Nat, and even liked him, she did not care for his humor sometimes. Her lusty figure did not seem to fit her all business attitude around the clinic. "He is convalescing in this room!"

The doctor and Jim looked at Nat as he followed Sally through the door.

"I'm sure glad you're here!" Jim declared.

"Why is that?"

"Doc thinks I should stay here at least a night!"

"And he should!" Alan added. "He has some broken ribs."

"Look doc, I said I would take it easy. I just want to go up to the dam to keep an eye on things. I won't do any lifting or try to run any foot races."

Alan was losing his patients. Damnit Jim your body has been through one hell of an ordeal! It needs to rest! And when I say rest, I mean bed rest!"

Jim looked at Nat. "Tell him you will go with me to make sure I don't do anything foolish."

"Alan, I'll see to it he doesn't do anything foolish. For starters, get me some rope so I can tie his ass to the bed."

"Ah Nat! I thought you were my pal."

"I am! That's why I'm going to make damn sure you stay in that bed until the doctor says you can get up and leave."

"You don't have to tie me down. I'll stay." He mumbled in defeat.

No sooner had the doctor and Nat left the room when they heard Jim roar at Sally. "I can take my own shorts off!"

"You shut up and lay still, or I'll coldcock you!"

They heard Jim mumble something, and a minute later Sally came out with Jim's wet clothes, including his shorts, and headed down the hall.

Alan laughed. "I didn't even suspect that he had a bit of modesty in him."

"I'll bet that's the first time a woman ever put him in his place."

"If he gives her any more guff, it won't be the last either."

"How are the others doing?"

"I sent all but Lisa and two others home. The three of them seem to have taken the worst beating outside of Jim. Lisa is worse than the other two. Somehow she got a bad cut on her back, and we all wound up with rope burns.

"How bad is that cut on Lisa's back?"

"Not too bad, but bad enough. It took a few stitches. I'm going to keep her here for a couple of days"

Sally walked past them carrying something which Nat didn't recognize because it was folded. Again they heard Jim roar. "You're not going to make me wear that goddamn thing! Get me some real clothes!"

Nat watched Sally close the door, and then there were more words, although Nat and the doctor couldn't make them out. A couple minutes later, Sally opened the door and calmly walked down the hall empty handed.

Looking into the room, Nat saw Jim sitting up in one of those little hospital gowns. Jim saw him. "What in the hell are you looking at?"

"That cute little dress you're wearing."

"Funny!" Jim said with disgust.

Nat turned back to the doctor. "Where is Lisa?"

"Two doors down."

"Thanks. Talk to you later."

Arn, Sarah, and Ellen were with Lisa when Nat came in. He walked over, took Lisa's hand then leaned down and kissed her on the lips. "Hi Angel! How are you doing?"

She blushed slightly then looked at Ellen briefly, then back at Nat. "A little weak, but Alan says I'll be alright."

"Well, Sarah and I have to get going." Arn stated. "I'm getting hungry. See you all later."

After they had left, Nat spoke to Lisa. "Alan said you received a cut on your back and rope burns."

"Yes I did, but I don't know how I got the cut. The rope burns form a circle all the way around me. They go right across my breasts."

Nat lifted the blanket. "Let me see how bad they are."

Quickly Lisa grabbed the blanket from his hand, and jerked it back down, turning a bright red. "Nat! I don't have any clothes on!"

"So? I've seen your boobs before."

Ellen looked Nat right in the eye. "Oh? When was that?" Then she looked at Lisa. "I didn't know you two had anything going."

Nat laughed. "Now don't go getting your tail feathers bent out of shape. You're jealousy is showing."

"I'm not jealous! I just didn't know about it."

Lisa took Ellen's hand. "Believe me. Nothing has been going on."

"Well, when did he see you naked?"

"I didn't say I saw her naked." Nat responded. "I said I had seen her boobs."

Ellen had a mischievous look in her eyes. "Uh huh! And you expect me to believe that's all you saw."

Lisa started crying. "Please Ellen. You have to believe me."

"I'm sorry Lisa. I believe you. I was just trying to give Nat a bad time. Not you."

"Let me explain."

"You don't have to explain anything. We all live in the same house. If that is all he has seen of you, then am surprised,"

Nat decided it was time for him to exit. "I think I'll go home and fix me something to eat."

"I'll be along very shortly." Ellen informed him. "Then I'll fix your supper."

Nat made some coffee as soon as he got home, and had just sat down with a cup when Ellen came in. He looked up at her. "I think I had better explain to you what happened."

"No. Let me explain something to you. This subject has never come up, but I think it's time it did. First of all, I do not claim you as mine. It's true, we have had sex together. But unless we make a commitment we are not bound to each other. To be honest with you, I hope that happens some day. Second thing is, Lisa told me after you left what happened. I am not so dumb that I don't realize that there is a shortage of men in this town. If you did have sex with Lisa, I would more than understand. She has desires just like anybody else. Now I'm not advocating that you can go bed hooping between our bedrooms, because neither one of us would put up with it. I'm not saying you would do that, because I know you well enough that you would not do it. But until there is a change in our situation, meaning you and I, and she should come to you. I would not have any hard feelings toward either one of you. Now! I've said my piece! I'll get supper cooked,"

The next three months brought much activity for the residents of Eagleton. As soon as Jim could get up and around, he was meeting with Charlie and Bill, to get ready to build a six foot wall from one end of the dam, across the top and on over to the spillway. During the days, the town was nearly deserted, as the people went down to the low lands to work the soil and put in crops for food.

The June evening was pleasant as Nat waked down to the river to set and smoke his pipe. Having just settled back to let his mind wander, he heard someone walking down the trail. Looking up he saw Alan. "Evening Alan."

"Evening. Mind I I join you?"

"Not at all. Have a seat."

Alan sat down and looked out across the river enjoying the tranquil scene laid out before him. "It's easy to see why you come down here as often as you do."

"Kinda grows on you. It's like Mother Nature casts a spell over your mind."

Neither one spoke for awhile, and then Alan broke the silence. "The folks have sure been putting in the hours to get the planting done."

"That they have. I've even seen you down there pitching in."

"Things have been pretty slow around the clinic lately. Just your usual cuts and scrapes. Although I did have a broken finger last month."

"Well if I'm not mistaken, it should pick up a little bit this month."

"You mean Sarah's baby?"

"Yeah. I'm kinda looking forward to another grandson."

Alan laughed. "What are you going to do if it's a granddaughter?"

"Hummm. I never even considered that possibility."

"You better give it some thought."

"You know something I don't?"

Again Alan laughed. "No, but from strictly a professional point of view, there are indications that it may be a girl. But I could be wrong. You can never know until it's born."

Nat thought about what he said for a few minutes. "Well if it's a girl, so be it. I'll accept her with just as much joy as I would a boy."

"By the way Nat. You ready to perform another marriage?"

Nat sat straight up and looked at Alan. "You decide on one of the women?"

"No,no,no. I'm not talking about me."

"Damn! I thought maybe you were going to break down and tie the knot."

"Not yet. Still giving it some thought,."

"Well, who do you think might be thinking about it?"

"Our resident ox.'

"Jim?"

"You got it!"

"I'll be go-to hell and back again. I didn't think any woman could tame that stubborn son-of-a-bitch!"

"Well it looks like one did."

"Who?"

"Sally."

"I should have known! Especially after the way she handled him that time you kept him in the clinic."

"You don't know the half of it. By the time I released him, he was saying yes ma'am and no ma'am to her."

"How serious is it?"

I think it's getting more serious by the day. If he is up at the dam when she leaves the clinic, she walks up there to see him, and several evenings they have just gone out for a walk. In fact, she has had him over to her place for diner quite often."

"I wonder what Sam thinks of this. You know he lives with Jim don't you?"

"Yes I know that. She has had Jim bring Sam along a few times for dinner. I asked Sam the other day if he agreed with what was going on, and the way he nodded yes, and the sparkle in his eyes, I knew he was all for it."

"He probably is!" Nat laughed. "Have you ever heard about their living arrangements?"

"No. I never gave it any thought."

"Well let me tell you a few things. The cooking is shared by them on alternating days. I asked Sam one day if Jim was a good cook, and he just looked down at the ground and shook his head no. Now on the other hand when I asked Jim about Sam's cooking, he said Sam made the best damn stew in the world, but Sam made it to damn often. Everything around the house is split evenly, more or less. But the best thing about them two living together is that Sam can't talk. When something doesn't go right for Jim, he goes home and rants and raves to Sam. Since Sam can't talk, he just shrugs his shoulders and lets Jim carry on till he gets it out of his system. They lookout for each other too, although sometimes I think it's more Sam looking out for Jim."

"You know that with Sally, he'll never get away with ranting and raving," Alan laughed.

"You got that right!" Nat agreed.

"Well anyway, prepare yourself for another marriage. Sally has got her sights set on him, so he doesn't have a chance."

"I'll be happy as a pig in mud to do that one. Sally is just what Jim needs.

"What about you Nat?"

"What are you getting at Doc?"

"Well, you and Ellen seem to be hitting it off pretty good. Why don't you two just match up and get it over with?"

"I don't rightly know. Something just doesn't seem right. She is a good woman, and I think a lot of her, but for some reason my heart isn't reacting like I think it should. But hang in there doc, it may just be a delayed reaction. Besides that, I don't see you rushing into anything yet."

"Lisa once told me that when the time came, my heart would tell me. So far my heart hasn't said anything."

Nat stood up to leave. "Let me know when your heart starts talking. Right now it's getting a little on the chilly side, so I think I'll head home.

"That it is. See you later,"

Chapter 14

Ellen and Lisa were washing the breakfast dishes as Nat sat at the table having coffee. He emptied the cup. "Any more coffee?"

"There is plenty." Ellen answered as she came over and picked up his cup. Just as she finished refilling the cup, there was a knock at the door. "I'll get it! She said.

She still had the cup of coffee in her hand when she opened the door and saw Will standing there.

"Arn just took Sarah down to the clinic! She is in labor! Will blurted out.

Without saying a word, Ellen took off out the door. Lisa sat a plate down on the edge of the counter and headed for the door, and before she even got to the door, the plate shattered on the floor. Lisa didn't even stop to look back as she shot out the door, hot on Ellen's tail.

Will hollered after them. "The pains are still five minutes apart!"

Nat came to the door. "How is she doing?"

"She's doing fine, but I'm not too sure about Arn tho'."

"Why?"

"He is as nervous as a long tailed cat in a room full of rockers."

"Did you say that the pains were still five minutes apart?"

"Yeah."

"Well, there is still plenty of time. Care for a cup of coffee?"

"Sure!"

As they went into the kitchen Nat looked around for his cup. "Now what in the hell did she do with my cup?"

"Ellen had a cup in her hand when she went out the door."

Nat looked down at the shattered plate. "Well, there you have it my boy. The official welcoming committee in action!"

Will couldn't help but laugh as Nat got two cups out of the cupboard and poured their coffee.

By the time Will and Nat arrived at the clinic, there was a group of about twenty people standing around outside waiting for the birth to happen. They all greeted Nat and Will as they approached and entered the clinic. Several more were inside including Jenny setting in a chair holding little Nat.

"Hello Jenny! Looks like little Nat is going to get a playmate."

"Yes! Isn't this exciting?"

"It sure is!" He remarked as he went down the hall.

Sally met him half way. "That's far enough!"

"I was just going to see how it's going."

"The doctor is taking care of everything, and I think he can get along quite well without you looking over his shoulder."

"Ah, I wasn't going to look over his shoulder. I was just going to check on Sarah."

"Sarah is doing just beautiful. Lisa and Ellen are in there with Arn, and that's more support than she needs."

"How much longer?"

"Not much. Now, you just turn yourself around and march right out of here."

"You're worse than some of those sergeants I had in the military!"

Sally put her hands on her hips and glared at him.

"I'm going! I'm going!" He went back out to the waiting room.

A few minutes later, little Nat started to cry, and a roar welled up outside thinking it was the signal that Sarah had the baby. Nat went to the door and stuck his head out, then shouted. "False alarm! That was just little Nat complaining about something!"

Everybody just laughed, and then somebody shouted back. "I guess we're just getting over excited."

No sooner had the doctor held the baby in his hands, and Arn realized its sex, he took off for the waiting room. He came to a dead stop, looked around, and just smiled.

Everybody looked back at him waiting for him to make the declaration.

Finally Nat couldn't take the silence. "Well?"

Suddenly Arn let out a yell. "Ya hoo! It's a girl!" Then everyone gathered around him shaking his hand and congratulating him.

A few minutes later it got deathly quiet as everyone looked past Arn. "What's wrong?" he asked as he turned around to see what they were looking at. Sally was standing there with a little bundle in each arm. Arn froze with his mouth gaping.

Jim put his arm around Arn's shoulder. "Well say something boy!"

"I don't believe it." He said in a low voice.

Jim pulled him over in front of Sally. "Seeing is believing!"

"Beautiful twin girls." Sally announced.

Arn fainted.

Nat and Jim quickly knelt down on each side of him. Jim looked up at Sally. "I do believe the boy has fainted!"

A few seconds later Arn came to and looked at Nat. "Tell me I'm dreaming."

Jim and Nat helped him up. Nat answered him. "You're not dreaming. Sarah gave you a beautiful set of twin girls."

Sally turned and walked back down the hall with Arn following her in a state of shock,

As Arn entered the room, the doctor looked up at him. "You okay, Arn? You look pale."

"She had twins."

Alan laughed. "I know. I'm the one that delivered them. Remember?"

Lisa and Ellen went over and gave Arn a hug. "Isn't this neat?" Ellen asked him.

"She had twin girls."

Lisa looked over at the doctor. Laughing. "I think he is in a state of shock."

"Well, you better sit him down in that chair before he falls down."

The doctor finished cleaning up then went into his office. Shortly Nat came into the office. "Did you know she was going to have twins, Doc?"

"I suspected it."

"Why didn't you say something?"

"Because it was only a suspicion."

"It doesn't matter anyway. They're both healthy. I think this calls for a drink. Got anything around here?"

Alan laughed. "Yeah! Coffee!"

"Anything stronger?"

"Nope!"

"I guess it's got to be coffee then."

As Alan poured them a cup of coffee, Sally came in. "Doctor, I put Sarah up in the first room. The sedation is starting to wear off now."

"Where is Arn?"

"He is still setting in the delivery room in shock."

"Where are Lisa and Ellen?"

"Lisa is with Sarah, and Ellen is trying to get Arn to say something besides she had twins. Sally said with a laugh.

Alan pointed at the little fridge. "Get an ice cube out of the fridge and drop it down the back of his shirt. He'll say something else."

She hurried over to the fridge and removed two ice cubes. As she headed for the door, Nat commented to her. "Why Sally! That gleam in your eyes makes me think that you have a bit of a sadistic nature about you."

"I do not!" She retorted and she went out the door.

A minute later they heard Arn. "Yeow! What the hell was that for?"

"To bring you back to reality!" Sally scolded.

"Where did Sarah go?"

"Up to the first room."

The doctor leaned back in his chair and placed his feet up on the desk. "You know Nat? I don't believe you ever mentioned whether you had any children or not.

"No. We never had any."

"Didn't want any or couldn't have any?"

"Couldn't have any."

"You or her?"

"I don't know. We never found out. We decided best it that way. I figured if she couldn't, it would tear her up not being able to give me a child. If I found out it was my fault, then I would have felt bad about not being able to get her pregnant."

"Before the war, there were clinics that offered artificial insemination. Did you ever consider that?"

"We discussed it once, and both decided that if we couldn't do it on our own, we would not seek outside help."

"To bad. Lisa told me that you loved your wife very much, and that she loved you just as much."

"Lisa never knew her."

"I know, but sometimes a woman senses things, and I'll bet Lisa was a hundred percent right. Was she something like Ellen?"

"Not even close. Why do you ask that?"

"Oh, just because you and Ellen seem to get along so well together."

"To tell you the honest truth Doc. Lisa is so much like my wife was that it gets scary. Maybe that's why I have kinda leaned towards Ellen instead of Lisa. I'm not sure I could handle having a woman that reminded me of my wife all the time." Nat stood to leave. "I think I'll take a walk, and then check back on Sarah"

"Okay. See you later."

Nat walked up the river for a short distant, then sat down on a rock. A few minutes later, a squirrel came out near him, stopped, looked at him as to say. 'Who are you?'

"Well, hello little feller." Nat spoke gently as the little animal starred at him. Then when it realized that Nat meant it no harm, it went about searching for food.

The squirrel made Nat think back to the little animal friends that hung around their house. Nancy had literally encouraged such pets. These pets consisted of squirrels, chipmunks, various small birds, an otter, and eventually Bandit. They even had a pet porcupine for a couple of years. It was getting so old it was having a hard time even moving around. Nancy had managed to feed and care for it for over two years before it succumbed to old age.

Old Thistle as they had dubbed him was lying dead on the porch when she had gone out to put the usual treats out for the animals. Nat had just gotten out of the shower when she walked into the bathroom carrying Thistle. Tears were pouring down her cheeks. "Honey? Thistle is dead."

"I see that dear. As soon as I get dressed I'll take care of him." He said in a matter of fact tone of voice.

"Do you have to be so cold about it?"

"I'm not being cold. I feel very bad about it."

"Well you sound like you don't care. She then turned and went outside.

He had come out of the house and found her sitting on a stump holding the porcupine. "I'm sorry if I sounded cold. I guess I just didn't know what else to say." Nat knelt down beside her and kissed her. "I'm going to miss him too."

She put her arm around him, and then laid her head on his chest. "Will you take him out into the woods and see that he is properly taken care of?"

"Of course I will." Then taking the animal from her took it way out in the woods and laid it beside a tree to let Mother Nature take care of her own.

Nancy was despondent for three days after that, but she never mentioned Thistle again. This was her way of coping with death. She never asked him how he disposed of the animals.

The following year Bandit came into their lives. Nat was out hunting when he saw four baby raccoons in a hollow tree. Thinking the mother was probably nearby, he went on. A few hours later as he was coming back with the deer he had shot, he checked on the raccoons. Their whimpering troubled him, so he looked around a little while trying to find fresh tracks of the mother. There was too much moss and leaves around for him to pick any tracks out. Wanting to be sure they were abandoned he went and got some fresh dirt and spread it around the tree. The next morning he went back to the tree and found no fresh tracks in the dirt. Gently he removed the four baby raccoons from the tree and took them home.

Nancy fussed over them and fed them the best she could, but three of them died. Bandit survived and became the terror of the household, getting into everything. It took two years, and a lot of patients to get Bandi half way trained to stay out of things, but in the end, he turned out to be the perfect pet. Except for some minor incidents, such as taking his peanut butter and jelly sandwich in on the bed to eat it, things went pretty smooth.

Nat's new friend seemed to be getting used to him sitting on the rock. It came right up next to his foot searching for food. Slowly he reached over to one side and picked up a fir cone, then dropped it in front of the squirrel. It quickly picked the cone up and scurried off into the brush.

Standing up, Nat slowly made his way back to the clinic to look in on Sarah and the twins. Lisa, Ellen, and Arn were still there when Nat entered. He kissed Sarah on the cheek. "Looks like Arn got cheated."

"What do you mean?" Sarah asked with a puzzled expression.

"Two babies, two breasts"

"Nat!" Scolded Ellen. "That's crude!"

Arn grinned. "I'll be glad to forfeit this time."

"I figured you would." Nat replied.

"You men are disgusting!" Ellen uttered in contempt. "Come on Lisa! Let's get away from those cads!"

Arn and Nat laughed as they hurried out the door.

Sarah reached out and took Nat's hand. "I want you to think of the girls as your granddaughters."

"I would love to." He looked up at Arn. "Do you have any objections Arn?"

"Hell no! You have been kinda a father image to us. You married us, and you have always stuck by us when we needed someone to lean on. Shit! It would be an honor if you thought of them as your granddaughters."

Nat swelled with pride. "Now I have three grand kids!"

Squeezing Nat's hand Sarah looked up at him. "The funny thing is that there have been a couple of times that I almost called you daddy. You have been so much like a father to me sometimes."

He remembered the incident at the dam. "Even when I scolded you for coming up to the dam that day?"

She laughed. "Especially that time. When you yelled at me to get going, I almost said yes daddy, but I caught myself. In fact, on the way into town, I was thinking that if I had said it, you would have gotten upset."

Nat chuckled. "No, I wouldn't have gotten upset, but I might have dropped the next sandbag on my foot. The funny thing is, Phill was standing next to me and commented that you forgot to say yes father."

"Oh he did not!"

"He sure did. The next time you see him, ask him."

"That's true!" Arn interjected. "I was talking to Phill the next day, and he told me about it."

"By the way. Nat asked, "What did you two decide for names?"

"Lisa and Ellen!!" Sarah said with a smile.

Nat started laughing. "What's so funny?" Arn asked.

"We now have a Nat, Lisa, and an Ellen. Somebody is going to have to get busy and come up with an Arn and a Sarah. Well, I think I better be getting a move on. I'm going down to the lowlands to try to find a double crib for my granddaughters, If I can't find one, I'll just have to make it myself."

"Bye daddy!' Sarah said with a sheepish grin.

Nat was smiling as he went out the door.

Nat was fleshing a deer hide when he heard a vehicle pull up in front of the house. As he walked around front, he recognized the pick-up as the one Phill usually drives, but it wasn't Phill. A man rolled down the window. "You Nat?"

The stranger got out of the pickup. Nat looked him over. The man was dirty looking with a heavy snarled beard which seemed to match the filthy buckskin clothes he wore. A bull whip was coiled and looped over one shoulder. The man also was cradling a rifle in his arm. "My name is Zack!"

"Pleased to meet you." Nat reached out to shake hands, but the stranger made no move to acknowledge the gesture. Nat lowered his hand. "What can I do for you?"

"You might offer me a drink. He then hooked one finger behind his lower lip and dug out a wad of snooze and threw it on the ground.

Lisa walked out on the porch to see what was going on. Nat looked up at her. "Would you bring us a cup of coffee?"

She looked at Zack without expression, and then went back into the house.

Zack's eyes followed her as she disappeared. "Mighty fine lookin' filly there. Your wife?"

Nat felt resentment towards the man's question. "Might be. Why?"

"Just askin'."

Nothing more was said as they waited for the coffee. Nat sat down on the steps, and Zack just stood there looking around at things. A couple minutes later Ellen brought two cups of coffee out. She handed one to Nat, then walked over and handed the other to Zack.

"Why thank you ma'am!"

She didn't answer him. Turning back towards Nat, she had a look of disgust on her face as she went past him and up into the house.

"Two little fillies! Now let me guess! You're hitched to both of them!"

"I'm not married to either one of them! Nat was getting riled.

"That's better yet!"

"Mister, I don't like your implications!"

"Didn't mean to rile you. Just makin' conversation. That's all."

"Well, pick another subject!"

Okay. How long you people been livin' here?"

"Over a year."

"Right fine lookin' town you got here. You all move up here from down below?"

"No. We came from all over. Where did you come from?"

"Oh, here, there, and everywhere. I been just travelin'. Covered a lot of ground. Been from California to up in Canada.'

"Pretty exposed, just wandering round like that isn't it?"

"Would be for most folks, but I'm good. Only the smart can do it. Gotta be quick too, and a good shot. I can shoot the eye out of a cat at a hundred yards."

"Have you seen many other normal people?"

"Yeah, I run into them every now and then."

"Are they trying to rebuild?"

"Naw! They is just fightin' to survive, but most of 'em won't make it, cause they ain't smart like me."

"Any large groups?"

"Found one 'bout a month ago."

"Where at?"

"Outside a big city, I think it was called Bellingham. Up in the hills east of it."

"How many people?"

"Oh, I recon' maybe a hundred."

Nat realized he was going to have to pry any information out. "Have they built a town?"

"Nope. Just a fort."

"What do you mean?"

"Just that. A fort. Kinda looks like a fort from the old western days."

"They live inside the fort then, I presume."

"You presume right. They got little shacks built inside. Kinda flimsy at that."

"Do they have many children?"

"A few. Mostly men tho'. You're the only man I seen here, outside the couple I met down below that let me use the pick-up to come up here."

"There are more."

"How many?"

"A few." Nat wasn't about to give him any more information. "How long did you stay there?"

"Not long. They weren't too friendly." Zack took another chew of snooze, then spit.

"How did you get over here?"

"Found me a boat a long time ago. Been gettin' around in that. I go inland every once in awhile. Especially when I hear there are people. I go to check it out."

"How come you never settled down?"

"Ain't found a place that meets my fancy yet."

"Have you come across many mutants?"

"If you mean the night creatures. Yeah I have."

"Very many?"

Zack thought for a minute, then spit. "Kinda hard to say. They're spread all over. Probably a few thousand."

"Any certain area where there are more of them than another?"

"A few places. Like northeast of Olympia, and south of Portland. Lots of 'em there."

"How are the highways in general?"

"Around the major cities, not worth a shit. But the farther you get away from the bombed areas, the better they get.

"What are your plans for the future?"

"Haven't made any yet. Mind if I look your town over?"

"Go right ahead, but don't start any trouble."

"You're wearing a sidearm there. You the law around here?"

"You might call it that. Just don't start anything."

Zack left to walk around the town, and Nat went inside.

"I don't like that man!" Ellen stated.

"He is a renegade!" Lisa added.

"Just the same, I can't run him off until he starts something. Which probably won't take long. Lisa, you take our truck and go down to the lowlands, and bring Jim and a few others back up here."

As Lisa went out the door, Ellen asked. What are you going to do?"

"Well, he made the comment that he didn't see any other men around here besides me. So, if other men start showing up, maybe he will just leave."

"What if he starts trouble before they get here?"

"Then I'll have to deal with it the best I can."

She put her arms around Nat. "I don't trust him. He looks like he would kill just for the fun of it."

"You're probably right." He went outside and finished up what he could on the hide, then came back in, and sat down with a cup of coffee.

A few minutes later, there came a pounding at the door. Nat arose and answered it. Alice was standing there with a frantic look. Nat! Did you know there was a stranger in town?"

"Yes. What happened?"

"He came into the supply house and helped himself to some of the things I was preparing. I told him around here we filled out a request sheet and signed it."

"What did he say?"

"Nothing! He just laughed, then came over and grabbed me and tried to take my clothes off. I got away and ran up here.”

"Are you alright?”

"Yes, but I'm not going back down there!”

Nat's blood was boiling. "You stay here!”

Just before he stepped off the porch, he heard Ellen. "Be careful Nat!”

Nat looked around for Zack, and finally found him on the edge of town sitting on a log eating on a freshly baked loaf of bread.

As Nat walked toward the man, he wished he had his rifle instead of just his pistol. "I want to talk to you!”

Zack stood up, tossing the bread on the ground and faced Nat with his rifle pointed at Nat's feet. "I figured you would show up as soon as that pussy went running to you”

"There was no call for what you did!”

"What are you going to-do about it big man?”

"You hit the road over there, and don't stop!”

"You're sure a stupid son-of a-bitch to give orders to someone that has the drop on you. I can raise this barrel and kill you before you even come close to clearing leather.”

Nat knew he was right, but he had to try to convince the man to get out of their town. "You kill me and the others will kill you.”

"I ain't scared of a bunch of women. What few men that are around ain't no match for me.”

"There are more than just a few around!”

"And you are a lying bastard! You got your own little harem here, and you don't like competition. Well, now you got competition, but you ain't much competition.”

"Don't press your luck!”

"Oh listen to the big man talk. Go ahead! Draw!”

Nat just stood there glaring.

"What these women need around here is a real man. Someone with real power. I'm going to take over this town, and you or nobody else is going to stop me. It won't take long to teach these women whose boss. All women like a man to treat 'em rough. Give them the whip a few times and they will love me for it.”

Nat knew that he was trying to anger him enough to get him to draw.

"Any men come around, and I give them all the pussy they want, and they will do whatever I tell them to do."

"You're not just sick, mister, you are mentally retarded!'

"Watch your mouth asshole, or I won't wait for you to reach for your gun!"

"Why wait?"

"I always let the other person make the first move, unless there is more than one."

"Like I said. You kill me and the others will kill you."

"You really like to think you're big. I've met a lot of men who thought they were big. Well, I shoot 'em and spit on 'em. There ain't no man big enough to beat me. I'm good!"

"The only way you're going to get out of here alive is to hit the road now!"

"I ain't leaving! 'Caus' I'm taking over your harem, and that black-haired bitch you got living with you will make a good town whore."

That was all Nat could take. Losing his self control, he reached for his gun, as anger raged.

Nat heard the explosion and saw half the man's head fly into little pieces, and the man flew sideways landing on his back.

Looking to his right Nat saw Silent Sam step out from behind a tree with a double barreled shot gun, still smoking. Sam walked over to Zack's body, and then leaning over it let some of his saliva dribble out of his mouth onto the body.

Nat quickly pulled himself together, then walking over to Sam, put his hand on his shoulder. "Thanks Sam! I guess I kind of lost my cool."

Sam leaned over the dead man and dribbled some more saliva, then looked at Nat with a twinkle in his eye.

Suddenly Nat realized what Sam was saying. "You earned the right to spit on him. He was the vilest man I ever met, and I hope I never meet another one."

Jim's truck came speeding up to them, sliding to a stop. Jumping out, he ran over to Sam and Nat. "What the hell happened?"

"He thought he was going to kill me and take over the town."

"So you shot him?"

"No. Sam got that pleasure."

Ellen came running up carrying a rifle. When she saw Nat she dropped the rifle, and ran to him, then threw her arms around him crying. "Oh Nat! When I heard the gun go off, I thought he had shot you!"

"Sam didn't give him a chance to. Just as the son-of-a-bitch went to shoot me, Sam shot him."

Lisa went over to Sam and put her arms around his neck and kissed his mis-shappened mouth. "Sam, you are a wonderful man. I don't know if we could make it around here without you."

As she let go and stood back, Sam had turned a beet red.

Ellen let go of Nat, then went over to Sam and kissed him also. "Thank you Sam. We all are glad that you are part of us."

That's right Sam." Lisa added. "Maybe we haven't really stopped to tell you how much we all love and respect you. In fact I'm sorry we have failed to do so. You have been so good to all of us, always thinking of everybody else, before yourself."

Sam looked at Nat with anguish in his eyes, and then a couple of tears trickled down his cheek. Nat walked over and put his arm around Sam's shoulder. "I know what you want to say, so can I say it for you?"

He looked at Nat and rapidly shook his head yes.

Nat looked at the others. "Sam wouldn't want to be with any other group of people. He feels like he is part of us and wouldn't want it any other way. He knows we accept him like a member of the family, and he really appreciates it. There is nothing he wouldn't do for any one of us."

Sam nodded in agreement.

Jim came over to Sam, then after hanging his head down for a few seconds, he looked up., "Sam, I'm more guilty than any of the others when it comes to not letting you know how much you're appreciated. We live together, and you always look out for me. You always have. Ever since we met." He then threw his arms around Sam and squeezed him. As Jim let go and stood back. Sam put his hand on Jim's shoulder and they looked into each other's eyes. There was no mistaking the bond between those two men.

As Nat started walking away Jim hollered at him. "What do you want us to do with this pile of shit laying here?"

"Put the son-of-a-bitch into the helicopter, and have Ken fly out over the water and throw him to the fish for food! Then somebody can go down and sink his god-damn boat!"

Sam caught up with Nat and pointed to himself.

"Go ahead Sam, if you want to do it. Check it for any weapons or any-thing else useful before you do it."

Nat headed for the house as Sam left to sink the renegade's boat.

Pouring himself a cup of coffee, he sat down, filled with anger at himself for being so stupid as to not take his rifle with him, causing him to nearly get killed.

When Lisa and Ellen came in, they saw that something was bothering him. "What's wrong Nat?" Ellen asked.

"Nothing!" He stood up, taking his coffee, headed for the door. "I just have to calm down I guess. I'm going to sit out on the porch."

A while later Sam drove up in front of the house. Nat saw that he had someone with him, but didn't give it any thought until Sam jumped out and hurried around to the other side of the truck.

Nat watched as Sam opened the door and brought a girl that looked like she was in her late teens or early twenties around the front of the truck. She was completely naked except for Sam's coat wrapped around her. Nat jumped to his feet as he saw how bad the girl looked. She was covered with bruises, and cuts, some of them had infection. Her hair had been cut to within an inch of her scalp. The skin around her wrists and ankles were raw and bleeding.

Sam pointed at the girl, then towards the lowlands.

"She was tied up on the boat?"

Sam nodded yes.

Lisa an Ellen came out onto the porch and saw the girl. "Oh, you poor girl!" Lisa cried, and they both ran down the steps to her.

"Where are you from?" Nat asked her.

She looked at the ground, but wouldn't speak.

"She is terrified!" Ellen commented, and then looked at Lisa. "Let's get her into the house!"

As the women took her into the house, Nat spoke to Sam. "Go get the doctor!" He then turned and went inside. The woman had taken the girl into one of the bedrooms.

Nat poured himself a cup of coffee and waited a few minutes, then asked if he could come in.

Ellen answered. "Not yet. We are still trying to get her cleaned up."

A few minutes later there was a knock at the door. He opened the door to see Sam and the doctor standing there. Alan looked at Nat. "Sam almost dragged me up here. Who got hurt?"

Lisa and Ellen have a girl in the bedroom that Sam rescued. She needs medical attention pretty bad."

"I'll get right in there but Sam didn't give me time to grab my medical bag." He went right into the bedroom. A few minutes later he came out. "She is going to have to come down to the clinic so I can treat her. What the hell happened to her? I can tell she has been tied up and beaten pretty bad. But where did Sam find her?"

That man that Sam shot today had her on his boat. When Sam went down to sink it, he found her."

"That man must have been demented to do that to her. She won't talk. Probably she is in a state of shock, besides being down right scared. Some of those cuts are infected pretty badly."

Lisa and Ellen brought the girl out wearing a robe. "I'm going down to the clinic with her!" Lisa told Nat.

"Alright. Let me know when she is ready to talk. I want to know how he came about taking her hostage. Also where she is from."

"I'll let you know."

They took her out and put her in Sam's truck. While Sam drove, Lisa sat in the seat with the girl, and the doctor rode in the back.

Ellen looked at Nat. "Where do you think she came from?"

"I don't know, but that guy mentioned a group over by Bellingham. Maybe he kidnapped her from there. Tomorrow morning, I'm going to have Ken fly me over there to look around."

"Can I go with you?"

"You can if you want to."

CHAPTER 15

Nat woke up as Ellen came out of the bedroom. "Didn't Lisa come in last night?"

"No. Knowing how she worries about someone hurt, she probably stayed with the girl all night."

He got up and pulled his pants on. "I better go down and check on her. Maybe Lisa found out more about her."

"I'll fix you something to eat first. If we are going to Bellingham, you better eat a good breakfast."

As soon as he finished eating he went down to the clinic. He met Sally as soon as he came in. "How is the girl that was brought in yesterday?"

"Out side of being physically abused, her health is pretty fair. Some malnutrition though."

"Has she said anything yet?"

"Not a word. Whatever happened to her was so traumatic that she is afraid of everybody, although she seems to be more at ease with Lisa near her. If she talks it will be to Lisa only at first."

"Can I go in to see her?"

"I guess. But please make it short." Sally started to turn around, but hesitated.

"Was there something else?" Nat asked.

"No. It's just that this is the first time you ever came in here and acted civil."

Nat laughed. "If you weren't Jim's girl, I'd swat you on the backside just so you wouldn't get disillusioned."

She glared at Nat. "Who told you I was Jim's girl?"

"Oh---I don't seem to remember."

"Did Jim tell you that?

"I told you I don't remember."

Sally was blushing as she turned and went down the hall. "You're impossible!"

Lisa was sitting in a chair next to the bed, and the girl was asleep. She signaled for him to be quiet as he came in, so he motioned for her to come out into the hall. As Lisa stood up, the girl's eyes quickly opened and she reached out and grabbed Lisa's arm.

Lisa looked down at her. "I'm not leaving you. I was just going to step out into the hall to talk to Nat."

The girl would not release her grip, and her eyes were filled with fear.

"That's alright." Nat said to Lisa. "We can talk here. I just didn't want to awaken her."

Lisa sat back down. "She still hasn't said a word."

"Well, maybe when she realizes that we all want to help her, she will talk. Until then, all we can do is show her we mean her no harm. Have you had any sleep yourself?"

"Yes. I laid my head down on the bed and slept some."

"That's not very comfortable. How about food?"

"Sally is going to bring some food in pretty soon."

"What I came down to tell you, is that Ellen is going with me over to the Bellingham area to see if we can locate that group the renegade told me about.

"How are you going?"

"I'll get Ken to fly us over there."

As Nat came out of the room he saw Alan. "Is she gonna' be alright?"

"I think so. It will just take a little time for the wounds to heal. Her mental wounds though, I'm not so sure of. She has been through one hell-of-a mental trauma. And you know, as well as I, that it takes time to get over that."

"Yeah, I know. Ellen and I are going to be gone for maybe a few days."

"Where are you going?"

"Over by Bellingham. That renegade said he had seen a group of people over there. Maybe he kidnapped the girl from them. I also want to see if I can talk them into joining us here."

"Well, good luck. Oh, by the way. Sam was in last night, and early this morning to check on the girl's well-being."

"Just goes to show you how much he cares about other people. Well, I have to get going. See you when we get back."

That night as Lisa was sleeping with her head on her arms lying on the bed beside the girl, she suddenly woke up feeling something touching her head. Lisa didn't move as she realized that the girl was stroking her hair.

After a few minutes, Lisa lifted her head. The girl quickly pulled her hand back. Gently, Lisa took the girl's hand and brought it up to the hair cascading over her shoulders. "That's alright, you go right ahead and touch it. I don't mind."

The girl cautiously ran her fingers through Lisa's hair. "So pretty."

"Yours will be again. I'm sure."

The girl reached up with her other hand and felt the short hair on her own head, and then tears ran down her bruised cheeks.

Lisa placed her hand lightly on the girl's cheek. The light from the doorway cast a soft glow on the girls face, and Lisa saw a deep sadness in the girl's eyes. She withdrew her hand. "Try to get some sleep now." Then laying her head back down, she silently cried herself to sleep, feeling a very deep sadness for the girl.

In the morning, Lisa lifted her head and looked at the doorway just in time to see Sam's face disappear. She then looked at the girl. Lisa saw that she was staring at the doorway.

During the day the girl seemed to have less fear when Lisa left to go to the bathroom or even get up and walk out of the room for a short while. It was that evening Lisa decided to walk outside and get a breath of fresh air.

While she was leaning against the side of the doorway, Sam came around the corner. He hastened up to Lisa, and then pointed towards the inside of the clinic. "She is fine Sam. I just came out to get some fresh air. You like her, don't you?"

Sam blushed slightly and looked down at his feet.

Lisa reached out and put her hand on Sam's arm. "I think when she learns to trust us, and starts talking, we are going to find out that she is a very nice girl."

Sam indicated that he wanted to write.

"Come on inside Sam and I'll get you a pencil and a piece of paper."

She got a piece of paper and a pencil off sally's desk, and gave it to Sam.

He picked up the pencil, and in clear handwriting wrote a note to the girl. 'I feel sorry for what you have suffered. Please get well and tell us who you are. We all want to be your friends---I want to be your friend. If I could talk, I would tell you how nice these people are. If you will let me know your name, I will write you another note.' He handed the paper to Lisa.

She read it, and then looked at him. "That is very nice Sam. Now why don't you take it in there and give it to her?"

Sam shook his head no, and hurried out the door.

Lisa took the note in and handed it to the girl. "It is from the man that brought you to us. His name is Sam, and he cannot talk because of being shot in the face."

The girl took the note and slowly read it. Tears came to her eyes as she finished reading the note, "Elizabeth." Then holding the note to her chest, she closed her eyes, and said nothing else.

Alan and Sally moved another bed into the room for Lisa to sleep in during the night. Lisa awoke and saw Elizabeth staring at Sam' note, but said nothing, and went back to sleep.

Sally awakened Lisa in the morning and asked her to come out to the waiting room. Sam was standing there when she came out. "Good morning Sam. Her name is Elizabeth."

Sam's eyes twinkled.

"That is all she said though. Are you going to write her another note?"

Nodding his head yes, he indicated for her to get him a pencil and paper. Upon receiving the materials he wrote another note. 'Elizabeth! That is a very beautiful name. I like it very much. When you get well, would you tell me more about yourself? If I can get you anything, or do anything for you, please let me know. Sam." He then handed it to Lisa, and went out the door.

She returned to the room and handed the note to Elizabeth. After reading the note, she looked at Lisa. "Tell him I will." She said in a soft voice.

Lisa was ecstatic with joy. Elizabeth had talked, and it was silent Sam that did it. She decided to let the girl talk when she felt like it, rather than try to draw it out of her. "Sam has already left, but I will be happy to tell him for you."

Elizabeth didn't speak for some time, and then she looked towards the doorway when she did. "He must be a very nice person."

Putting her hand on Elizabeth's arm, she smiled. "He is loved by everyone. Sam is one of the gentlest people you could ever want to know. He will be stopping by to check on you around noon. Do you want me to bring him in to see you?"

Quickly she put a hand up to her short hair. "No!"

"Okay. I won't, but I have to go see the doctor. I'll only be gone for a few minutes."

When she came out of the room, she saw Jim tip-toeing away from her down the hall with a bouquet of flowers held behind his back. "Jim! What in the world are you doing?"

Jim froze in his tracks for a few seconds, and then turned around. "Uh---uh---nothing." He still held the flowers behind him.

"Don't give me that Jim! You are not one to go sneaking around with flowers hid behind your back for nothing. Who are they for?"

"Uh---the new girl?"

"Wrong! You already went past her room."

Jim was starting to get uneasy as he shifted from one foot to another. "Well---I was just going to ask the doctor which room she was in." He brought the flowers around in front of him. "Uh---do you think she might like them?"

Lisa laughed. "She probably would if they were for her. The only trouble is, I don't believe for one second that they are for her.

Just then Sally came out of a room behind Jim. "Jim! What are you doing here? You told me last night that you would be up at the dam all day."

Jim looked around as if looking for a place to hide. Then he opened his jacket and started to stuff the flowers underneath.'

Lisa quickly reached out and grabbed his wrist. "Oh no you don't! That would ruin them!"

"Ruin what?" Sally asked as she walked up beside them. "Flowers! This makes three days in a row that you have brought me flowers." She took them from him and looked closely and smelled them. "And each day they are more beautiful. Thank you Jim."

He turned beet red, and glanced at Lisa. Then facing Sally hung his head down. "Ah, they ain't much."

"They are to me. Now you just come over to my place for supper again tonight!"

Lisa smiled. "I won't tell a sole Jim, but I do have a favor to ask you."

He was glad to have the subject changed. "What?"

"Could you go into Port Angeles and look around in the store for a wig?"

"Huh?"

"A wig! You know, to wear on one's head."

"What do you need a wig for? There is nothing wrong with the hair you got."

"It's not for me silly! I want you to find me a dark brown, long haired wig. Is that asking too much?"

"Well, I don't know."

"You don't know what?"

"I ain't never done nothing like that before."

"I know what she wants it for." Sally stated. "So you just go down there and at least try to find a nice one. It's for a good cause. Now get a move on, or no more meals until you do!"

"Okay! I'll see what I can come up with."

After Jim left, Lisa looked at Sally. "I think you caught yourself a very good man."

Sally laughed. "I know I have. In fact, he wants to get married, but I'm enjoying his efforts to convince me."

Just before lunch, Sally came into the room. "Ken is out there and he wants to talk to you."

"I heard him land. Did he say if anything was wrong?"

"No, but he doesn't act like anything is."

She went out to talk to Ken. "Where are Nat and Ellen?"

"They stayed over there. Nat talked the people into coming over here to live. They figure to be here in three or four days."

"Why so long?"

"Well, they have to round up enough boats, and pack what they want to bring."

"How many people are there?"

"Seventy-nine."

"That's good! Are you flying back over there?"

"No. I've got to get up some crews to start building more houses for those people. I just stopped by to let you know what's going on. See you later."

"Bye! Thanks."

Sam came by at lunch time again, and Lisa went out to see him. "Elizabeth said to tell you she will. Sam, if you come by this evening I think she just might want to see you. No promises though. Do you know what I'm saying?"

He shook his head yes.'

"Just in case she does want to see you, I want you to find some flowers someplace, and bring them with you."

Eagerly Sam shook his head yes.

Lisa got him some more writing material. "Here! At least tell her something, even if it's only hello."

Sam wrote. 'Elizabeth, I just stopped by to make sure you are okay. I will come by again this evening. Sam.' He handed the note to Lisa, then touched her cheek. Nodding thank you, he went out the door.

Lisa delivered the note to Elizabeth. As she read the short note, tears sprang to her eyes. Then again she reached up and touched her short hair. Rolling over, she then buried her face in the pillow and cried herself to sleep.

A couple of hours later, Sally came into the room. "Jim is back from down below."

"Did he get what I asked for?"

"He sure did! You have eight to choose from!"

Lisa turned to Elizabeth. "I'll be gone for about a half hour. If you need anything, just call for Sally, and she will be right here."

"Please hurry back! Elizabeth pleaded with fear in her eyes.

Lisa rushed home, took a quick shower, then gathered up her makeup, and went back down to the clinic. Gathering up the wigs, she went into Elizabeth's room. "It's time to see if we can't make you feel better!" She then deposited the things on the bed.

Quickly Elizabeth grabbed one of the wigs and put it on her head, then stroked the hair that fell over her shoulders. She looked up at Lisa with an inquisitive look.

"It looks beautiful! Now let me put some make up on your face to cover the bruises." Carefully Lisa applied the make up to Elizabeth's face. After she finished, she stepped back and looked at the girl. "You look absolutely beautiful. I'll go get a mirror for you to look at yourself with."

As soon as she took the mirror from Lisa and looked at herself, she touched the hair, then her cheeks. "So you really think I look alright?"

"Of course you do!"

Just then Sally came in. "Oh! It looks like we have a new patient! And a mighty pretty one at that?"

Elizabeth lowered her head. "You both are so kind. Thank you."

Suddenly Lisa got an idea. "Sally! Elizabeth looks like she is exactly the same size as Jenny. Would you mind going up and asking her if Elizabeth can borrow some of her clothes?"

"I would be more than happy to! I'll be back as quick as I can!"

"Why are you going to all this trouble for me?"

Lisa took her hand and smiled. "To show you that we care about you and we want you to feel comfortable around us. Also, we want you to accept us as your friends."

"But you don't even know me."

"That is not as important as the fact that we can help you, and give you a place to live. We are like one big happy family here, and we want you to feel like you are part of the family. As far as knowing you, well, I think I know you well enough to know that you are the type of person we want in our family."

"Are all of the others as kind as you and Sally are?"

"Every single one of them! And like I told you before, Sam is one of the kindest. Another one that is super kind and gentle is Nat. He is the one that Sam took you to first. Right now, Nat is our leader. We all look to him for leadership, although he has decided to turn the leadership over to the people."

"You love him, don't you? I can see it in your eyes."

"He belongs to Ellen, the other woman you met when Sam brought you to us. Ellen and I are very dear friends, and I wouldn't do anything to hurt her."

Nothing more was said until Sally returned with the clothes. "She sent enough for five changes." Sally laid the clothes down, and then picked up a dress. "Look at this cute green dress!"

"Oh! I like that!" Elizabeth said with excitement. "Can I try that one on?"

"Honey, you can wear whichever one you want!" Sally laughed.

Lisa and Sally went out of the room while Elizabeth got dressed. "What do you think?" Sally asked.

I think she is going to be just fine. I sure hope she lets Sam come in to see her."

"If she does, Sam will be struck down by her beauty. That, I'm sure of!"

"I hope you are right."

A few minutes later Elizabeth called out that she was dressed. When they went back in, she was wearing the green dress, and looked stunning.

"My words!" Exclaimed Sally. "You are the best looking woman in town!"

Elizabeth blushed." You are being to kind."

"I agree with her!' Lisa added. "You are absolutely beautiful!"

The doctor walked in at that time. Seeing what was going on, he looked around. "I thought we had a patient in here. Where did she go?"

Lisa laughed. "Doesn't she look gorgeous Alan?"

"This is my patient? Well! I must say that I've never had a more beautiful patient!"

Elizabeth blushed profusely. "Thank you doctor."

"I think that come tomorrow morning, I shall allow you to de discharged." He then turned and left.

Tears came to Elizabeth's eyes. "I don't have any place to stay."

Sally handed her a tissue. "Now don't go ruining your makeup. You are welcome to stay at my house. I have an extra bedroom. Besides that, I live by myself. And don't worry about being alone. During the day when I come down here, you can come down with me and help around here. I'm sure the doctor would be very happy to have the extra help."

Elizabeth threw her arms around Sally and gave her a hug, then turned to Lisa and hugged her also. Both of you are so nice. How can I thank you enough?"

"You already have!", Sally answered. "I better get back to work, or the doctor might think he can run this place without me."

After Sally had left, Lisa and Elizabeth sat and talked, with Elizabeth asking about Eagletown and the people living in it.

Sally stuck her head in the doorway. "Lisa? I think you better get out here on the double."

When Lisa went into the waiting room, she couldn't believe her eyes. The first thing she saw was the biggest bouquet of roses she had ever seen in her life. Sam stood there in a white shirt, black pants, and black shined shoes. There were so many roses that he could hardly hold them in one arm. "Sam, those roses are beautiful, and so are you! Let me go ask Elizabeth if you can come in and see her."

She returned to the room. "Elizabeth. Sam is out there, and he has something to give to you. Is it okay for him to come in?"

"Do you think I look alright?"

"You definitely look alright."

"What do I say to him?"

"Anything you want. He would just be happy hearing your voice."

"Okay! But I'm nervous."

"So is he!" She went to get Sam.

"Sam, I think the Princess is ready to meet a Prince!"

Blushing, Sam slowly walked into the room. Just inside the door, he stopped and stared.

Elizabeth walked over and stood in front of him. "Do you like the way

I look Sam?"

He slowly nodded his head yes, and then he held the flowers out to her.

She had to use both arms to hold them. "They are the most beautiful flowers I have ever seen in my life Sam. No one has ever given me flowers before. Thank you! Thank you for bringing me here."

Lisa patted her on the arm. "I'll be right outside the door if you need me."

When Sam came out of the room, he went straight outside, walking as if on air.

Sally looked at Lisa. "Bingo!"

Lisa laughed and went back into Elizabeth's room. She was sitting in a chair holding the roses. "I'll put them in a vase for you."

"Let me hold them a little longer. Please?"

"You can hold them as long as you like, but if you don't put them in water before too long, they will start to wilt."

"Just a little longer, then we can put them in a vase."

"Well? What do you think of him?"

She was silent for a moment. "He can say so much with his eyes. I really like him."

"He likes you too!"

Nat had Ken fly over the Kitsap Peninsula, Seattle, and then north to Bellingham. None of them spoke as they viewed the total destruction spread out beneath them. The whole area looked like one huge garbage dump full of rubble. Everett had been completely leveled by a direct hit. Bellingham from the air looked like one huge traffic jam had occurred in the final troughs of death. Just about every intersection had a wreck.

As they turned east, Nat spotted a cemetery. "Set down in that cemetery over there."

"What's down there?" Ellen asked.

Nat looked at her. "Just memories."

Ken landed and shut the engine down as Nat got out. He turned and looked at Ken. "You didn't have to shut it down. I'll only be a few minutes."

"Take your time. I'm just going to give it a check over while I have the chance."

"Do you want me to go with you?" Ellen asked.

"No, I want to go alone. You stay here with Ken."

They watched as Nat walked nearly to the other side of the cemetery, then he stopped at a grave and stood there looking down at it.

Ellen looked at Ken. "I wonder who is buried there?"

"Got me! Must be someone pretty special for him to stop and pay his respects"

Nat read the marker. Dorthey Williston---born March 1st, 1929, died July 9th, 1987.

They had been out working in the garden early, taking advantage of the long summer days to get things done. A light drizzle had been in the air for the first couple of hours, but the sun had broke through by ten o'clock and it promised to be clear skies for the remainder of the day.

Standing up and rubbing the small of his back, Nat looked at Nancy. "I vote that we go inside and take a break."

"I vote the same way." She came over and put her arm around his waist. "This is the best garden we've had."

"It sure is, and next year will be better yet. We will have the house completely finished by this winter too."

Just as they sat down at the table to drink a cup of coffee, they heard a plane circling overhead,. Nat looked at Nancy. "I wonder if some pilot is having trouble and looking for a place to land. If he is, he won't find any place around here. I'm going out to check."

He grabbed his binoculars and went outside. The plane came down low making a pass over the cove then gained altitude again. Nancy came out and stood beside him. "What do you think he's up too?"

Nat watched the plane through the binoculars as it leveled off then, making a turn, started flying parallel to the beach. As they watched, someone jumped from the plane. The parachute opened immediately. At first, it looked like they might land on the beach, but a stiff breeze suddenly came up and carried the parachutist inland.

Handing the binoculars to Nancy, he started in the direction of the parachute. "Whoever it is, they're going to wind up in a tree."

As Nat jogged along, keeping his eyes on the parachute, he realized that whoever was jumping should have worn a diver's suit because they were coming down in the middle of the water in back of the dam.

The parachutist had landed in the middle of the reservoir by the time Nat arrived at the dam.

"Help me get out of here Nat!"

"Jer! You crazy asshole! What the hell are you trying to do?"

"Just get me out of here! This damn water is cold."

Nat put the row boat into the water and rowed out to Jerry. As soon as he helped Jerry into the boat, they pulled the parachute in with them. Nat started rowing toward shore. "Would you mind telling me why you dropped in on us?"

"Nancy's Aunt Dorthey died."

Nat was silent for a moment. "When?"

"Yesterday morning."

"Do you know what the cause of death was?"

"A drunk driver ran a stop sign and smashed into her. It happened the evening before yesterday. She was in a coma right up to her death."

"Who is handling the funeral arrangements?"

"Nancy's mom."

Nat was quiet as he beached the boat and helped Jerry out. They draped the parachute over a branch. "We'll hang it up in a tree to dry after we get you dried out. You talked to Nancy's mom?"

"Yeah, briefly on the phone before she left to catch a plane to fly out from Maryland."

As they approached the door, Nancy came out. Why Jer! What a pleasant surprise!"

"Yes Ma'am."

"Just look at you! You're soaking wet. We'd better get you dried off." She took Jer into the bathroom, then, after showing him how to run the dryer, she gave him a robe of Nat's to wear while the clothes were drying.

She came into the kitchen as Nat was pouring himself a cup of coffee. I asked Jer why he came up here and he said that you would tell me. Nat? What's wrong?"

"Aunt Dorthey is dead."

Nancy stood immobile as she turned pale. "No----" suddenly the tears streamed down her face as Nat set his coffee cup down and put his arms around her, holding her tight. "How?"

"An auto accident."

"When did it happen?"

"Night before last. Somebody ran a stop sign and hit her."

Prying herself out of Nat's arms, she turned, and ran into the bedroom and threw herself on the bed, sobbing uncontrollably.

Jerry came into the kitchen. "She's taking it pretty hard isn't she?"

"I knew she would. She loved Dorthey as much as her own mother. How did you find out about it?"

"Well, after you got married, I stopped in to visit Dorthey every once in a while, as you know. I also got to know Nosey Matilda. Anyway, Matilda got a hold of me right after she called Nancy's mom and asked me if I could get word to you and Nancy somehow. After telling her I would try, I asked her for Nancy's mom's phone number. Mrs. Coleton and I had never met but she knew who I was from Dorthey and Nancy's letters. She agreed to hold the funeral until next Saturday to give me a chance to try and locate you and give you time to get there."

Nat thought for a couple of minutes. "This is Tuesday. If we leave early tomorrow morning, we can be in Vancouver by late tomorrow afternoon. We can get my Land Rover out of storage and be in Bellingham by dark. Is your car in Vancouver?"

"Yeah, I left it at the hotel I stayed in last night. After explaining the situation to them, they said I could leave it there for a couple of days. They were real nice about it too. I offered to pay for the parking and they refused to accept any payment."

They talked for a while longer and then Jerry's clothes were dry. As Jerry went to get dressed, Nat went in to check on Nancy. Sitting down beside her, he stroked her hair. "We will be leaving in the morning for Bellingham."

She didn't answer, so he went on. "The services will be on Saturday. Your mother is making all the arrangements."

Nancy looked up with tear-stained eyes. "Will daddy be there?"

"Not if he thinks I might be there. You know how much he was against you marrying someone who fought land developers."

She sat up and wiped her eyes. "I know. That's why he wouldn't even let mom come out to meet you." Nancy put her arms around Nat and laid her head on his chest. "I'm sorry he feels the way he does about you."

"It's not your fault. He believes in what he does just like I believe in protecting nature the way I do."

"But he didn't have to be so stubborn about letting mom come out to meet you."

"Well, at least I was able to talk to her on the phone as long as we called her."

"I know, and she really enjoyed talking to you. In several of her letters, she said she wished that, somehow, she could meet you."

"Too bad it has to be this way, but at least she's finally going to get the chance."

Nancy stood up. "I'd better go see if Jerry's clothes are dry."

"He's already getting dressed." Nat stood up to leave the room. "I'd better get out there so I can show him around."

"Alright. I'll be out a soon as I put some fresh make-up on." She looked into the mirror. "Oh! I look terrible!"

Nat came into the kitchen as Jerry was pouring himself a cup of coffee. "Grab your coffee and let's get out there and hang the parachute up so it can dry. Where did you get it?"

"At the airport where I hired the guy to fly me up here. It's bought and paid for so I'll leave it here. Maybe Nancy can make something out of the material."

After the parachute was put up to dry, Nat showed jerry around the place. Entering the house, they saw that Nancy had fixed them a lunch. As Nat and Jerry sat down, she came over to Jerry. "Thank you for going to all this trouble to let us know about Aunt Dorthey. We really appreciate it."

"That's okay. I'm just glad I was able to do it."

"Do you still work for the Forestry Department?" She asked.

"Sure do! It's been twenty-five years now."

Nancy put lunch on the table and sat down. "Have you settled down with one woman yet?"

"No way! I'm enjoying my freedom too much. Besides that, I wouldn't want to ruin my image of a foot-loose and fancy-free man."

Nancy looked Jerry right in the eyes. "Jer', when we lived down there, I saw just what kind of person you are. You spent most of your spare time working with the different scouting groups and under-privileged children. The few times you did go out on dates, from what I heard, you were a perfect gentleman and a splendid man for women to go out with. I'll bet that if you got married, you would be the ideal husband for any woman. I think you should find a woman to share your life with."

Jerry looked at Nat. "Help me out of this Nat."

"No---she's absolutely right."

After a short silence, Jerry declared. "You folks sure have a nice place here."

Nancy laughed, "Okay! We'll change the subject."

As the sun rose in a clear sky, Nat put their luggage on the boat while Nancy fixed some food to take with them on the journey to Vancouver.

The trip took all day and they arrived in Vancouver at five in the afternoon. They picked up Jerry's car then had dinner before getting Nat's Land Rover out of storage.

It was just about dark as they drove into the driveway at Dorthey's house and the lights were on. "It looks like mom is still up." Nancy stated.

With Jerry carrying the suitcases, Nat rang the doorbell. As soon as the door opened, Nancy threw her arms around her mother and kissed her on the cheeks. "Oh mom! I'm so happy to see you again."

Nancy's mother was tall, slim, and beautiful. Most of Nancy's features had been passed on to her from her mother.

Nat and Jerry stepped inside and, as Jerry set the suitcases down, Mrs. Colton pulled away from Nancy and walked over to Jerry. She held her hand out to Jerry and, as he took it, looked him up and down. "You must be Nat!"

"Oh no, ma'am! I'm Jer'! That's Nat!" he exclaimed, nodding toward

Nat. "But thanks for the compliment."

Turning to face Nat, she looked up at him. "I'm terribly sorry!"

"That's all right." He laughed. Taking her hand as she held it out, he bent down and kissed her on the cheek. "I'm very happy that I finally have the chance to meet you."

"For some reason, no one ever mentioned how tall you are." Stepping back a little, she looked him over. "You are a very handsome man. It's easy to see why Nancy was attracted to you, but, she has always had good taste."

"Mother! You're embarrassing me!"

"I'm not trying to embarrass you dear. I'm complimenting you."

Nancy put her arm around Nat's waist. "His real beauty is inside, and I love him very much."

"So you have told me in your letters. I have a full pot of coffee made. Would anyone like a cup?"

"I could go for one." Jerry stated. "By the way Mrs. Colton, is it okay for me to sleep on the couch tonight?"

"It's perfectly all right with me, but I think Nancy is the one you should ask."

Why should he ask me?"

"My dear, Dorthey left her entire estate to you because she had no children of her own. You have always been as close to her as you have been to me."

"Didn't she leave you anything?" Nat asked. "After all, you were her sister."

"Dorthey and I discussed that several times. Like I told her, there is nothing I need. My husband may have his faults, but he is a very good provider. It was my idea for Dorthey to leave everything to you, Nancy"

Nancy started crying and put her arms around her mother. "You shouldn't have done that."

"Well, I did! And, I don't have any regrets about doing it either. Tomorrow we will go down to her lawyer's office and he will give you a copy of the will. Another thing you will have to do as soon as you get a copy of the death Certificate, is go to the bank and open the safety deposit box. In there you will find her insurance policies and also other important papers.

The insurance policies are rather large. Anyway, we'll talk about that to-morrow. Right now, I want to get to know my son-in-law a little better. Let's sit in the kitchen and talk over coffee."

CHAPTER 16

Ellen startled Nat as she put her arm through his. "Ken wants to know how much longer?"

"We can go now." Taking one last look at the grave marker, he turned to go.

"She must have been somebody very special to you."

"Dorthey was my wife's aunt, and yes she was very special."

As Ken started the helicopter, he asked Nat. "Which way from here?"

"Just zigzag north and south, working our way east. That renegade said that the settlement was built like an old fort. It shouldn't be too hard to spot from the air."

It was nearly two in the afternoon when they had located the settlement which was built in the middle of a large field. From the air, small garden plots could be seen close in next to the walls of the fort-like structure. Inside of the rectangular compound were rough-built sheds which served as living quarters for the people. On each corner of the walls were mounted two large searchlights.

As they landed in the field about two hundred yards from the structure, a pickup with three men riding in the back carrying rifles, drove out and stopped a short distance from them. None of the men disembarked from the truck, choosing to point their rifles at the helicopter and wait for whoever was aboard to come out into the open.

Ken looked at Nat. "They sure don't look like they are ready to welcome us with open arms."

Nat looked them over. "They're just being cautious. I can't say as I blame them either. Go ahead and shut this thing down. Ellen, you stay in here with Ken and stay alert." He then slid the door open and jumped out onto the ground.

When Nat had covered half the distance to the truck, the driver got out and walked toward Nat. "What's your business mister?" The man asked as he met Nat.

"You the leader of this colony?"

The man hesitated for a moment. "No, Big Henry is. Who are you?"

"My name is Nat. I'm the leader of a settlement over on the Olympic Peninsula. Would you take me to talk to Henry?"

"How many others are in that eggbeater?"

"Two---a woman and the pilot."

"They armed?"

"They are, but we didn't come here to start any trouble."

"That's good because we got enough troubles already without somebody coming along and giving us more. You all can get into the back of the truck and I'll take you to see Big Henry"

Nat motioned for Ken and Ellen to join him and the three of them got into the back of the truck as the driver got back in and drove them up to the huge gates. As they waited for the gate to be opened, Nat noticed that the walls were pretty close to being fifteen feet tall. A man stood guard on top of the wall with an automatic rifle, watching them with curiosity as the truck pulled inside.

Coming to a stop in front of one of the small buildings, Nat, Ellen and Ken clamored out of the truck as a huge man came out the door. The man was as tall as Nat, but much more muscular, looking as if he could pick up a bull ox and throw it a good distance.

Reaching his hand out, Nat looked him in the eyes. "You must be Henry."

"That's me! He shook Nat's hand. "What can I do for you?"

"My name is Nat and these two with me are Ellen and Ken. We flew over from the Olympic Peninsula where we have built a small town."

"Well, come on into my home. It's not much, but it keeps us dry and warm"

The building was only a one-room shack with a wood stove against the wall opposite the door. A large double bed was against the wall on the right and on the left was a kitchen table and chairs. At the stove was a woman cooking and a girl of about nine or ten was standing beside her. Both turned and looked as the others entered.

Henry gestured toward the woman and child. "My wife Marie and daughter Heather." He looked back at Nat. "You folks drink coffee?"

"We all do." Ellen answered.

"Marie, pour our company some coffee. Nat, you and the others go ahead and have a seat." As they sat down, Henry started the conversation. "You say you built a town?"

"That's right. We have a population of well over a hundred. Included in our town is a medical clinic with a doctor, a teacher to teach our children, and we also built a dam to furnish us with electricity."

"How do you protect yourselves from the night creatures?"

"We call them mutants. Our town is situated up a valley in the mountains. The snow pack helps protect us on three sides most of the year. So far, we haven't had to contend with any attack from them. We send parties out periodically to search for them and kill them. This summer we are concentrating on attacks across the Straits of Juan de Fuca by using the helicopter."

"You mean to tell me that you actually go after them?"

"It's better than waiting for them to come to us and catch us off guard."

"I like your line of thinking but it would be totally out of the question for us to try that."

"Why is that?" Ken asked.

"Several reasons. One, we lack the manpower. Secondly, we have plenty of weapons and ammunition but not enough to supply an attack. We have to use it sparingly so we have enough when we need it to ward off an attack."

"How do you protect your searchlight?" Nat inquired.

"They are covered with bullet-proof glass. Those lights are one of our best assets when an attack occurs. We run generators at night and keep four of the lights scanning the area all night. There hasn't been an attack for nearly six months now."

"How many people do you have living here in your settlement?" Asked Nat.

"Seventy-nine now. When we first started out, we had a little over a hundred, but radiation sickness took the others. Have you had much of that problem?"

"Not too much, although we lost four babies at birth due to the radiation."

"We lost one last year that way. In fact, the mother died not too long ago from radiation sickness. It was sad too. She suffered a lot. This doctor you got---is he pretty good?"

"Excellent, as far as we're concerned. We are very fortunate to have him in our town. He is always jumping in to help whenever he can on any work that has to be done too."

Henry thought for a second. "A doctor that isn't afraid to use his hands for labor is a rare doctor at that. There have been a few times around here when we sure could have used a man like that."

Nat felt comfortable talking to Henry, as if he had known the man for years. "What line of work did you do before the war?"

"I was a logger down by Darrington. What about yourself?"

"I took an early retirement, so to speak, and was living up in Canada. Before that I was a Special Investigator for the Department of Natural Resources."

"What did a Special Investigator for the Department of Natural Resources do?"

"Kept land developers under control. If they wanted to develop a certain area, I would go in, spend as long as needed, then report to the Department of Interior whether or not that particular area could be developed. If I said no, then that usually ended that developer's plans."

"How did you decide whether or not if it could be developed."

"Many things entered into my decisions. Usually, the first thing I checked was the animal life, then the plant life. After spending a lot of time checking on the wildlife population and the plants that they relied on for their existence, I checked other things such as soil, water run-off, and the possible damage to the environment if it were developed,."

"Sounds like a lot of work went into a decision. Now I know what happened when there was talk about the possibility of a development and then you didn't hear any more about it."

While Nat and Henry continued talking, Marie took Ken and Ellen out to show them around, leaving Heather to tend the fire and pour coffee as needed.

Henry looked at Nat. "What I would like to know is how come you folks came to be flying over here?"

"We heard about your group."

"From whom?"

"A renegade that called himself Zack."

Henry thought for a moment. "I remember him. That man gave me bad vibes as soon as he showed up. It only took me five minutes to make up my mind that I didn't want him around here."

"How long did he stay?"

"He didn't! I ran him off. That son-of-a-bitch was bad all the way through. Did he give you any trouble?"

"He tried, but it didn't work, so he wound up getting himself killed by one of our most honored townsfolk."

"Glad to hear it---people like him doesn't deserve to live. I have no use for those renegades. All they do is prey on the good folks that are trying to make it in what is left of this world."

"He was the first one to ever show up in our town and I hope he was the last."

"It would be nice, but don't hold your breath. From what we've seen, there are quite a few of them out there running around."

"Well, they can just stay out of our town. We have no use for them."

"What made you decide to come over here?"

"To be honest with you, we came over to ask you folks to move over to our town. All the folks in our town are like one big family and we are try-ing to build a new society. We feel that, the more of us who join together, the better the chances of survival. Sooner or later, the mutants are going to start banding together, and when that starts to happen, it will mean trouble for small settlements like this one and ours."

"As I mentioned before," Nat continued, "we can offer you medical help for the sick and an education for the children. Also, we will build you homes with two or three bedrooms, whichever you need. Another thing we have done is to implement a farming program to feed all of us and others that may come to join us."

"Are you the ruling authority?"

"Kind of. They all look to me for their leadership. That will change at the end of the year. I've convinced them that they should rule themselves instead of depending on one person." Nat went on to explain the system they had decided on for the ruling authority.

When Nat was finished, they sat in silence as Henry thought about what had been said. Finally, Henry reached a decision. Standing up and running his fingers through his hair, he looked at Nat. "You have made us a very gracious offer Nat. This evening, I would like to call all our people together and have you repeat what you have told me and offer them, as a group, your offer. As for myself, I am intrigued at the idea of joining you folks. I have been the ruling authority here since the beginning and, to be honest with you, it has been one hell-of-a-hard job for me. The only reason I'm doing it is because no one else wants it. The worst part of it is that I'm not a ruler of men. I can boss a logging operation, but I have a difficult time seeing to the needs of a community, settlement, town, or whatever. That's just not my cup of tea. If we all decide to join you, just give me a job to do and I'll work my ass off to get it done, but leave me out of the politics."

Nat stood up and, shaking Henry's hand, smiled. "If you folks join us, you got a deal! Right now, we are in the process of building the dam a little higher. The man in charge of that is called Jim. I think you and he would really hit it off, and I know he could use a man like you on his crew."

"You seem to be a very perceptive man Nat. If you say I'll get along with this Jim, then I'm sure I will. As far as the meeting this evening, after you're finished talking, I will cast the first vote to move to your town. Have you given your town a name yet?"

"We sure have. It's called Eagletown.

"Well, even if they decide not to move, I would still like to come and see this Eagletown for myself."

"You're welcome any time you want to come if the rest decide against moving."

"As I told you before, I'm the ruling authority here, but I'm sure my vote will weigh heavily on the rest of the voters. What's the man-to-women ration in your town?"

"A lot more women than men."

Henry laughed. "Make sure you point that out at the meeting. That one point is liable to make up their minds to move. Let's go outside and I'll show you around and introduce you to some of the people. Once you get to know them, they are one hell-of-a-great bunch."

The tour lasted until supper time and included their gardens, defenses and supply system. The two men talked about their lives before and after the war and their desire to see a strong come-back of the normal people. By the time the tour was completed, both men had a great admiration for each other. Henry, with his wife and daughter, had been camping deep in the Cascade Mountains when the nuclear attack had hit. If it hadn't been for his knowledge of the woods, he felt they wouldn't have made it. The heat from the explosions had caused some of the snow pack in the mountains to melt quite rapidly causing the rivers and streams to swell past flood stage. His truck and camper had been parked next to a stream so it was swept away and they had to hike out. As time passed, they met others and slowly banded together for protection. The fort-style settlement had been Henry's idea. He designed it and they all helped build it. Henry sort of fell into the leader position as time went on and none of the others wanted to accept the position.

That evening everyone gathered around a large bonfire to listen to what Nat had to say. After he finished, there was much talking among the people for about fifteen minutes then Henry stood up and had them quiet down.

All eyes were on Henry as he spoke. "These people have made us an offer, but if you think about it for a minute, you will realize that it is more than an offer. It is a way to the future. The future of our children, their children and future generations to come. They have started a society which is what is needed to survive in this destroyed world---yes destroyed! But not totally. It can be re-built. These good folks have made the move to start the re-building process. I would like to join them and work with them in their struggle to re-build. Let me be the first to cast my vote. I vote we pull up stakes and move into a town with others who share our dream of a future."

He had no more sat down next to Nat when a voice yelled from the crowd. "Let's move!" Soon, the entire group was chanting. "Move! Move! Move!"

Henry looked at Nat. "Well, I guess that settles it. Your town just increased its population by seventy-nine."

Nat laughed. "And you said that you weren't a leader. That little speech you made was spoken like a true leader of men."

"All I did was speak from the heart. I meant every word I said." He then stood up and got the crowd's attention again. "Tomorrow we start packing! Tonight we celebrate. Let's show these fine people what kind of citizens they are getting. Those with musical instruments go get them."

Within a half an hour, four fiddles, two guitars and a set of drums were making music. Henry grabbed Ellen and started the dancing as Marie took Nat's hand and pulled him out to the dance area. The men took turns dancing with Ellen while the women kept Ken and Nat busy. A couple of hours later, Nat and Ellen wound up dancing a slow dance together.

She laid her head on his shoulder. "Isn't this the neatest thing? I have never had so much fun in my entire life. These people are fantastic."

"They sure are. There is no doubt in my mind about them fitting in with the people of Eagletown."

"I think we should build a place to have dances and have a dance every Saturday night."

"After we get houses built for these people you go right ahead and suggest it. I'm going to send Ken back tomorrow to get crews started on the building. You can either go back with him or you can stay here and help with the moving."

"I'm staying with you."

The next morning, Henry called everyone together. "I've led you good folks for some time now and you all have been great followers. I'm proud of the whole lot of you. This move we are about to undertake is going to take co-operation from everybody. Now we can't go off half-cocked or it might turn into a nightmare. This move is going to have to be organized and handled properly. I don't feel capable of organizing and leading you through this move. Nat, here, is capable of doing it so I'm turning the leadership over to him. I'm asking all of you to give him your co-operation as well as you have given it to me in the past. Thank all of you for the support you have given me." He then turned to Nat with a tear in his eye. "They're good folks. I know you will be proud to lead them to your town."

"I'm sure I'll be just as proud of them as you are Henry." He turned to the crowd and held his hands up for silence. "Before I start handing out jobs, let's hear three cheers for Henry!"

The group roared out five cheers for Henry and various people shouted words of praise for him. Tears of pride streamed down Henry's face as Marie handed him a handkerchief.

As soon as the group quieted down again, Nat started assigning jobs to different persons. Ten men were sent to locate boats to transport them over to the Olympic Peninsula. Another crew was sent to locate vehicles to haul the people and their belongings down to the docks by Bellingham. Still another crew was sent to find containers to pack the belongings into. The rest were to start packing whatever they wanted to take with them.

By that evening, everything needed had been acquired except enough boats. The crew that had been searching for the boats reported that they were having a hard time finding boats that were seaworthy enough to make the trip safely but another day of searching might turn up the needed boats.

The next morning, Nat and Henry walked around the compound checking on the progress of the preparations being made. Nat looked up at the searchlights. "I think what we will do is have a small crew come back over here with the helicopter and bring those lights over to Eagletown. We could position them in strategic places in the valley for part of our defenses if we should ever need them"

"Sounds good to me. You know, some day this place might be a tourist attraction for the future generations." Henry laughed.

"It just might be. If it is, I hope they get the history right and give you the recognition as the founder of it."

"That's a good one! Me being mentioned in history books."

"I don't see anything wrong with that. This settlement was your creation.

You brought the people into it then guided them through a very difficult period of time. Some of them might not have made it if it wasn't for your support and leadership. By doing what you did, you set yourself apart from the others. That's what puts you into the books as part of a history."

"Ah! You make it sound like I'm a hero or something. All I did was do what I felt was important for our survival. Nothing heroic."

"I'll bet these people think of you as a form of hero. Your wife and daughter surely think of you as a hero and I'm sure your descendants will speak of you with much pride. A couple of hundred years from now, every child studying history will probably consider you as one of the founders of our new society."

"How are they gonna know about us? There aren't any books being printed and probably won't be for some time. By the time somebody gets around to printing a book about all this, names will be forgotten."

"Don't be too sure of that Henry. As a matter of fact, you just gave me an idea. When we get to Eagletown, I'm going to talk to Howard. He's our teacher. I'm going to suggest that he head up a project to get everyone to write what they can remember about their past and their experiences up to now. Then, he can put it into a book. I'm sure we can locate a printing press somewhere. I also think that someone should start a book to record all our events as they happen the way they happen. That way, our descendants won't have to speculate as to how we rose from the depths of a man-made hell and built what I hope is a new and better society."

"Sounds like a good idea to me. I hope he can do it."

That evening everybody was packed and ready to go except for their bedrolls and spirits were running high. The people felt like they were moving from the past into the future. While Ellen and Marie sat inside talking, Nat and Henry sat out on the porch enjoying the warm evening. Heather was playing tag with four other children as they watched in silence.

Finally, Henry commented. "It seems like it's been so long since Heather has been able to go to school. Before the war, she was the top student in her class. She loved school more than any other kid that I met. This Howard fellow. I hope he is a good teacher because Heather is a good student. It sure is going to be nice for her to go to school again. Marie and I have been trying to teach her but we aren't any good at giving her the education she needs."

"I'm sure you will find him very competent as a teacher. He has set it up so he teaches the first six grades in the afternoon and the rest in the morning. School is taught eleven months out of the year with two weeks off in the spring and two weeks off in the fall. That way, the kids can help during planting and harvesting."

"I like that concept."

Early the next morning, everybody started loading the trucks up and by nine o'clock, the group started for the boats. Traveling to the boats only took an hour and as soon as they arrived the belongings were transferred to the boats. The boat loading took just about two hours to complete.

Nat gathered everyone together before setting out. "We have a little over fifty miles to travel to get to Port Angeles. The tide is just about in right now so that means we will have about six hours of outgoing tide to help us. We have to stay together as close as we can. I'll be in the lead boat so I can set the pace. If any problems arise for anyone, signal as quickly as you can. Each boat is to pick someone to be a spotter. The spotter's job is to watch the other boats for signs of distress. If all goes well, we will be docking in Port Angeles before dark. We have nice weather and light winds so it should be a fairly smooth crossing. Now, let's get on board and cast off!"

Within fifteen minutes, every boat was out on the water heading for their destination. The trip went smoothly all the way and, as they passed Dungeness Spit, Ken flew over them and headed toward Port Angeles. Nat said to Henry. "That means that they will be waiting for us at the docks to transport us up to Eagletown."

"You folks have a place to put all of us up?"

"Everybody will have to share the houses we already have built until we get more done. Before I came over to your settlement, we had started twenty-five houses. I told Ken to get another twenty-five started. With all this extra manpower, it shouldn't take long to finish all fifty houses."

"We are all good workers, so just tell us what to do and we will do it."

"I'm counting on that. You, Marie and Heather will stay at our house until yours is done."

"You and Ellen have any kids?"

Nat chuckled. "No. As a matter of fact. We aren't even married."

"Oh! I guess I just assumed you were. That's why I put you two up together. I'm sorry."

"Don't be. We sort of have a relationship going even though it's an unusual one. She has her own bedroom and I sleep on the couch. We share the house with another woman. I'm just as close to her as I am to Ellen but in a different way. The other woman's name is Lisa and you folks will really like her. She also has her own room but, for now, Ellen and Lisa will share one bedroom and you and Marie can have the other. I'll put a cot up in your room for Heather to sleep on."

"I sure hope this Lisa doesn't feel like we are intruding on your hospitality."

"She won't. She is a wonderful person and likes to help people in any way she can."

As they pulled into the docks at Port Angeles, a large crowd was waiting for them with plenty of trucks to transport the new residents up to Eagletown. Nat eased the boat up to the dock and Ellen threw Jim a line to tie the boat up. Jim stood on the dock as Nat and Henry came ashore.

"Welcome back! Jim roared as e slapped Nat on the back. "We are as ready as we can get on such short notice."

"Jim I want you to meet a man that is going to be working for you. This is Henry. Henry, this is the man I told you about."

They shook hands as Jim looked Henry up and down. "Damn! As big as you are, I'd be afraid to give you an order. I'll just ask you nicely when I want you to do something."

Henry laughed. "Don't let my size scare you Jim. If you have an order to give me, just give it to me and I'll do it."

"If you say so. I just hope you never get mad at me and hit me over the head. If you did that, it would take all day to dig me back up."

Nat punched Jim on the arm. "If you ever got him that mad, then you would deserve to get driven into the ground, but right now, let's get these boats unloaded. There is not a hell of a lot of daylight left."

The sun was just getting ready to sink over the horizon as they finished unloading the last boat. Nat and Henry rode with Jim when they pulled away from the docks.

Nat spoke to Jim as they got underway. "Is the construction getting underway all right?"

"Shor' is! I pulled the crew off the dam to get the ball rolling."

"How is the extension on the dam coming along?"

"Well, this will delay it a bit but not so much that we can't get it finished before winter sets in again. With all this extra help, maybe I can still run a small crew on the dam."

"I would like to work with you on that crew." Henry volunteered.

Jim glanced at him. "You're hired! When you get settled in tomorrow, have someone bring you up to the dam and I'll explain what we are doing. Then, I'll put you to work. In fact, you can stay at my place tonight if you want.

"Thanks for the offer, but I along my wife and daughter are going to be staying at Nat's house which he has so graciously offered to us."

"Married, huh?"

"You betcha! And I wouldn't have it any other way. You against marriage?"

"No way! Might make that step myself some day."

"You got somebody lined up?" Henry asked.

Jim glanced at Nat. Then, after a couple of minutes of silence, changed the subject. "You know Henry, you folks are going to like Eagletown. The people are just fantastic."

"So I've been told. From what I've seen so far, it's the absolute truth. I'd kind of like to look the town over before I come up to the dam though. If it's all right with you."

"That's fine with me. Take your time and meet the people that you are going to be living and working with."

Jim pulled up in front of Nat's house and stopped. As they clamored out of the truck, Phill's truck pulled up in back of them with Ellen, Marie and Heather. Nat turned to Henry. "We can unload the trucks in the morning after a good night's sleep. The lights are on in the house so Lisa must be home. Come on in and meet her."

Just as Nat reached for the door, it flew open and Lisa was standing there. "I have fresh coffee made and---oh!" She looked up at Henry. I see we have some company also."

As they stepped inside, Nat introduced them. "Lisa, this is Henry and this is his wife Marie." Putting his hand on the girl's shoulder, he continued. "This little gal is their daughter, Heather. A new student for Howard. I've invited them to live with us until a house is completed for them."

Lisa shook hands with them. "Well, welcome into our humble little home. Please make yourselves as comfortable as you can. You can take my bedroom and I'll share the other with Ellen. Can I offer you a cup of coffee?"

Your sure can." Henry answered. "And we will graciously accept it."

Lisa turned to Heather. "And I'll bet you would like a cup of hot chocolate."

"Yes ma'am."

Ellen came around from in back of the other. "I'll help you."

"Anything I can do?" Marie asked.

"Well, if you like, you can help with supper. I had already started it but now we will have to put on some extra. I didn't know we were having company."

"Just show me where things are and we will remedy that in a hurry." Marie laughed as she followed Lisa and Ellen out into the kitchen.

Heather walked over to Nat. "When do I get to start school Mr. Nat?

He patted her on the head. "Tomorrow afternoon if you want. In the morning I'll take you down to the school and introduce you to the teacher. Is that okay with you?"

"Yes sir!" She then headed for the kitchen.

"I told you she liked school." Henry stated.

"I think Howard is going to really enjoy having her as a student."

Lisa brought coffee in for the men. "Nat, I have the most beautiful story to tell you."

He took the cup from her. "If it's about Sleeping Beauty, I've heard it."

"No silly! She playfully punched him in the stomach. "It's better than that."

"Well then, let's hear it."

"It's about Sam!"

"Sam?"

"Yep!"

Nat looked at Henry. "Sam is a very special person around here. He got shot in the face and can't say any words. You will meet him tomorrow." He turned back to Lisa. "Go on! I'm all ears."

"Sam's got a girlfriend."

"A what?"

"Will you quit interrupting me? A girlfriend."

"Who?"

"Elizabeth!"

Nat shook his head. "I'm afraid I don't know her."

"She is the girl Sam brought to us off that renegade's boat. Her name is Elizabeth."

Nat looked at Henry again. "I forgot to ask you. Has anybody from your group come up missing in the last few weeks?"

"No. If there was, I would have known it right away. She is not from our group."

He then asked Lisa. "Did she say where she is from yet?"

"No, not yet. But anyway, she and Sam have grown fond of each other. You should have seen the armload of roses he gave her. They were so beautiful."

"Where is she staying?"

"For right now, she is going to stay at Sally's house. During the day, she will go down to the clinic and help out around there."

"That's the perfect setup if I ever saw one,"

"Why do you say that?" Lisa questioned.

"Well, with Sally and this Elizabeth living together and working together and Jim and Sam living together and Jim being sweet on Sally and Sam being sweet on Elizabeth, well it's a perfect setup."

"You know about Jim and Sally?"

"Yep!"

"How did you find out? I didn't find out until after you left for Bellingham."

"I don't remember."

Nat!" She scolded,. "You do too remember! Now who told you?"

"I heard it whispered in the wind."

"You rat!" She stood up and headed for the kitchen. "No sense in me asking you again. I should have known that you wouldn't tell me."

The next morning, the job of sorting the newcomer's belongings out was accomplished with ease because Nat had assigned each person a number which was written on the containers. Most of the containers were placed in storage until it was needed for later as the houses were completed.

Nat kept his word with Heather and took her down to the school. He motioned for Howard to come outside. "Howard, I want you to meet a star student. This is Heather and she came in last night with the folks from Bellingham. She loves school and can't wait to start."

Howard took Heather's hand. "Well, this is truly a pleasure. I will be very happy to have you as one of my students. It gives me a great thrill to be able to teach a student who has a thirst for an education. Heather, you just be here at one o'clock and I'll introduce you to the other kids. At that time, I'll also give you your text books that we are using. What grade were you in?"

"I had finished the fourth grade, sir."

"This afternoon I will give you some tests. Maybe we can move you up to the sixth grade. How does that sound?"

"Really?"

"That's what I said. Is that okay with you?"

"Yes sir!"

"Where are you living now?"

"With Mr. Nat. So are my mother and father."

That's a fine place to be living,. I'll see you this afternoon then."

"Yes sir,."

"Do you have a couple of extra minutes Howard?" Nat asked.

"Yes. The class is having a half hour to do some extra studying."

"Well, I came up with this brainstorm the other day and I would like you to give it some thought."

"Okay, what is it?"

"I would like to see you start a project to get each person in Eagletown to write a short biography of themselves and then have you put it into a book. I'll see if the scavenger crews can locate a printing press when they are looking around or maybe they have already seen one and can get it up here to use. Then I would like to see you or someone else as capable as you to be the town historian and record the events that happen as time goes on so the future generations will have an accurate history."

"I like the idea. I'll definitely give it some thought."

"Thanks! Well, I have to get going. Talk to you later."

Okay. See you later.

Chapter 17

It was two weeks later and Nat was with a crew tearing down a house on the bluff.

"Hey Nat!" Phill called out. "Look out on the water. Doesn't that look like a small boat drifting without power?"

Nat looked where Phill was pointing. "It sure does. Get a pair of binoculars out of the truck."

Phill quickly ran and obtained the binoculars and gave them to Nat. "It's a boat alright! Why don't you take a truck down to the docks, then go out and check it out. Use Sam's because we are loading yours right now."

Phill headed out for the docks and took one of the boats with an outboard motor. Upon reaching the drifting boat he saw a young man lying in the bottom. He could tell that the man was still breathing. Phill quickly tied a rope on to the drifting boat and headed back into the dock. On the way in he waved his arms hoping that the others would see him and go down to the docks.

Nat had been watching, and saw Phill waving his arms. "Let's go guys! Phill is indicating a problem!"

They jumped into their trucks and sped down to the docks. Nat and the others arrived at the dock before Phill. As Phill got to the dock, he threw a line to them. "There is a man in the bottom of the boat that is barely alive!"

As soon as the boat was secure Nat jumped into the boat. The man tried to talk but his mouth was to dry. Nat spoke to him. "Don't try to talk right now." Turning to the others he hollered. "Bring me some water!" One of the men got Nat some water and he gave the man a small sip of water.

The man's lips were cracked from the lack of water, and he was extremely weak and was unable to sit up by himself.

They stabilized the boat and Nat picked the man up and handed him up to the others. Nat had them put him in the seat with Sam driving with Nat holding the man between them. "Drive like hell and go straight to the clinic!"

Upon arriving at the clinic, Nat carried the man inside. Alan met him in the outer room. "What happened to him Nat?"

"We found him floating out in the Straits!"

"Get him in room one, and put him on the bed!" Alan then immediately started treating him. "Sally isn't here right now. Do you think you could go get her for me?"

"You bet!" Nat stated as he headed for the door.

A few minutes later, Sally came through the door. "Nat said we have a new patient that is badly dehydrated!" She came over to look at the man.

Elizabeth was right behind her, and as soon as she saw the man she shrieked. "Johnny!" And ran to the side of the bed and crying bent over and lifted his head. "I'm so glad you are still alive."

Alan gently pulled her back. "Don't make him talk right now. He is in bad shape and needs to rest. He is young and should recover quite rapidly."

"But he is my brother!"

A few minutes later Nat came through the door to check on the man. When he saw Elizabeth crying he looked at Alan. "What happened?"

"This young man is Elizabeth's brother. His name is Johnny." Alan stated.

Nat walked over to Elizabeth. "Can we have a talk?"

She looked up at him with tears in her eyes. "He is my brother and I thought he was probably dead."

Why did you think that?"

"There were only a few of us left when that man kidnapped me." She shuttered at the mention of the kidnapping. "He came into our place and Johnny ran him off." She continued. "A few days later I was walking along the trail next to the beach when out of nowhere he grabbed me and knocked me out. When I came to I was in his boat tied up." Elizabeth started shaking and sobbing.

Nat put his arms around her and held her. "You don't have to tell me anymore about that part. Where were you taken from?"

As she wiped away the tears she told him that they worked at a small private resort on the west side of Vancouver Island.

"Could you show me on a map?"

"I don't think so because it's not on any maps I saw. Johnny could show you right where it's at."

"Good! I'll ask him as soon as he is able to show me. You go back to his side and I'll check back later to see how he is doing."

"Thank you sir."

"It's Nat. Not sir."

"Okay."

Nat went home, and as he entered, Ellen, Lisa and Marie were fixing supper. He went out into the kitchen,. "Well we had quite a surprise today." Nat announced.

"What's that?" Asked Ellen.

"We rescued a man today that turned out to be Elizabeth's brother."

The women looked at each other. Lisa spoke first. "That must make her very happy. How did it happen?"

Nat explained everything to them.

"Maybe we can fix him some chicken soup to give him some nourishment."

"You better check with Alan first."

Lisa piped up. "I'll go down and ask." She then went out the door.

As soon as Lisa got to the clinic she found Elizabeth and gave her a big hug. "I'm so happy for you and your brother being reunited."

"Thank you. The doctor says he's going to be alright."

Just then the doctor came into the room. Lisa asked him if it was okay to fix him some chicken soup.

"Not now. But tomorrow you can, but make sure the chicken is cut small and don't give him more than a cup at a time. He's young and he will recuperate nicely."

"Thank you doctor." Then turning towards Elizabeth. "If you want a break, I'll be glad to sit with him for a spell."

"I'm doing fine, but thank you."

"Well, I'll go back home. If you need anything, please get word to me. Bye."

The next day Nat, Ellen, and Lisa went down to the clinic.

Alan greeted them. "Good morning."

"How is Johnny doing this morning?"

"He is doing great! He's even sitting up on the side of the bed."

"Is it okay for us to visit?" Lisa inquired,.

"You sure can. It looks like you have plenty of that chicken soup with you. I'll be glad to help him eat it."

"Like you said. There's plenty."

As they walked into the room Johnny looked at them. "I really want to thank you for rescuing me."

Nat spoke. "I'm glad we were able to. You were pretty near death. Do you feel up to talking?"

"I think so, but I'm still pretty weak."

"Good! I'll be right back."

Nat left and came back with a map of Vancouver Island. "Your sister said that you lived on the west side of the island."

"That's right."

"How many of you lived there?"

"Lately twenty some people, that is all that's left? We started out with about eighty people. As we tried to leave we were killed off by night people and a few killers during the day. As time went by we were attacked mostly at night. We seemed to lose one or two every time we were attacked. I agreed to try to go for help by myself as I felt I had the skills to make it on my own. When I started down the Straits of Juan de Fuca my motor broke down. I don't know how long I drifted back and forth in and out of the straits. Several days tho'."

"I want you to show me on the map just where you was located." Nat laid the map out on the bed.

"Right here! It doesn't show too good on the maps. It's a really small cove. At the end of the cove is a small private resort. Most of the survivors worked there, and the rest lived close by or were guests"

"It seems to me we need to rescue the rest of your group. I'm going to get up a party to go up there and bring them back here." Nat stated.

Johnny looked at Nat. "I'm going with you!"

"Let's see how you feel when we get ready to go,.."

Two days later Nat had a group ready to go up on the west side of Vancouver Island. The doctor gave Johnny the okay to go along.

Lisa opted to stay home, but Ellen insisted on going.

The next morning they started out with eleven boats. Johnny stayed on Nat's boat to show the way. Weather was relatively calm so they made good time. They had taken the chase boat with them in case they needed it to ward off any opposition.

It was getting late in the day and they realized that they would not make it by dark. Nat spoke to Johnny. "We had better find a cove for the night."

"Okay. It's going to take a couple hours to get there."

They located a secluded cove to drop anchor in for the night. Not too long after dark they heard a couple boats going by heading north.

Johnny turned to Nat. "I'll bet they are heading to our cove for another attack."

"Well, we just have to do something about that! Let's get in the chase boat and chase them down."

"Isn't that kind of dangerous Nat?"

"Not really. Just come along and see how this works."

They took off after the two boats. Johnny was surprised how fast the chase boat went. As they closed in on the boats which were running side by side, Nat turned on the high power spot lights shining them on the occupants As soon as the lights hit them they tried to shield themselves from the bright lights. The men on the chase boat opened fire killing the mutants almost instantly. Both boats started going in circles with no one to steer them. The chase boat pulled up alongside one of the boats. Hank then threw a stick of dynamite into the boat and the chase boat headed towards the other. When they were about thirty yards from the first boat it exploded. They then closed in on the other boat and did the same thing, blowing it to pieces.

On the way back to the other boats Johnny commented. "That's about the coolest thing I've ever seen."

The next day they reached the cove where the survivors were. The people were happy to see Johnny. He explained to them what had happened to him since he left, and finding his sister. Everybody agreed to start out the next morning. That gave everybody a chance to decide what they wanted to take with them and get everything loaded.

They had just bedded down for the night when shots rang out. Those with guns took positions and started shooting back. How many mutants couldn't be determined. From the flash of gunfire there must have been at least twenty of them.

Nat and Ellen went outside and got behind a long log that had been driftwood. After about a half hour of shooting, it stopped. Nat hollered to get back inside. He looked over at Ellen who was about ten feet from him. She didn't move. Nat hollered again for her to get back inside, but she still didn't move. He ran over to her and rolled her over. She had been hit three times. Once in the neck, once in the chest and the other was in her arm. As Nat checked for a pulse he knew she was dead. Picking her up, he carried her body into the resort and laid her down on a couch. As he held her hand, Hank came over and put his hand on Nat's shoulder. "I'm sorry Nat."

Nat nodded. "Thanks Hank." He then let his chin rest on his chest. Down deep he knew that this could happen every time there was a shoot out. It could have been him or Lisa, Arn, Sarah or anyone else that was a member of their group. To have it actually happen was a wakeup call for Nat. Questions went through his mind. How was he going to break the news to Lisa and the others? How is it going to affect the town that she was such a part of? He knew he would be taking her body back to Eagletown to be buried. Is it time for him to move on? Should he quit going out on rescue missions?

The next morning they were loaded and out on the water at daybreak. Nat let Johnny pilot the boat while he stayed below with Ellen's body,.

Just before dark they pulled into Port Angeles. Phill had been watching with binoculars for them and by the time they docked there were plenty of vehicles to transport them to Eagletown.

As Nat's boat pulled up, Jim was there to catch a line. "How did it go Nat?"

Before Nat said a word Jim realized that something was wrong. "We lost one of our own!" Nat said with sorrow.

"Who?"

"Ellen."

Jim and everybody else fell silent. Nobody knew what to say.

"I'll need help bringing her body up to the truck."

Jim and Phill leapt down onto Nat's boat,. "We'll do it Nat." They went below and brought Ellen's body up and put in the back of Jim's pickup truck.

As they drove up to Eagletown, nothing was said. Jim pulled up in front of Nat's house. "Jim, I don't want Ellen left in the truck all night. Would you take her down to the clinic and ask Alan if you can leave her there for the night."

"Sure Nat."

Just then Lisa came out on the porch. One look at Nat and she knew something was wrong. "What's wrong Nat?"

"Ellen is dead."

"No! It can't be. Where is she?"

"In the back of the truck."

Lisa ran down to the truck and looked in at the body. She started crying as she looked at Ellen. "Oh my God!" Lisa reached down and brushed a lock of hair back off Ellen's face.

Nat came down and pulled her back and she turned and threw her arms around him and sobbed uncontrollably.

"You had better get going Jim."

Word spread throughout the settlement like wildfire. Before long people were showing up at Nat's house to offer their condolences. After a while Nat asked everybody to leave and give him some time alone.

When everyone had left, Lisa asked Nat. "Would you like me to stay with someone else tonight?"

Nat put his arms around her. "No. Having you here gives me some comfort. Just let me hold you for a few minutes."

She asked. "Would you like me to get you anything? A cup of coffee? I could fix you something to eat."

"I'll try a cup of coffee." He stated as he released her.

Heading for the kitchen she told him. "It will take a few minutes. I'll put on a fresh pot."

"Thank you." Setting down in his chair he pulled out his pipe from habit. Before putting tobacco in it, he stopped and looked at it. He was still turning it over and over in his hands when Lisa brought his coffee. Looking up at her he tried to smile. "At least I still have this to remember her."

She leaned over and kissed him on the forehead. Yes, and for the short time we knew her we have a lot of beautiful memories. I'm going to fix us something to eat. I know we don't have much of an appetite, but we really should try to eat anyway."

That night neither one of them could sleep much. During the night Lisa came out to Nat and they just sat there holding on to each other dozing off.

A knock at the door woke them up. Nat got up and answered the door. It was Arn and Sarah. As soon as they came in, Lisa hugged Sarah and they both just sobbed.

"Jim asked me to let you know that the burial will be at noon."

"Thanks Arn."

"You know Nat, this is so hard for me to accept. I guess I'm still in a state of shock."

Nat put his hand on Arn's shoulder. "I think we all are. Even if in the back of our minds we knew this was a possibility. It's going to take time to get over it. We have to move on somehow."

"Well, I understand, but it's not going to be easy for me. I guess Sarah and I better get going so we can get ready."

The burial took place with everybody in Eagletown present. Many people related stories about themselves and their association with Ellen. The number of nice things said showed how much of an impact she had on people's lives. Nat and Arn were too choked up to speak.

After the burial, Nat walked down to the river to think. About an hour later he heard someone behind him. Turning around he saw Johnny standing there. "Have a seat Johnny."

Johnny sat down by Nat. "Nat, I'm truly sorry for your loss. Somehow I feel somewhat responsible."

Looking right at Johnny he spoke. "I do not want you to feel one bit responsible. We didn't have to go on that rescue mission, but the people in Eagletown are the type of people that cannot live with themselves as long as they know someone needs their help. Your group needed our help. The fact that Ellen got killed is not your fault or anyone's fault in your group. So I don't want to hear any more about fault. Is that clear?"

"Yes sir!"

They sat and talked for quite awhile, with Nat asking Johnny more about himself. He admitted that he had learned about survival on his own. Some from books and some from his mother who raised him and loved to camp out in the wilds. Nat came to admire the man for is knowledge of the land and the wildlife that lived on it.

Time had gotten away from them and it was getting late. "I think we had better call it a day. Thank you for taking my mind off Ellen's death for a spell."

Coming into the house, he saw Lisa just setting there staring into the fire in the fireplace. He went over and sat beside her and put his arm around her shoulder. "I'm sorry I left you alone"

"That's okay. I needed sometime to myself to think."

"That's not too good some times in a time of sorrow."

"I know, but sometimes it can be good."

"Maybe. You know yourself better than anyone."

"Where have you been?"

"Down by the river talking to Johnny. I like that man. He has a very good knowledge of the outdoors. I'll bet him and Arn really hit it off. They have quite a bit in common."

"Arn needs someone to be close to besides you." She said.

"Why do you say that?"

"If anything happens to you, he will need a close friend to lean on. He has always leaned on you."

"I guess you're right."

"Have you given any thought as to what you are going to do?"

"I have, but I haven't come to any decision yet."

For the next few days Nat was relative quiet, as he was deep in thought. He knew he had to make a decision. Either he stayed at Eagletown or he goes back to his home in Canada. There were a lot of advantages to staying here. One is Lisa. He has become quite attached to her. If he left, she is the one he would miss the most. The only trouble is that he couldn't ask her to go with him because all of her friends are here. Anyway, she is probably more interested in Alan. He is a good man and it would probably be a good match.

Nat himself wasn't fond of being around a lot of people. That's why he had moved to Canada in the first place. He was lucky that Nancy wanted to enjoy that way of life with him.

The decision was finally made. As he came into the house, he called Lisa out into the living room from the kitchen.

She came out with a cup of coffee for him.

"I've made my decision and I want you to be the first to know. This has not been an easy decision to make, but I'm going back home in Canada. My main reason is that I think I'll be happier there. When we started out it was to get revenge on the mutants. I had no idea that this many people would be amassed. It became a situation of helping these wonderful people to their salvation. This has happened. They really do not need me to lead them anymore. There is several men here that can lead if need be. Once their government is established they are well on their way to success."

Lisa just sat there with tears running down her face. "I think I understand what you are saying and I really wish you the best if that is what you want." Deep down she wished he would ask her to go with him. She felt if she asked him, he would feel obligated to her and say yes and she would become a burden to him.

Choosing her words carefully she spoke quietly. "You will be missed by every person here. You have touched each and everybody's lives. Everyone here loves you more than you can ever know. I will not try to talk you out of it. That would be stupid on my part. You have been such a close and dear friend to me, and helped me in so many ways, but I want whatever you want. Thank you for everything." She gave him a hug and kissed him on the lips.

Early the next morning, Nat and Lisa walked out on the porch as Jim drove up to give him a ride down to the dock. Nat threw his gear into the back of the truck. Turning around he walked back to Lisa and he gave her a big hug. "Bye Lisa." He then got into the truck and they headed for the dock.

Nothing was said at first. Jim broke the silence. "You know Nat, we are sure going to miss you. I'll bet Lisa will miss you more than anybody else."

"What makes you figure that?"

"Just a hunch. The look on her face when you told her bye."

"We've lived together for quite a while, and became somewhat close. I was more attached to Ellen so I don't think Lisa had any designs on me."

"Well, I think you're wrong."

Just before casting off Nat shook Jim's hand. "When I need supplies I'll be back, so this isn't like saying good bye forever. At least that way I'll be able to see how everybody is doing."

"Good luck, Nat! Bye."

Nat made good time and arrived at the cove before dark. Pulling into the cove he saw his boat was still tied to the dock. Tying up at the dock he cautiously looked around. After checking the boat he left at the dock, he took his binoculars and looked at the house. The door was closed and all the windows looked intact. Taking his shotgun he crept up to the house. He spent quite a bit of time checking all around the outside of the house.

It appeared that no one had been here, so he carefully opened the door pushing it open with his shotgun. Nothing happened so he crept inside. After listening for a few minutes he came to the conclusion that no one was in the house, but he checked every room just in case.

Being satisfied that no one was around, or had anybody been there as the house had not been ransacked, he set about lighting fires in the fire places and the cook stove.

The next morning Nat set about tearing up the false floor and bringing things up from below to start setting up house. That afternoon he went up to the dam to check it out. After opening the valve to the power plant, he went to the switch shack and threw the switch and the light in the shack came on.

Heading back to the house he thought that tomorrow he would clean the screens.

It was about two weeks later when he was coming back from hunting and had bagged two grouse. It was still daylight but starting to get dark. As he broke out of the woods he saw smoke coming out of the cook stove chimney.

Cautiously he crept up to the house fearing that maybe a renegade might have found his place. Nat pushed the door open and stepped inside. Seeing no one he crept toward the den. Suddenly he stepped on a board that creaked. Almost immediately he heard someone paying the piano to the music of 'Walk in the Wild Wood'.